I0549439

The Angelic Gene

By Steve Goodwin

© 2013 Steve Goodwin

ISBN: Paperback 978-0-9873784-7-7
ISBN: eBook 978-0-9873784-6-0

Published by Software Development Pty Ltd
Brisbane, Queensland, Australia

All characters and events appearing in this novel are fictitious. Any resemblance to real events, or persons living or dead, is purely coincidental.

Acknowledgements

This section is growing longer with each novel as the community of fans grows. First, I wish to thank everyone who supports my novels. Your kind words, reviews, and social media interaction are cherished. Some names of regular supporters come to mind so I'll mention them individually: Sandra, Marsha, Lachelle, Sharyl, Kutemba, Tony, Janice, Sean, Isabella, Ruth, June, Christina, Jade, Sue, Shirley, Joyce, Kelly, Jeanette, Sheena, Larry, Mahi, Brian, Jennifer, Lis, Robert, Vivien, Stewart, Patricia, Valerie, Glynda, Jon, Christine, Delilah, Anne, Terry, Amberwren, Louise, Jari, Karen, Nathan, Fiona, Brenda, Irene, Blanca, Steve, Jason, Mark, Kirk, Lisa, Kara, Vicki, Andrea, Linda, Robert, Cara, Donna, Doris, Mary. If I have missed your name, be assured that I value your interactions.

A special thank you to Wendy Moss and Pete Scott, proofreaders of *Elijah Hael - The Genetic Code* and *The Angelic Gene*. And a warm thank you to Nathan Rippingale for his many contributions during proofreading *The Angelic Gene*.

Thank you to the cover model for this novel, Jennifer Douglas, and her photographer, Christina Cheang.

All the reviewers who have left reviews on Amazon, Goodreads, and other places across the Internet, you have my deepest respect. The reviews help in many ways, and I hope you continue to take the time to write them. If I had one wish, it would be for each reader to leave an honest review. They not only help motivate me in my writing but also help carve the direction of future stories. I get a glimpse into the way people are interpreting my writings, which, at times, are quite surprising. I love seeing the different perspectives people take on my stories.

i

For those who have contacted me personally to discuss my writings, Peter Younghusband, Wendy Moss, Donna Gooch, Pete Scott, Chad, and others: I thank you for taking the time to engage in conversations that have allowed me to grow as a writer.

Thank you, Linda Breen, for helping with some background research on Fuller Church.

Scott, my editor. I can't thank you enough for being part of my writing journey. You have helped me grow as a writer and spiritually. The summaries, the edits you put forward, and words of advice are invaluable.

To my in-laws, Val and Bruce Perkins, thank you for your ongoing support with my novels and diligent proof reading of *The Angelic Gene*.

To my Wife, love you, and thank you for putting up with my long hours in front of the computer and reading my drafts.

Last but not least, thank you to my daughter Jessica, the light of my life. Her smiles lift my spirits to encourage my writing. In many ways, the young girls in *The Angelic Gene* story are based on some of the playful tendencies I see in her. Love you, Jessica.

Author's Foreword

Now the acknowledgements are over I'll take a brief minute to talk about this novel. While this is technically the third novel in the Elijah Hael series, it is a prequel to *Elijah Hael*. As such, the novel can be read first, second, or third. A reader will benefit from reading the work third or first and will be moved in different ways as a result. If you are new to the series, this novel is a great place to start.

The Angelic Gene is set in an earlier time than the previous two novels, between 1860 and 1878 in England. It was a challenge from the start as research involved ensuring I only included items that existed in those times. I quickly discovered I could not use such simple things as glass coffee tables and garbage bins.

Most places in the novel are real, including travel distances between them. This presented challenges on a number of fronts. One was to ensure a certain degree of historical accuracy, and another was to ensure the travel distance was feasible with the transport systems available in those times. This is not to say that I have not taken a little artistic license with some of it (I certainly have) to create a more exciting and wondrous story.

If you know Sophia from the first two novels, you will find a younger version of her in this novel. This will give you insight to Sophia's background through several twists and turns. A few surprises await you and no doubt you will see a few connections with the other two novels. I am looking forward to seeing who picks them out.

I hope you find the journey as fascinating through reading as I did while writing. God bless and enjoy.

Chapter 1 - Beginnings

London, 1862

Rain drenched, in the middle of the night, a handsome solitary man in his mid-thirties burst through the weary large oak doors of the bleak St Thomas Hospital cradling an unconscious pregnant woman in his arms. He staggered forward, each determined step more trudging than the last, leaving a trail of blood on the floor behind him, until at last he collapsed onto his strained knees. Two nurses—one senior nurse, one younger—ran towards the defeated man as he shouted, "Help, you have to save her! The future depends on her survival!"

The sodden man carefully placed the motionless woman on the well-trodden white tile floor and then collapsed onto his side, revealing the bejeweled hilt of a dagger protruding from his back.

The senior nurse, Angela, crouched beside the pregnant woman, placed two fingers on the smooth white skin of her neck, and pressed lightly. The younger nurse checked the man's wrist for a pulse to confirm what his open yet vacant eyes told them. "He's dead," she said.

Angela nodded. Under her aging fingers, every second grasping for life, Angela felt a faint arterial rise. "This one is alive, but her pulse is very weak."

A third nurse rushed a stretcher down the corridor to them. The three nurses acting as one carefully placed the pregnant woman onto the portable bed. They carried her into a nearby examination room—sterile and claustrophobic—and transferred her onto the hard wooden surface of an operating table.

"Right," Angela said, "the doctor will be here soon." She turned her attention to an orderly. "Peter, call the police and put up some screens around the dead man in the foyer."

"I'm on it," Peter replied.

Minutes later, middle-aged Dr. Gregory rushed in clad in his full-length white coat. "What do we have here, Angela?"

"A young woman, quite pregnant, who was brought in by a man who subsequently died. She appears to be in a bad way herself." Angela nodded toward the woman on the table. "Her pulse is weak."

"Grab some smelling salts," Dr. Gregory said as he approached the woman and began a visual scan for any wounds. "Let's try to wake her up." The youngest of the three nurses scuttled out of the room.

The woman, who appeared to be in her early thirties, was quite beautiful. Her closed eyes were in perfect balance with her rather petite nose and slender mouth. She looked like a sleeping princess awaiting a kiss from a handsome prince. Her raven black hair was fine as spun silk and draped around her shoulders and down the sides of the operating table. Her long white cotton dress was marred with a chaotic pattern of blood splatter.

"Not her blood," Dr. Gregory muttered, without looking up from examining her.

"I would say," Angela said, calculating the degree of her baby bump, "that she is likely around eight months pregnant, possibly more."

Dr. Gregory shrugged. "Likely. So, how did the man who brought her in die?"

"Most probably by the dagger in his back," Angela said. "The Bobbies, I should say police, are on the way to investigate."

The doctor pushed back her eyelid and was surprised such that his eyebrows raised by the striking emerald-green color of her eye. Even in an unconscious state, her eye seemed like a doorway into a secret luscious green garden bustling with mystery. The room's bright light reflected in her fully dilated pupil. As if frightened, the dark black disc of her pupil constricted. He began feeling around her ribs, abdomen, and upper thighs searching for any sign of physical trauma. "No wound on her person," he said. "Physically she seems fine." He continued the examination, ran his hands along the sides and top of her head. "No swelling, no apparent bruising." He sighed, shaking his head. "Does she have a name?"

"I'm sure she must," Angela said, "but not one that we know."

"I say," Dr. Gregory said, eyebrow still raised.

Angela blushed at her sarcasm but stood staring at the motionless woman's face, lost in admiring her beauty.

A younger nurse named Eleanor added, "She is wearing a gold bracelet. The top is inscribed with 'Sophia.' That might be her name."

"Hmm," Dr. Gregory mumbled, nodding. The nurse who had left the room returned with a small ceramic vial of white crystals. She held the bottle under the unconscious woman's nose. After a few seconds, the woman's face contorted and her eyes opened. She raised her arm, pushing away the hand holding the vial under her nose. Then, at once, she let out a deafening cry of pain and clutched her belly.

"She is in advanced labor," Dr. Gregory shouted. "Quick, prepare for a birth."

Eleanor fetched a steel bowl, filled it with warm water, and gathered several rags.

The woman's breath was frantic and ragged between cries of pain as her contractions increased. "Breathe steadily," Angela said as she gripped the woman's hand to try to comfort her.

A stream of blood began to flow from between the woman's legs and down the side of the table. "She is hemorrhaging," Dr. Gregory shouted, fumbling for some cloths.

Angela winced as the woman squeezed hard on her hand. She thought about pulling her hand away, but seeing simultaneous terror and distress in the woman's eyes she decided to grit her teeth and bear the discomfort. *It's the least I can do*, she thought. From past cases, she knew well that women who hemorrhage during childbirth rarely survived.

Another contraction, and the woman heaved and let out a loud glass-vibrating screech that tensed the eardrums of everyone in the room. The pores of her sweltering forehead released additional moisture, forming beads of sweat that soon joined to create little rivulets of distress.

Eleanor dabbed the woman's forehead with a damp cool cloth. Blood began seeping from the woman's nostrils and ran around the corners of her anguished lips. The nurse wiped the initial trails away. Within moments, the creeks of blood turned into steady rivers that turned the whites of the cloth crimson. She gestured for Dr. Gregory to look.

He replied, his brow slumping, "Do your best to take care of it."

The woman's strained eyes cut to the red soaked rag as she experienced another contraction. Once the contraction passed, she seized the nurse's wrist, glared at her with conviction, as if reconciled to her own fate. "Leave it!" Then her voice softened as she said, "Save the baby."

"Crowning. I can see the head," Dr. Gregory announced. "One more push should do."

The woman gasped for air, but her lungs, drowning in her own blood, found no oxygen. All color washed from her cheeks, leaving behind skin pale as a snow-peaked mountain. Summoning all her might, she tried to push. With stubborn abandonment, her body did not respond. She mumbled, "No. Not like this," as her eyelids drew down.

"Stay with me," Angela urged, sensing the woman's hand go limp in her grasp. "The baby is nearly here." No response. The room was then quiet as a graveyard as Angela checked the woman's pulse. She closed her eyes, shook her head. "She is gone, doctor."

"Right, then let's do our best to save the baby," he replied.

Chapter 2 - Sophia

Two weeks later

A wave of frenzied rapping drew the attention of Sister Mary to the sturdy front door of the *Saint Juliana Of Pavilly Orphanage For Girls.* "Whoever could it be at this hour?" she said. She rubbed her hands together, trying to infuse warmth into the ends of her fingers. She cupped her hands in front of her mouth, took in a deep breath, and then exhaled the steamy air to warm her palms.

"Whoever it is had better have a quite good reason for disturbing us at such an ungodly hour," Sister Catherine replied as she stood in the kitchen kneading dough for the children's breakfast.

Sister Mary trudged her way to the door, feeling each stride in her arthritic knees. At the entrance, the rusty holders squealed as she slid the large iron bar across to free the large oaken door. A bitter breeze greeted her, numbing her face as the early morning sun peeked through the opening. Seeing no visitor, she scanned her eyes up and down the lane. A typical early winter's dawn. Nobody about. The uninviting cold kept sensible people indoors at this time of day. A light coat of virgin snow covered the street, the stairs approaching the doorway, and the wooden handrails surrounding the entrance. "Nobody here?" shouted Sister Mary.

Just as she was about to retreat, she heard a little alerting cry below. She cut her eye downward to the source of the sound. A brownish hand-woven wicker basket rested on the straw welcome mat. Inside the basket, peeking over the top of the white woolen blanket, were the emerald green eyes of a baby—eyes that caught Sister Mary's gaze and held it. Then the baby made a little gurgling sound, as if to say, "Who are you?" while making a cute expression that caused the ends of Sister Mary's lips to curl into a tender smile. She crouched down and picked up the basket. "Now who do we have here," she mumbled, scanning up and down the vacant street a second time in search of whomever left the newborn.

Nobody. Oddly, there were no footprints or signs of activity. Snow was falling, but not so heavily as to have covered up footprints. She shrugged, and stepped back inside the orphanage. Using her weight, fighting a gust of wind, she pushed the door closed with her back. She then hurried to Sister Catherine carrying the basket. "Catherine, look, a baby."

Sister Catherine peeked into the basket. Short black strands of hair covered the baby's head. "She is so cute," Sister Catherine said, lifting up the blanket covering the baby. Embroidered in black wool on the baby's small white cotton shirt was the name Sophia. "I guess her name is Sophia," she said.

"That's a fine name," Sister Mary said, wondering why anyone would leave a baby as perfect as this. When mothers left their babies due to poverty, the newborn arrived naked or wrapped in rags. The basket and clothes alone ruled out poverty. "I guess we have a new member of the orphanage."

"I guess we do," Sister Catherine replied.

Sophia's flailing arms reached out and wrapped her small hand around Sister Mary's finger. "Oh, look, her fingers are so tiny," Sister Mary said. A strange tingling sensation flowed through Sister Mary's finger, up her arm, and spread throughout her body leaving goose bumps in its wake. The feeling was pleasant and lent a sense of comfort and relief. Oddly, the arthritis pain in her knee, which had plagued her since she turned fifty six years before, at once eased. She thought about mentioning the sensation to Sister Catherine but decided it may have simply been the joy of Sophia's touch. A placebo effect.

"Where are we going to put her?" Sister Mary asked, wiggling her finger back and forth, playing a kind of tug-a-war with Sophia.

"I can dig out the old wooden cot in the attic," Sister Catherine replied. "It'll need a dusting. We can keep the cot in our room to avoid waking the other children during the night when she needs a feed."

Sister Mary beamed. "That sounds lovely." It had been some time since she had the pleasure of caring for a baby. The orphans, commonly labelled "abandoned children," came from a variety of backgrounds but typically entered the orphanage after the age of four because the parents were too ill or too poor—thanks to bank closures and businesses folding—to provide for them. Saint Juliana of Pavilly Orphanage was one of the better orphanages in which a child could end up. It had nothing in common with the many orphanages in which the violence and neglect were so horrific that the children preferred running away and taking their chances on the street.

The sound of Sophia breaking wind followed by a pungent smell changed Sister's Mary expression from one of joy to distaste. She screwed up her nose. "Oh, I think Sophia has made a delivery of her own."

Sister Catherine let out a small laugh. "That's my cue to go search for the cot. I'll let you handle the delivery, dear."

"Not all duties of a mum are pleasant, are they?" Sister Mary said, lifting Sophia from the basket and planting a feather light kiss on her forehead.

After changing Sophia, Sister Mary took her to their bedroom to check on the progress of Sister Catherine and the cot. On entering the room,

Sister Mary was surprised to see the cot fully set up. The room, which had an air of holiness, contained two single beds, one on each sidewall; a small window opposite the door; a rather old worn cupboard that had seen better days; an oak dresser with a large oval mirror above it; an oil painting of Jesus at the Last Supper hanging above the bed; a wooden crucifix nailed on the back of the door; and a ceramic statue of Mother Mary sitting on the dresser. "You were quick, Catherine," she said.

"Thank God the cot wasn't too far packed away in the attic," Sister Catherine said, wiping down the sides of the cot with a damp cotton rag. "I only had to move a few things to be able to drag it out. A few more swipes here and her bed should be ready."

Sister Mary rested on her bed cradling Sophia, rocking her gently back and forth. Sophia's eyelids opened for an instant and then struggled with an invisible weight pulling them shut until at last they lost the fight. They repeatedly tried again, opening a little less each time. "Looks like our little girl needs a rest."

"Well, I think her bed is ready," Sister Catherine replied. The basic cot was of simple design: Four barriers made from painted white timber slats, similar to a picket fence, surrounded the base. Inside a dainty pillow rested atop a soft straw mattress covered with a hand-crocheted white blanket.

Sister Mary carried Sophia over to the cot and placed her gently under the blanket. Sophia began to whimper, obviously preferring the arms of Sister Mary and the gentle comforting rocking motion.

"Oh," Sister Catherine said, opening a small brown wooden box on her bed from which she retrieved from an old mobile. "I found this." She held up the mobile, a large wooden crucifix tethered to a string. Attached to each side of the horizontal beam of the cross were three strings, equally spaced and each two inches in length, from which dangled smaller crucifixes. Sister Catherine stood on the cot and attached the mobile to a small hook protruding from the ceiling so it dangled above the cot. Sister Catherine gave the large crucifix a quick spin. Sophia's gaze was drawn to the cross and her crying settled. The smaller crosses danced their own style of courting, rotating in different directions as the main crucifix revolved. Before long, Sophia's eyes closed and she fell into a peaceful sleep.

Sister Mary whispered, "Well, we had better be finishing breakfast. The children will be awake soon." Sister Catherine nodded. Together, they left the room. Sister Mary glanced over her shoulder, beaming with grace as she watched Sophia resting so tranquilly. "It appears God has blessed us with another little one."

"That it does," replied Sister Catherine. "That *it* does."

Chapter 3 - Miracles

1875 - Thirteen years later

The mid-afternoon sun vanished behind dark clouds, growing in height and width, like grungy soapsuds expanding in sloshy water. These suds, though, were black and menacing. A flash of light erupted, followed by a jagged streak of bright light darting to the ground several miles away. Shortly afterwards, the earth rumbled. "We need to get back to the orphanage," Sophia said. She was sitting next to Anne on the wooden platform of the treehouse with her legs dangling over the side.

Anne gazed towards the heavens. Her eyes widened in alarm. "Ooh, those clouds do look awful. Perhaps we should stay here."

For nearly a month, Sophia and Anne had been busy building their home away from home, a comfortable treehouse nestled in amongst the large branches of an ancient sprawling maple. Several planks of rough wood secured by a tattered rope and set between two large branches formed the floor. The source of their building materials was an old lumber mill on the eastern side of the forest, which, according to legend, was haunted by ghosts at night. Sophia had used her graceful well-mannered speech and sweet innocent smile on the owner, a Mr. Brumby, who rarely refused her requests to take off-cuts and other scraps. For the roof, they had gathered hornbeam branches, which they weaved together and secured to higher branches to create a small dome over the wooden floor. There were no walls other than the surrounding leaves and branches of the maple tree. To climb into the treehouse involved mounting a waist-high branch, pulling up to a higher branch, and then jumping across to the wooden floor, which was about four feet off the ground. Their next planned task was to build a ladder to make entering and exiting easier.

"I don't think our hideout will offer us much protection from the storm," Sophia said, looking at the porous ceiling of Hornbeam branches that formed the roof of the treehouse. She imagined the ceiling being peeled off by gusts of wind tearing through the trees.

Anne's voiced quivered. "But what if we get struck by lightning?"

Sophia recalled an adoption day at the orphanage four years earlier, when both girls were nine. Anne, who was two weeks younger than Sophia and had come to the orphanage at the age of four, had looked into Sophia's eyes with a look of fear and sadness and said, "But what if we get separated?" Over the years, their friendship had developed into a tight sisterhood. Some people actually mistook them for sisters since they were of similar height and build and both had striking green eyes and black hair. On every adoption day Anne and Sophia huddled towards the back on the room away from the other children so as not to be seen by parents looking for a child to adopt. Most children wanted to be adopted, but not Sophia and Anne, who feared being separated.

Only rarely did a couple want to adopt more than one child, and then it was only two children under four. Whenever a prospective parent expressed interest in one of the girls, they would pretend to fight and act like uncontrollable children. That day four years earlier, however, their stunt had not worked: Sophia was chosen. Tears cascaded down Anne's face as the adoptive male parent dragged Sophia by her arm out of the orphanage.

Sophia had other ideas. Before boarding the waiting carriage, she stomped on the man's foot. He turned, yelled an obscenity, and slapped the child across the face with such force it sent her tumbling across the paved street. Sister Mary came charging out of the orphanage at once with a closed umbrella in hand. She approached the man and wacked him first on the left shoulder, then on the right, and proceeded to poke him in the gut, while yelling, "You get out of here and don't come back. You should never treat a child like that, no matter what she has done!" Sophia had run back inside the orphanage and cuddled Anne in the corner of the adoption room, where she whispered, "We'll be fine. Nothing will separate us."

"We'll be fine," Sophia said, as another lightning bolt split the bruised sky. She lowered herself over the side of the treehouse and dropped to the ground. "Come on."

"Okay," Anne said. She followed Sophia down from the treehouse.

While waiting for Anne, Sophia tied the laces on her new off-white saddle shoes, which hurt her feet. After wearing them for a day blisters would form on the back of her heels. She never complained because it was so rare to receive anything new at the orphanage. The only distinction between the left and right shoe was where her big toe had started to stretch the leather. Anne had the same shoes, except hers were beige.

"I'm ready," Anne said.

Her shoelace tied, Sophia dashed through the forest, swerving left and right to avoid the trunks of various kinds of trees, ducking under branches, hurdling small logs, evading loose rocks, and leaping minor crevices just waiting to trip her up. Anne, breathing heavily and falling further behind, yelled, "Sophia, wait! Slow down. I can't keep up."

Hearing Anne's plea, Sophia paused, scanned the hostile sky, and said, "We need to keep going. The storm will be here soon."

"But I can't," Anne said, bending over, clutching her knees, and drawing in a deep breath, "run as fast as you."

Sophia knew that she was much faster than Anne, even when she was only moving a third of her maximum potential, as she was then. Her speed and dexterity often annoyed others, so she had learnt to forcefully tone down her agility. Sister Mary and Sister Catherine often called her "Speedy."

After Anne caught her breath, they ran through the forest together at a pace comfortable for Anne, until stopping abruptly at the edge of a deep ravine nicknamed *dead man's gorge*. "We need to cross quickly," Sophia said, retreating a step from the edge and thankful she had been running at Anne's pace or she might have toppled over. "Once the rain starts this creek will quickly turn into a raging river."

Anne bobbed her head as if stuck between yes and no.

Sophia put her hand on Anne's shoulders and looked her in the eyes. "You can do this." This was not the first time she had crossed the ravine and Sophia wondered what troubled her. They typically crossed at a much shallower point to avoid the treacherous steep sides.

"Okay, but don't rush me," Anne replied. She began to side-step down the rocky steep wall of the ravine, leaning steeply to one side to counteract the slope. Within a few feet of the top, Anne's leading foot landed on a loose rock and she began to slide, picking up speed. She tried leaning inwards to slow her momentum but overdid it and tumbled forward as her feet regained traction. She landed with a cruel thud on her left shoulder. From there she rolled, bounced, tossing and turning alternatively off her elbows and knees, picking up new bruises and cuts on each uncontrolled rotation.

Sophia chased after her, trying to think of a way to slow Anne's fall and coming up empty. Then she heard a loud snapping sound, like a branch being broken, mixed with Anne's pained cries. She watched as Anne came to an abrupt halt at the bottom of the ravine and lay in the cold shallow waters of the creek. Anne's cry rang out over the sounds of the distant thunder as the creek water around her turned red. At the midpoint of her lower leg between here the knee and foot, a jagged bone protruded from the broken skin.

Sophia rushed down, heart racing, limbs trembling, and knelt beside Anne, wondering what to do. The storm was fast approaching, the intervals between the loud claps of fierce thunder shortened and bright flashes of lightning lit the dark sky. Sophia realized the flooding rain was mere moments away. She thanked God in her thoughts they were upstream of the storm. "Apart from your leg," Sophia asked, "do you have any other pain?"

Between gulps of uncontrolled sobbing Anne replied, "I hurt all over, but mainly my leg."

Sophia gently rolled Anne onto her back to enable a better view of her leg. The broken shinbone protruded about an inch from the surface of the breached skin. From the reddish color of the surrounding water, Sophia could tell Anne had lost quite a bit of blood. Feeling a strange draw, Sophia placed her right hand just below the protruding bone and her left hand on Anne's thigh. A white glow started to form around Sophia's hands. At first startled, Sophia pulled her hands away, until, sensing the mysterious draw for a second time, she placed them back on Anne's leg. Slivers of white light streamed from her hands into the open wound. Anne began to shake, as if she was having a seizure, as the obtruding bone slowly retracted through the open wound and disappeared into Anne's flesh. The skin above formed over the gash and in a matter of seconds all signs of a wound vanished.

Anne stopped shaking. She glanced down at her leg. She dug her feet into the creek bed, pushing herself away from Sophia. "Are you a witch?" she said, her voice shrill and eyes wide.

"No, at least I don't *think* I am," Sophia replied, rotating her hands in front of her own gaze wondering how she had just done what she did.

Anne rose to her feet. "I feel great." She patted herself down seemingly searching for injuries. "But how—" She shot Sophia a look and shrugged. "How did you do that?"

Raindrops began to fall, lightly at first and then without warning in great sheets. "I don't know," Sophia responded. "We should keep this a secret." The water in the creek bed began to rise. "Quickly, we must get out of this ravine, Anne." Sophia reached out and offered her hand to Anne. After a moment of hesitation, Anne took Sophia's hand. With Sophia taking the lead, hand in hand they clambered up the opposite side of the ravine.

The intense cleansing rain washed the blood from Anne's clothing and body. No sign of injury remained; it was as if her fall had never happened. Side by side they ran, holding hands, back towards the safety of the orphanage. Lighting struck regularly around them followed by the deafening boom of rumbling thunder. Neither the flashes nor sound bothered either of them. Sophia's mind was still lost in reconciling the healing event. As they approached the orphanage, Sophia spotted Sister Mary calling out and running towards them, holding a sheet of fabric above her head as if to keep herself dry from the hammering rain. The three of them huddled together under the makeshift umbrella as they moved swiftly to the warm dry comforts of the orphanage.

Anne and Sophia appeared as two drowned rats. Their long black soaked hair dangled over their shoulders and down their backs. The waterlogged clothes they wore stuck like glue to their shivering cold bodies. Water dripped leaving large puddles on the floor.

Sister Catherine approached with a towel. "What on earth have you two been up to?" She shook her head as she patted them down with the towel. "You're lucky God and his angels watch out for you. You could have been killed in that storm."

Teeth chattering, in unison they replied, "We're sorry, Sister."

"I'll go prepare a warm bath for you," Sister Mary said with a little smile as she turned to make her way to the upstairs bathroom. Sophia heard Sister Mary mumble as she shook her head, "Those two, always up to something, will be the death of me."

Chapter 4 - Runaways

Several Weeks Later

The ocean seemed restless, irritated by an uneasy wind whipping in ever-increasing gusts. Sister Mary, standing on the shore in bare feet, allowed the granules of the warm sand to squirm between her toes as she watched the unsettled waves crashing against shore. Somehow something was not right on this day, however, for the peaceful place she came to in her mind during her afternoon nap was troubled.

Another gust of aggressive wind immersed her. She clutched her veil to prevent it from being swept away. "Mary," a powerful and sincere male voice sounded from behind her. Startled, she spun around and found standing behind her a handsome man, perhaps in his late thirties, dressed in a dazzling white suit. His appearance and demeanor were amiable appearance, and charisma radiated from his warming smile and his deep ink-blue eyes. The sensation of being close to him, even in a dream, seemed familiar to Mary, like being close to Sophia. In the shadow of his broad-rimmed white hat, his hypnotizing stare captivated her. She blushed and made to turn her eyes away, but couldn't. She wondered why the unruly wind had not claimed his dignified hat as she fought to cling to her veil. *I'm dreaming,* she thought. *Anything is possible.*

"Who are you?" she asked, eyes narrowed.

"Diniel," he replied, with a single nod. "It's a pleasure to meet you, Sister Mary. Your work protecting the infants does not go unnoticed."

"Unnoticed by *whom?*"

Diniel looked towards the darkening sky and made another single nod. "Mary, there isn't much time. They have located Sophia. You need to help her flee."

Mary shook her head, pondered why this mysterious man was giving her orders. Her brows lowered. "Who? Why?"

"The storm is coming. Here, take this." Diniel held out his steady palm on which rested a silver crucifix glowing with a faint white aura. It was attached to a loop weaved of snowy cotton thread. "Give this to Sophia."

Mary reached out and took the necklace. "How? This is a dream. When I wake up it will be gone."

"I must go," he said. "Do as I say. The future depends on her survival."

"Wait," she said, her tone a little impatient. "What is going on?" The squalls increased. Mary's feet began slipping in the soft sand. She leaned into the cold harsh gusty wind to help steady herself. Diniel once again gazed upwards. Black charcoal-colored clouds filled the intimidating sky. A single bolt of intense lightning forked from the darkness, momentarily blinding Mary. The strike connected with Diniel, consuming him in a radiant white explosion of energy: he vanished.

After her sight restored, Mary cut her eyes across the beach searching for Diniel. Unable to find him, pressing her knuckle against her lips, she returned her concerned gaze to the ocean. Volatile waves, triple their normal size, crashed threateningly into the beach. Every second surge travelled far enough up the sands to soak her ankles. As the cold foamy water retreated, the shrewd rip of the sea around her feet tried to drag her into the enraged ocean.

Distant screams mingled with the sound of booming thunder twisted through the wind. The cries for help grew louder as the rumbling in the clouds softened and her surroundings began to fade. Mary began to rock, very methodically, back and forth. She opened her eyes to find Anne pulling at her shoulders, tears welling in her eyes, shouting desperately, "Wake up."

"Steady down, Anne," Sister Mary said, taking Anne's hands from her shoulders. "What on earth is the matter?"

Anne pulled at her hands. "Come quickly! He has Sister Catherine."

As Sister Mary rose from her favorite napping chair, a silver cross necklace fell to the floor. She reached down and picked it up. "This can't be," she muttered.

"What?" asked Anne, tugging at her arm. "You need to come quickly."

"Okay, Anne, I'm coming." Sister Mary followed Anne out of the sitting room and to the top of the stairs. The sight below turned her stomach. Sister Catherine was kneeling before a man whose face was concealed by a long red cloak trimmed in gold. Surrounded by a faint red mist, his hand gripped Catherine's forehead. Her mouth was open at a peculiar angle and appeared paralyzed as the man shouted in a menacing yet measured tone, "I'll not ask you again, where is Sophia?"

"Come quickly," Sister Mary whispered, dragging Anne out of sight of the man below. "Where is Sophia?"

"She is in our room under her bed, hiding from the man."

"And the other children?"

"They're with Sister Margaret. They went to the park. Me and Sophia didn't want to go."

"Sophia and *I*," Sister Mary corrected, trying with fierce intent to stay strong. She fought the tremors of fear that threatened to shake her, knowing that for the children's sake she had to keep her composure. "Quiet now, let's make our way to Sophia." Together they hurried to Sophia's bedroom as a shriek of agony echoed up the stairwell behind them.

"Will Sister Catherine be okay?" Anne asked.

Sister Mary knelt on one knee in front of Anne. Trying hard to keep the desperation in her heart from showing on her face, she said, "Yes. Whatever happens, God will look after her. You needn't worry." She told herself to do likewise, although she struggled to trust her own words as Sister Catherine's screams hampered her thoughts.

* * *

On seeing the feet of Sister Mary and Anne enter the room, Sophia slid out from under the bed. She ran directly to Sister Mary and hugged her tightly. Mary held the silver necklace up, said, "Sophia, take this. It will help protect you." Then she placed the necklace over Sophia's head so that the crucifix dangled over her chest. "Now Sophia, you need to go, leave this place, and don't return."

Sophia bit down on her lip to calm its quivering. Tears welled in her eyes and, though she tried to hold them in, they broke free. "Why? Have I done something wrong?"

"No, not at all, you beautiful child," Sister Mary said. She placed her hands on the sides of Sophia's head and wiped her tears away with her thumbs. She bent down and kissed Sophia on the head. "Come now, Sophia, you must go." Sister Mary then walked over and unlatched the bi-fold bedroom window and pushed it ajar. The gap between the two windowpanes was just wide enough to provide a passage out onto the shingled roof of the kitchen below.

Sophia stammered. "But, I, I d-don't w-want to go!"

"You have to, Sophia. Danger is present, and we have to keep you safe."

"Where should I go?"

"Seek shelter in the forest. Wait there a day or so, and then return, and we will find a better place for you."

Sophia was torn. She didn't want to leave the Sisters, the orphanage, her adopted siblings, and especially Anne. This was her home. Yet the anguish in Sister Mary's eyes helped Sophia make a decision. "Okay," she said.

Anne pulled on Sister Mary's robe. "What about me?" Anne said, apprehensive.

"Come with me, Anne," Sophia said. The statement came from her instinct to protect her best friend. "We'll be fine. Nothing will separate us."

Anne scrambled over to Sophia's side and looked at Sister Mary. "Please, please can I go with Sophia?"

Sister Mary seemed to weigh the request for a moment before saying, "Yes, it's probably for the best. Hurry now." She gently pushed them towards the window. "Be careful. May God's angels watch over you."

Sophia stepped through the window and onto the gently pitched roof. Once she got a stable footing, she reached back inside the window and helped Anne through. Together, taking care to be silent, they crawled towards the roof's end. Sophia glanced over the edge and calculated the drop to be nearly twice her height. She swung her legs over the side, put them together, and allowed herself to drop feet-first, bending her knees to absorb the impact. She hit the ground, fell forwards onto her hands, stood up, dusted off her palms, and gazed up to see Anne, peering rather sheepishly over the edge of the roof.

"I can't make that drop, Sophia," Anne whispered, chewing at her thumbnail.

"Hang on a second." Sophia surveyed her surroundings. After finding nothing suitable to help or serve as a ladder, she looked up at Anne and shook her head, whispered, "Lower yourself over the edge." After hesitating for a moment, Anne lowered herself over the side of the roof. Sophia grabbed her around the knees. "It's okay, I've got you. You can let go." Anne released her white-knuckled fingers. Anne's weight took Sophia by surprise and propelled her stumbling backwards. She tried to regain her footing but failed and fell onto her back with Anne crashing on top of her. Stuck under the weight of Anne sitting on her chest, Sophia gave her a gentle nudge and strained to say, "You can get off me now."

After gathering her thoughts—no doubt relieved that she had survived the fall—Anne hopped off Sophia's chest and stood up. "Sorry, Sophia." She reached out and helped Sophia to her feet.

"It's okay, Anne," Sophia said, smiling gently, "at least you had a softer landing." Deep down, Sophia was quite proud of Anne's bravery.

Holding hands, they made haste into the sheltering forest.

* * *

Sister Catherine, steeling herself against the physical pain racking her body, remained faithful as the shrouded man shouted, "I will not ask you again! Tell me where the girl is, and you can all go!" She shook her

26

head defiantly. A tear rolled around the corner of her contorted mouth. She clutched the wooden crucifix hanging from her neck in her right hand. She felt the tips of his fingers tightening against her temples as the red energy circling his palm grew brighter, more intense. After several seconds, the red glow dimmed and he removed his hand and shouted, "Die then."

Her muscles slackened, and she collapsed to the floor, overcome with pain, barely conscious. The man raised his hands and roared. The sounds of doors and windows slamming shut echoed throughout the orphanage followed by a few seconds of eerie quiet. Utter silence created an illusion of time stopping. Through her blurred vision, in what looked like slow motion, flames erupted from the base of the walls. Then time appeared to resume as the smell and sound of burning wood filled her senses. In a moment, the walls were ablaze in raging fires. The man faced the orphanage entrance, paced to the burning door, and then, as if the wood was made of liquid, passed through.

Moments later, Sister Mary came charging down the stairs and crouched beside Sister Catherine. "Can you rise?"

"I think so," Sister Catherine murmured, even though her muscles screamed *no*. She took hold of Sister Mary's hand and used the little strength she had remaining to rise to her feet. She leaned into Mary's hug and together they lumbered into the lounge room in search of a way out through the fire. It was no use. There was no breach for escape in the intense fire covering the walls. Navigating became increasingly difficult as smoke permeated the remaining oxygen and limited visibility. In the middle of the lounge, the two Sisters collapsed to their knees. With imminent death approaching, they closed their eyes, clutched their rosary, and began to pray. "The Lord is my strength and my shield; my heart trusts in him, and I am helped."

As life began slipping away, Sister Catherine noticed the appearing of a pearly glow, bright as the sun, which turned into a white shimmering oval-shaped portal. A man stepped forth from the radiant light.

"Diniel?" Sister Mary said.

"Yes, Mary, I'm here. Do not be afraid." He crouched in front of Sister Mary and Sister Catherine, took one of their hands in each of his, and prayed with them. A sense of peace flowed through Sister Catherine. All the fear she harbored vanished. Mary collapsed, conquered by the toxic smoke, and within seconds Catherine followed.

Chapter 5 - Mr. Brumby

The afternoon sun blended into the distant horizon and darkness overtook the tall trees of the forest. A swirling wind rustled the branches in high-pitched whispers and shadows seemingly stalked the girls. "You're doing great, Anne," Sophia said. "Only a little further now."

"Where are we going?" Anne's strides were labored, as if each of her feet were laden with a twenty-pound weight.

"To the shack near Mr. Brumby's Lumber Mill," Sophia said, as she snapped some branches blocking her chosen path. "We can hold up there for a day." A little deeper into a denser part of the forest, past several stalwart trees, they came to a shallow creek with water steadily flowing under thin sheets of forming ice. "Not far now. This creek leads directly to the shack."

In the fading light, Sophia stayed close to Anne as they navigated their way along the creek's edge, taking care not to step into the icy water. In the distance, the graying timber shack that straddled the creek like a bridge with only one entrance came into view. After crossing a few rickety wooden steps that wobbled under their weight, Sophia pushed the rusted door handle. The old hinges groaned, as if straining to support the heavy door. Their entry sent several grey mice scurrying through the gaps in the timber that lined the base of the walls. Not much inside—just six hay bales, a pitchfork, a gritty old glass windowpane overlooking the timber mill, and dusty cobwebs strung in the darker corners of the ceiling.

Sophia went straight to work. She pulled hay from the bales and used the soft strands to make two thick mattresses. "There we are. It's not the best bed you have had, but it's not bad."

Anne dropped onto the makeshift bed and tried to bounce. "It'll do nicely."

Sophia stuffed some strands of hay into the cracks of the walls to keep out the mice and other creatures—rodents, snakes, and insects. She shoved the two leftover hay bales behind the door to prevent anyone attempting to enter.

"How long will we stay here, Sophia?"

Sophia heard a quaver in Anne's voice and sensed her fear. Sophia knew that, ever since the day she healed Anne's leg, she had become the girl's rock, not merely a friend but someone she trusted and in whom she found comfort and protection. "Until the morning." Sophia gazed out the frosty window at the rising quarter moon peeking over the roof of the lumber mill. Her warm breath created patches of moisture on the glass that made it seem as though the surface of the moon was melting. "What are you feeling, Mr. Moon, happy or sad?" she mumbled, tilting her head from side to side.

Just then the handle on the door of the shack turned, the knob whining with a squeal of neglect. Encumbered by the hay bales, the door stubbornly resisted opening. Whoever was at the door pushed harder. Sophia's eyes widened and her heart thumped like a charging elephant. She grabbed the pitchfork and rose prepared to fight off the unwanted intruder. Anne huddled in the corner.

"Sophia, Anne? Are you in there?"

It was a man's voice, deep and bellowing, and Sophia recognized it after an instant as the voice of Mr. Brumby. "Yes, Mr. Brumby," she said, as yellowish light fluttered in through the partially open door. She exhaled a sigh of relief as her thumping chest resumed its gentle padding. She silently thanked God, rested the pitchfork against the wall, and then shoved the hay bales blocking the entrance into the corner.

Many times in the past, Mr. Brumby had left treats for them in the shack knowing that once or twice a month the girls came to the shack to play. Even though the Sisters had warned them against ever taking food from strangers, Sophia trusted Mr. Brumby. In fact, he was one of the few men she did trust after being struck by the man who had tried to adopt her. She had first ran into Mr. Brumby one day as he stood behind the local church house with welling sorrow in his eyes. He was standing before two gravestones, one etched *Jill Brumby 1838-1869*, the other *Jane Brumby 1863-1869*. Speech had eluded him that day. Sophia had wanted to ask who Jill and Jane were, but sensing his pain she had waited and asked Sister Mary that evening. Jill was Mr. Brumby's wife and Jane, his only daughter. The two had both passed away within weeks of one another after contracting tuberculosis. Sister Mary had told her that Mr. Brumby carried sadness on his shoulders ever since. All he had left in the world was his black border collie Dash, a shorthaired creature of joy who had a white patch over her right eye and would follow the man everywhere he went. Over the years, Sophia discovered that Mr. Brumby's lonely dismayed eyes illuminated with a little glint of joy whenever she and Anne came around.

Mr. Brumby stepped inside carrying an old metal lantern by an iron-ringed handle, rocking back and forth in his right hand. In his left was a brown paper bag. The flickering flames cast a buttery tint over Mr. Brumby's face that extenuated his depressed brown eyes. "What on earth are you two doing here at this time of the night?"

Anne sat upright on her bed content to watch as Sophia did the talking. In one rapid breath, Sophia said, "There was trouble at the orphanage. Sister Mary told us to hide out in the forest for a day. I thought this would be the best place to stay for the night. We can go if it's not ok—"

"No. It's okay." Mr. Brumby gazed at Anne and then turned his attention back to Sophia. "You can stay, of course. I only noticed you were here because Dash seemed to sense something in this direction."

"Sorry, Mr. Brumby," Sophia said, looking down at the floor. "We really should have asked, but night was falling and—"

He waved away her explanation with a little flutter of the bag in his hand. "You needn't stay out here. It'll be freezing tonight. You can come stay in my house, in the spare room."

"Could we?" Anne leapt to her feet, clapping her palms together.

Sophia bit her lip. "I'm not sure, Mr. Brumby," she said, her voice low. She scratched the side of her neck. "We might be putting you in danger."

"Nonsense, Sophia," he said, shaking his head. "Does anybody know you are here?"

"No, but Sister Mary knows we went into the forest."

"Come on," he said, gesturing towards the door. "All will be fine."

Anne took a step toward Mr. Brumby, but Sophia paused, let her eyes move from Anne to the walls of the shack and then finally back to Mr. Brumby. "If it's okay with you, Mr. Brumby," she replied, biting the tip of her fingernail, "I would prefer to stay here. I do appreciate your kindness."

Mr. Brumby appeared conflicted, as if he was torn between wanting to help directly by providing proper shelter and yielding to her heartfelt request. He paused for a moment before saying with a slight frown, "Okay, Sophia."

"Thank you, Mr. Brumby." Sophia stepped up to him and circled him with her arms and gave him a warm hug.

"Well, at least take these," he said. He set the lantern on the floor and reached inside the paper bag and retrieved two chicken-and-cheese sandwiches. "Fresh from the local town store," he said, his eyes sparkling with a hint of joy, as if taking a reprieve from their usual muted grief. "I'll cook myself up something different. Not much of an appetite for chicken and cheese tonight."

Anne snatched one of the sandwiches, said, "Thank you." She took a bite and while chewing a mouthful of sandwich said, "Thank you, Mr. Brumby." He struggled not to let his lips upturn. Sophia accepted the second sandwich with a gracious thank you.

"If you girls need anything, I'll be in my house behind the timber mill." He picked up his lantern, stepped outside and pulled the door closed.

As her eyes readjusted to the dark interior of the shack illuminated only by the pale moonlight through the frosty window, Sophia wondered if Mr. Brumby would go check on the orphanage to find out what was happening. She hoped that, if he did, he would wait until the morning. After returning the hay bales behind the door to prevent unwanted guests, Sophia and Anne sat down on their hay mattresses and finished eating their sandwiches.

Before long, they both lay back and stared at the ceiling of the dusty shack, watching the spiders move about their cobwebs. The arachnids were busy wrapping the insects that Mr. Brumby's gas lantern had lured into the shack. The captives shook frantically in the webs, fighting for their life, trying to escape. After Anne fell asleep, Sophia lay with her eyes closed but still awake, resting but staying alert.

For Sophia, the discomforting night was long. Every unexpected noise roused her attention. Every ominous shadow drew her watchful eyes. When the consoling sun began to rise, casting vibrant light through the shack's window, Sophia experienced a sense of relief. She continued to rest, allowing Anne to sleep until she heard the distressed wail of a dog barking in the direction of the lumber mill. One impatient bark after another punctuated piercing howls. Sophia peered through the fogged window trying to locate the source. No luck, for the pleas for attention seemed to be coming from the other side of the lumber mill. Most likely, from Mr. Brumby's house.

Anne rolled onto her side and then hastily flipped to the other, covering her ear with her shoulder. A moment later she turned onto her back. "Is that a dog?" she said, rubbing her eyes before rising to a sitting position.

"I think so," Sophia replied.

"Should we go see what it's all about?" Anne said, stretching her arms.

"Okay, but we need to be very careful."

Very carefully, they slipped out of the shack and, using the barking as a beacon for direction, headed towards the lumber mill. As they came around the side of the lumber mill, Mr. Brumby's house came into view. The front door of the two-story timber house, ripped from its hinges, lay out on the front lawn. "Stay here, Anne. I'll go have a look."

"But, I—"

"No buts," Sophia interrupted, pointing to the ground. "Stay here." Anne leant against the side of the mill with her arms folded across her chest. Her downturned smile told Sophia she was unimpressed with the order.

Sophia darted over to the sidewall of the house and then, crouching under the windows, sneaked slowly around to the front and onto the front porch. She peeked around the corner of the door and saw Mr. Brumby lying motionless on the floor. Next to him, snuggled into his side, was Dash who let out the occasional howl. Without waiting, Sophia rushed inside to attend to Mr. Brumby. Dash quieted her barking to a soft moan. Sophia placed her ear near Mr. Brumby's mouth, checking for the sound of breath. None. She shook her head gravely, wondering what to do next. Dash, her eyes reflecting Sophia's own grief, placed her head on Mr. Brumby's stomach.

Sophia's head jerked in the direction of a deep, corrupt voice. A man with a face dark as night hidden in the shadows of his red gold-trimmed cloak advanced down the stairs. "You are a hard girl to track down, Sophia." He raised his right hand. A red sphere rotating with charged energy formed on his palm. Dash charged at him, growling, as he continued down the stairs. Sophia rose to her feet, but before she could retreat, a red energy beam projecting from the sphere struck her violently in the chest. The beam lifted her as if she was weightless to within a hair's breadth of the ceiling. Dash leapt at the man, jaw open ready to bite. He extended his left arm and thumped the poor dog, the strike sending her tumbling backwards across the floor until she came to a painful halt near the entrance. She lay there unmoving, whining in pain.

"Sophia, Sophia, Sophia," the hooded man said. "You are one of the last. I have been hunting your kind down for some time. One by one, I have eliminated you."

"Who are you?" Sophia said, struggling to move against the force of the red energy holding her high up in the air.

"His name is Mephistophelian, but he is known as Mephis," a stranger wearing a white suit and a broad-rimmed hat said as he entered through the front door and stepped over Dash. The stranger knelt and placed his steady hands on Dash. Seconds later, Dash leapt to her feet, tail wagging, and sat attentively next to the doorway.

"You cannot interfere here, Diniel," Mephis said, turning his focus to Diniel while holding Sophia restrained near the ceiling with his beam. "Your God doesn't allow you to interfere in human affairs."

Diniel raised his hand. "It seems you forgot to the read the fine print." White bolts of energy shot out from his fingertips like lightning bolts and struck Mephis in the shoulders, propelling him backwards into the railings of the stairwell. The red beam holding Sophia disintegrated into tiny particles that dispersed. She fell to the floor. "Firstly, Sophia is a minor." Diniel raised his other hand. A single ball of white energy discharged from his palm. "Second, things are changing." The sphere collided into Mephis' chest, the force compelling him to one knee.

From his half-standing position, Mephis raised his left hand and jetted a red beam of tunneling energy towards Diniel. Diniel responded with a white energy beam—the two continuous beams collided and exploded into a fiery pink ball. The center point of the collision moved back and forth as if in a fierce tug-of-war match.

Arm shaking, Mephis seemed to exert more energy causing the explosive point to move closer to Diniel. In reply, Diniel, gritting his teeth, used his other arm to buttress his elbow, stabilizing his arm shooting the white energy. The conflict point inched towards Mephis. Diniel yelled, "Get out of here, Sophia! Go now, run!"

In a state of confusion mixed with fear, and with a hundred questions rumbling in her mind, Sophia did not question the order. She rose to her feet and on shaking legs scrambled out of the house. Dash followed as she returned to Anne. "We have to go," she said, grabbing Anne's arm, virtually dragging her from the wall. The three of them, Dash, Anne, and Sophia fled into the forest.

* * *

"You can't win, Diniel. You know that," Mephis bellowed as the red beam began to engulf the white. Diniel stumbled backward, the force seemingly overpowering him. Mephis rose to his feet, raising his other hand. A second beam of red energy extended, this one connecting with Diniel. The white beam faded as Diniel propelled backwards through the doorway. He lost his hat as he landed on the damp grass outside. He squirmed, trying to regain his strength, as Mephis approached.

"Have you any last words, Diniel?"

"There is one thing you'll never understand about some humans, Mephis—something that separates them from evil like you."

"And what is that, Diniel?"

"They are prepared to die," he replied as he wriggled backward along the ground, "out of love, to protect each other."

"Yes, that can be quite intolerable, as I have found with the Brumby fellow and others," Mephis said. He pulled a jagged-blade assassin's dagger from under his coat. "What about you, Diniel," he said, admiring his red glowing dagger, "are you prepared to die for them?"

"If it came to that, I would." Diniel concentrated hard on the front door of the house lying on the ground while continuing to draw Mephis' focus. The large piece of wood began to flutter, and then careered through the air and into the back of Mephis' head, knocking him forward to the ground. Diniel rose as he gestured a symmetrical figure eight symbol with his hands. A white glowing portal, shimmering and oval shaped, opened before him. He picked up his fallen hat and put it on, glanced back at Mephis, and then stepped through the gateway. The portal condensed to a single bright white dot and then vanished.

Mephis rubbed the back of his head as he gathered himself to his feet. He peered into the forest, tracing the outline of his dagger's blade with his fingers, mumbling, "Well, well, Sophia, looks like you have a friend."

Chapter 6 - Burned

The direction they ran was inconsequential to Sophia. Her only objective was to put as much distance between Mephis and them as possible and fast. All her questions—*Who is Mephis? Who is Diniel?*—could wait.

"Why - are - we - running?" Anne said, between gasps for air.

Sophia planted her feet and slid to a stop on the loose undergrowth of the forest. The air was filled with a medley of rustling wind, chirping birds, and buzzing cicadas. She faced Anne. "We should be far enough away now." Dash sat next to Sophia with her tongue dangling from her mouth, panting heavily.

Anne stood with hands on hips drawing in deep breaths. "Away from *what?*"

"It doesn't matter. But we must keep moving." Sophia wondered: *Where can we go?* A smell wafted past her nose, a scent of burning wood and … something else. Something foul, an odor she had never experienced before. "Can you smell that, Anne?"

"Yes, faintly." Anne drew in a deeper breath. She screwed her nose, pinched it, and exhaled through her mouth, as if to reverse the breath she drew. "It smells terrible!"

Trying to find the source, Sophia gazed skyward. The stand of tall sturdy trees blocked her view. "Wait here." She strode to the base of a silver birch tree. "I'll have to climb." Reaching up, she grabbed the lowest branch and heaved herself up. From there she mounted the next higher branch, then the next, staying close to the trunk, as she navigated the ascent. Far below, Anne, the size of a toy doll, chewed on the ends of her fingernails while staring up at her. As she broke through the tree's canopy, the source of the odor became visible. A gloomy cloud of black and grey smoke bellowed aimlessly upwards in the light breeze from the direction of the orphanage.

An empty feeling gnawed the pit of Sophia's stomach. Dreadful thoughts consumed her. *Is the orphanage burning? Did Mephis do to the Sisters what he had done to Mr. Brumby?* She lost her footing on the slick branch and began falling. Below, the cry of her name erupted from Anne. Falling ever faster, Sophia's world went black as her fear engulfed her senses, yet she refused to succumb to it and, by reflex, reached out and caught hold of a wooden limb. Hanging by her hands, fingernails tearing into the bark of the branch, she strained and pulled herself up and sat in the crotch of the limb. She paused a moment to allow her shaking hands to settle and catch her breath. Then crossed herself as she would when entering church and whispered, "Thank you." Carefully, she descended the silver birch.

As Sophia made the final small leap to the ground, Anne raced to her, arms wide. Sophia opened her arms and let Anne wrap her arms around her. She then closed her arms around Anne tightly and squeezed hard. Anne said, "Thank God you didn't fall."

"Oh, that was nothing," Sophia replied. But it was something. She closed her eyes and with her inner voice said *Thank you* a second time. "Did I scare you?"

Anne squeezed her tightly. "Maybe just a little."

"We have to keep moving," Sophia said. "The smoke appears to be coming from the orphanage."

Anne pouted as her eyebrows drooped. "The orphanage?"

Sophia unclasped Anne's arms from around her waist and pushed her away gently while keeping hold of one hand. Together, they trekked through the forest towards the orphanage.

The rank odor thickened until it became so vile that Anne pinched the end of her nose shut and breathed only through her mouth as they proceeded to the edge of the forest that surrounded the rear of the orphanage. Through the gaps in the trees, Sophia witnessed what she feared most. Smoke, black as a witch's cauldron, danced up from the burned remains of the orphanage. A single wall, charred black, remained standing at the far right. Inside the smoldering remains, only the staircase had survived the gluttonous flames, though a few steps were missing and the railings were burnt away.

Police patrolled the skirts of the orphanage and kept onlookers behind an imaginary line. Firemen armed with axes scoured the burnt remains. Sophia's gaze was drawn to something to her left, something dreadful that made her stomach ache and burn as it were a sponge having been violently wrung out. The scene so devastated her that her strength vanished and her legs buckled under her weight and she fell to her weary knees, heaving. Green bile rioted from her stomach, shot out of her mouth, and puddled on the burnt ground. Another lurch. Tears wet her cheeks as she struggled to collect herself. Anne stood silent, fixated on the scene. Two large black bags lay on the sidewalk and from the outline of the contents she knew what, who, they contained.

Dash came alongside Sophia, sat beside her and began licking the tears from her cheek. Sister Mary and Sister Catherine were her parents, mothers and father, whom she loved. Sophia stroked Dash lightly across the side of her head. Sophia felt responsible for the devastation all around her. She blamed herself for the death of her family and of Mr. Brumby. They were dead because Mephis wanted her. If it weren't for her, they would still be alive … all of them: the Sisters, and Mr. Brumby.

Fog started to infiltrate her thoughts. Her vision blurred. Her mind spun, as if she twirled madly on the spot fifty times and suddenly stopped. Her eyes stared vacantly at the sky. The image of black smoke masking the sun blurred and then faded into a scene of murky blackness. She passed out.

* * *

Voices, familiar tones, woke Sophia from her slumber. Lying on her back, her eyes opened on a clear blue sky framed by a canopy of gently swaying trees. She rolled her head in the direction of the voices. Up in her treehouse she saw Sister Mary and Sister Catherine sitting with their legs dangling over the side of the floor board. "Up here!" Sister Mary shouted.

Sophia closed her eyes, thinking: *This can't be real.* After a few seconds, she opened her eyes and took a second glance. Towering above her with his hand outstretched, Diniel blocked her view. "Come: Get up," he said.

She reached out, grabbed his hand, and allowed him to pull her up. "Where am I?"

"A place created from your memories," Diniel replied.

"Oh…" Sophia gazed around. "This looks just like Anne's and my hideaway in the forest. Our treehouse."

"It is. It is a place where you feel safe."

"Oh," Sophia repeated. She directed her sight towards the Sisters. "And they are here, too?"

"Yes. They are with me for now."

"Oh." Sophia's eyebrows lifted, her lips pursed. She was at a loss for words. The sky grew dark as rain clouds formed amongst the roll of distant rumblings.

"Don't be upset, Sophia. You bear no responsibility for what happened. Sister Mary and Sister Catherine are fine. Trust me, they are."

Raindrops began to fall. Sister Mary whipped out an umbrella seemingly from thin air. "You are such a show off, Mary," Sister Catherine muttered as Sister Mary sprang the latch on the parasol causing its pure-white tarpaulin to spring to life.

"That's nothing," she said. "Watch *this*." Sister Mary then floated off the side of the treehouse. "I'm flying." Sophia's jaw dropped as Sister Mary glided through the air.

"Stop messing around this instant, Sister Mary," Sister Catherine said, slapping her hands down on the wooden floor by her sides. "Nuns are not meant to fly."

Sister Mary, twirling her umbrella, floated across the sky. "I think children would find a magical flying nun fascinating."

"I rather think not," Sister Catherine huffed.

Sophia shook her head. This was not the first time she had seen Sister Mary and Sister Catherine debating. In many ways, watching the two argue with such mock sternness amused her. On this occasion, although she was mesmerized at the sight of Sister Mary sailing through the sky suspended from the stem of an umbrella, Sophia sided with Sister Catherine, who made a valid point. Nuns are not meant to fly. But … on the other hand, she did think a flying nun was rather neat. So Sister Mary might be onto something with the "flying nun" business. Sophia's cheek muscles tightened pulling her somber lips into a tiny smile. The dark clouds began clearing, and the rain ceased. She looked to the sky. "Did … the weather just respond to my mood?"

"Yes," Diniel replied. "In this creation."

"Will you always protect me against Mephis?"

Diniel gazed towards the heavens. "I'm afraid, dear, that I've already done too much."

"So where do I go, Diniel? What do I do now?"

As Diniel began to speak everything grew dimmer until it faded into a blackness. The weird spinning sensation returned, overcoming her as she heard the words echo around her thoughts. "Seek out Jeremial of the Order of Esdras."

* * *

Sophia opened her eyes. Anne, with weeping eyes, stood over her. A tear momentarily bulged in the corner of Anne's eye before falling onto Sophia's lips and slipping to the tip of her tongue. The salty sensation stimulated her taste buds. "It's okay, Anne. I'm here." She rose, then reached out and pulled Anne towards her. "We'll be okay," she said, rubbing Anne's back.

"What are we going to do now?" Anne asked, dropping syllables from the words in her snivels.

"Find Jeremial of the Order of Esdras."

"Who's he?"

Sophia retreated out of her embrace with Anne, shaking her head. "I have no idea."

Chapter 7 - Mephis

Jack descended the wooden steps, some of which creaked as if complaining about being disturbed, leading into the basement of an ordinary Whitechapel home. In the basement, illuminated by the glow of gas lanterns, Mephis sat at a tanned oaken table scrawling on scrolls with a quill. Without his shrouded hood on, Mephis' auburn eyes contrasted with the pale white skin of his well-aged face, an oval elongated by a low-set jaw and bald head. On Jack's approach, he set the quill down and turned his soulless eyes to the man. "So, Jack, did you get it?"

"Yes, Master," Jack replied, shuffling his feet towards the desk on which he placed a black leather doctor's bag.

The left corner of Mephis' mouth raised, creating a deep crevice that bisected his cheeks. "Well, well, Jack, you might have a place with me after all."

"Thank you, Master," Jack said, bowing his head. "May I ask why Master needs the human remains?"

"It appears that my target, Sophia, has attracted the attention of Diniel and his ilk. For what reason I do not know. However, it may make the task of assassinating her by direct measures more complicated. Nevertheless, with the use of sorcery, I may be able to achieve my goal by other means."

Jack nodded. "I see, Master." Before Jack met Mephis, he believed magic to be mere illusions and nothing more. Now he knew different. Mephis, a sorcerer by definition, used magic, not ordinary magic but dark magic that draws power from red energy—a force invisible to humans created by their negative emotions or in more precise terms *sin.* When abundant red energy was absent, Mephis drew the energy from the remains of humans stained by depravity to perform his devilish spells.

Mephis rose from behind his desk and strode over to the far wall strung with dozens of hand-drawn portraits in the shape of a genealogical family tree. All the sketches had an X scrawled across them in red ink except one at the end of a long list of descendants: A picture of Sophia. Jagged red lines crisscrossed the whites of Mephis' slightly bulging eyes as he stared at her image. "I've waited an extremely long time, Sophia, to end your line."

"Master, why is Sophia so important?"

Mephis stared blankly at Sophia's portrait as he spoke. "Her kind spread a white energy that drains the red energy, which is my power. The less power I have, the more difficult it is for me to create the gateway to the Underworld to allow my brethren of Shadows to enter this realm."

"The same energy you use on me, Master?"

"Yes, Jack," Mephis replied, nodding slowly as if he found the question disagreeable, "the same energy that keeps you alive."

Jack placed his hand on his belly and traced around the large lump growing beneath his skin. The day the doctor told him he had an incurable disease he offered his soul to anyone, or anything, who could extend his life. Soon afterwards, he ran into Mephis at a local pub. For nearly two decades, he has been Mephis' personal slave in exchange for perpetual remission of the malignant tumors inside his body that threatened to end his life.

Mephis returned to his desk, picked up the doctor's bag, removed an object wrapped in a blood-stained white cotton rag, and placed it on the middle of a small altar in the corner of the basement. Six candles, their golden holders inscribed with unrecognizable symbols, were set along the sides of the wooden altar. Two tall candles stood at either side of a grey stone tablet that rested against the back wall of the altar. Jack gazed at the phrase *cor aut mors* chiseled across the tablet. Though his limited Latin vocabulary impeded his understanding of most of Mephis's incantations, he understood this phrase to mean Heart or Death. Your choice between Heart—moral values, duty, and loyalty— or Death—to matter to no one, to have no integrity. The tablet appeared to offer a choice when harnessing its power. Jack discerned all too well the choice Mephis made.

With the end of his finger, Mephis touched the wick of each candle to start a flame. After all candles were lighted, he placed his hands on either side of the cloth wrapping and began chanting. Each spoken word carried a sense of power, an invisible force, vibrating glass jars on the shelf.

Jack wondered what the unintelligible words meant as he watched a thick purplish fog form between the two candles standing in front of the stone tablet. An image appeared inside the fog. A wood yard. The picture inside moved, as if they were viewing the scene from someone else's eyes, striding between the stacked logs. A brown snake as long as a man's arm slithered into view.

Mephis rolled his shoulders, squinted, clenched his teeth, and rubbed his hands together. "Let's see how you deal with this, Sophia." He began a new chant, this one more ominous. A scarlet glow formed around the cloth covering the human remains. As his chanting continued, the glow turned into dancing streaks of red energy circling the cloth. His chanting grew louder and faster as he passed his hands over the top of the cloth. His head lurched backwards, and he let out an agonizing wail as the red energy diverted into his palms. Several seconds passed as his body shuddered with the influx of energy that continued entering his body through his palms. Then in an instant the red energy vanished and he regained his normal composure. The bloodied cloth lay abandoned on the altar, the sacrifice within consumed. The purplish fog dispersed. "Clean up the altar, Jack," Mephis said, returning to his desk.

"Master, what did the spell do?" Jack asked as he began cleaning the altar.

"A little embellishing." He glared at Jack with pupils fully dilated, as if demon possessed. "Something I wouldn't need to waste my powers on if you had done your job thirteen years ago."

Jack tilted his head down and shuffled his feet. "I will not fail you again, Master." He wrestled to believe his own words. He was not convinced that, in the same situation, he would carry out the task as commanded.

Mephis' pupils flinched to black dots no larger than pinheads as the red blood vessels in the whites of his eyes reddened. "You had better not!"

Chapter 8 - What now?

Followed closely by Anne and Dash, Sophia trekked through the trees towards their secret treehouse hidden in the depths of the forest. *How do we find Jeremial?* she contemplated. Focusing all her mental energy on trying to find a solution to that problem drowned darker thoughts about Mephis and about Mr. Brumby and the Sisters' demise. For that, she was thankful. The single-minded pondering gave her stomach respite from constant churning.

Suddenly, Anne sprang in front of her, blocking her way forward. "Books! We might be able to find out about Jeremial through books!"

Sophia's eyebrows fidgeted as if they were tussling between good idea, bad idea. "But where are we going to find books that contain information on Jeremial?" She paused, pulled at the lobe of her ear trying to jog her memory. "What was it again … the Order of Esdras?"

"Last year Sister Mary took me to the Order of Cistercians, a monastery in London," Anne said, bouncing on the tips of her toes, seemingly overjoyed with her recollection. "She called them the 'White Monks.' They had a whopping library, full of all sorts of books."

Sophia edged closer to Anne. "Do you remember where it is?"

"Hmm, sort of, let me think." She rubbed her chin before continuing in a more buoyant tone. "It was near a big park, um, Hyde Park. Sister Mary took me there to see the gardens after we left the monastery because I was well-behaved while waiting for her to finish her tasks."

In the back of her mind, Sophia wondered how Sister Mary had managed to keep Anne's intrinsic curiosity at bay, in a library of all places, without her getting into some sort of trouble. It wasn't that

Anne was disobedient just curious and a little mischievous in her curiosity. Knowing Anne well, Sophia pictured her wanting the book on the top shelf of a two-story bookstand and climbing up the shelves without a ladder to reach it. Book in hand, she would look down, realize her height, and freeze. At that point, she would cry for help. It was just such exploits that had led Sophia to give her friend the pet name CTL, short for *Charge in Think Later*. Bringing her thoughts back to the present, Sophia asked, "What did Sister Mary do there?"

"I'm not sure," Anne said, shaking her head slowly left and right, pursing her lips. "She just said she had business to attend to."

They resumed walking. "I don't know, Anne. It's a long way into the heart of London on foot, a good day's walk at least."

Sophia contemplated Anne's idea as they progressed deeper into the forest. The more she did, the more the concept seemed to be their best option.

With a jubilant leap, Anne said, in a higher pitch than normal, "I know! We could take the Shillibeer from town."

"The Omnibus?" Sophia's head jutted back. "We can't afford a ticket."

"It's large. We might be able to sneak on."

Sophia glanced towards the early morning sun hiding behind a thin sheet of whitewashed cloud. "It'll be worth a try." She stopped, changed her course towards town, and resumed striding through the forest, quicker now, with a purpose and direction. Before long, though, the undergrowth thick with many species of fern grew denser and inconsiderate of their trespassing. They trudged through the shrubs, pushing leaves aside, stomping lower vegetation to the ground. Dash appeared to have an easier time, maneuvering amongst the underbrush, vanishing at times, below the leaves of the various plants. After an hour of driving through the dense foliage, they came to the small creek, which Sophia recognized as the waterway that led to the shack near the lumber mill. The foliage-free banks of the creek provided a welcome reprieve and easier path to follow. Half an hour later, on approaching the shack, they heard muffled voices from some way off. Sophia squinted into the distance to locate the sound. "There's police across the field near the lumber mill. They'll be checking on what happened to Mr. Brumby."

"But … why?" Anne said, allowing the word to drag longer than it should. "Is Mr. Brumby okay?"

Sophia looked at the girl, thinking: *Does Anne need to know Mr. Brumby is dead?* A dilemma. The ordeals over the last twenty-four hours created enough emotional weight to topple a resilient mind, never mind Anne's fragile, loving conscience. Sophia had little doubt that the turmoil bothered Anne more than she was letting on. But she did have the right to know, for Mr. Brumby was as much Anne's friend as he was her own. She decided at the moment to change the subject. "We'll sneak around the back of the lumber mill, through the wood yard. We'll climb over the fence and come out at the side of the dirt road leading into town."

"But what about Mr. Brumby?"

"Come on now, we've got to get to London. We can talk about him later."

The color drained from Anne's face, leaving it whiter than normal, and Sophia knew that Anne had come to her own conclusion as to the welfare of Mr. Brumby. "I'm sorry, Anne," Sophia said.

They walked a short while in silence until they came to the wood yard. "This is creepy," Anne said, gazing up at the intimidating stacks of logs.

The stacks were set close to each and formed log walls several times taller than the girls.

"Yeah, it kind of feels like we are mice in a maze," Sophia replied, skipping over a muddy puddle. Stiff gusts created disturbing screeching noises as the wind passed through the lumber piles. Sophia added, "Glad the sun is up."

Dash barked aggressively as if to sound a warning. Both Anne and Sophia turned their attention to where she barked. Sophia retreated as a long brown snake three times longer than she was tall and wider than her forearm slithered from the darkness between the wood lots. The treacherous snake hissed, its antagonistic pink forked tongue darting in and out, as it slivered towards them.

Anne, motionless, whispered, "What kind of snake is that?"

"I don't know. I've never seen one this big before," Sophia said, shifting only her eyes for something she could use as a weapon against the beast. "It's not from around here."

Teeth bared and growling, Dash charged. In defense, the snake, mouth open, fangs dripping with death, lunged. Dash leapt backwards, avoiding the strike. Sophia darted over to the right-hand side of the snake, dived into a forward roll while grabbing an arms-length branch. Without warning, the snake struck as she proceeded to rise from the roll. With her newly acquired stick, she deflected the attack of the serpent's head of to her left. Venomous spittle splashed across her arm. Sophia climbed up the stacked logs of the woodpile as if it were a ladder. The snake wasted no time in pursuing her; it rose up using its body to extend itself.

On reaching the top log, Sophia turned and poised on the edge. Trying to halt the snake's ascent, she struck out and swung the stick like a hammer towards the snake's head. She missed and lost her balance and tipped forward. With both arms spiraling in reverse circles, terrified, she attempted to regain her composure, but failed. Unable to stop the forward momentum, she toppled towards the snake. As she fell, she reached out and grabbed the snake's body, a foot below the head, and squeezed as tightly as she could, as if grabbing a fireman's pole. Under Sophia's weight the snake fell to the ground hissing and spitting as it struggled to free itself. Unable to find release from Sophia's grasp the snake wound its long body around her torso. After a few loops, the snake tightened its grip on Sophia.

As the tension of the serpent's coil began to squeeze her chest, Sophia's breathing became difficult. She tossed around her options. *If I let go the snake will surely bite, but if I keep holding on the snake will crush my ribs.* Dash joined the fight and wrapped her teeth around the snake's tail. She dug her front paws into the ground, reared backwards, and pulled on the extent of the snake attempting to draw the spineless creature off Sophia. Her efforts were in vain. Dash's strength was no match for the snake's great power. Sophia stabbed at the snake with the stick she wielded, but its thick-scaled skin defended against her thrusts. Her breathing started to labor. Her strength began to wane. The snake increased the contraction as if sensing approaching victory.

Armed with a sharp-pointed stick of her own, Anne moved herself in front of the snake. Her arm shaking, too scared to watch, she covered her eyes and jabbed the stick towards the serpent. The snake hissed, jaw fully extended, its exposed poisonous fangs dripping, and lunged towards her. Blinded by her own hand, Anne gallantly thrust the wobbly stick forward directly into the snake's approaching mouth. By fluke of the random movement, the stick penetrated the unprotected skin of the creature's upper jaw and passed into the brain. Uncontrolled and powerless, the snake wriggled and released its grip and Sophia wormed herself free.

After rising to her feet, Sophia ran to Anne and hugged her tightly. "Thank you." Dash watched Sophia and Anne embrace, tilted her head to the side, and made a slight contented murmuring sound.

"Is it dead?" Anne asked, her body trembling.

"I think so," Sophia responded, glancing back at the snake as it wriggled aimlessly, weakly. Her eyebrows raised in disbelief. She moved to one side of Anne and faced the snake. With her arm outstretched, she pushed Anne backwards as if to shield her, while retreating from the snake. Black smoke, thickening, began rising from the creature's skin while at the same time appearing to melt into the ground, until the venomous reptile vanished completely.

"How did it disappear?" Anne asked.

"I'm not sure." Sophia knelt down and ran her hand across the dirt where the snake had seemingly melted, shaking her head. "We have to keep moving. There are forces around that do not want us to find Jeremial."

"You'll get no argument from me."

They resumed navigating between the woodpiles heading towards the fence around the lumberyard.

On arriving at the base of the six-foot timber fence, Sophia moved into position to climb over. The cross beams at the two-foot and four-foot marks made an easy ladder to clamber up the side. A bark from Dash made her pause, however. "Hmm. How are we going to get Dash over the fence?" She checked the fence. The well-weathered palings were grey in color and some quite contorted. She pushed a paling where the base appeared to come away from the lower crossbeam. The paling moved outwards. After a few more shoves, the top nails gave way and the slather of wood fell to the ground on the other side. She tried the same strategy on the paling next to it, but that one was tough and wouldn't budge. She tried the one on the opposite side. It gave a little. Anne joined Sophia in thumping the bottom of the paling with their palms. Each time the paling moved slightly further away from the lower beam until at last it popped free. They did the same at the top, and the paling gave way. Dash, Anne, and Sophia squeezed through the gap created by the fallen palings and followed the dirt road leading from the lumber mill into town.

Chapter 9 - Town

As they reached the outskirts of Ashford, the sun was high in the sky and warmed their cheeks, but did little to fill their stomachs. They hadn't eaten since Mr. Brumby, the kind gentleman, had given them his chicken-and-cheese sandwiches. "Is that your stomach, growling Anne, or Dash's?"

"Mine. Sorry, Sophia," Anne replied, rubbing her stomach.

"We'll have to do something about that in town."

Sophia's eyes cut to the distant bell turret of the church in the center of town. She pointed in the direction. "That is where we will go. We can rest and be safe there."

On the town's main street, crowds of people, shoulder to shoulder, pushed and shoved around the many farmers' market stalls hawking all kinds of baked items, livestock, fish, fruits, vegetables, and cut meat. The smells that filled the air were heavenly. A little farther down the road, they came to the entrance of the church. Constructed of ragstone with bath stone dressings the church appeared to be one of the sturdier structures in town. Other buildings, mostly of medieval design, consisted mainly of aging wood.

Sophia turned to Dash. "Wait here." Dash, seemed to nod in obedience and then lay down and curled up on the ground next to the front entrance. Sophia followed Anne through the large doorway of the church. Several rows of empty pews, on both sides of a main walkway, faced a lectern centered on a pulpit in front of the far wall. Above that, a wooden crucifix spanned from floor to ceiling. Light penetrated the stained-glass windows in the church's clerestories and cast multi-colored God rays through floating dust particles, which created an ambience of cordiality.

"It's so quiet," Anne said.

"You wait here, Anne. You'll be safe. I'll go get us some food from the markets."

"But you have no money."

"Just wait here. Don't leave," Sophia said, gazing into Anne's curious eyes and thinking telling Anne to sit tight was rather like telling a playful puppy to stay.

Outside the church Dash walked beside Sophia as she paced down the market street. With her hair disheveled and clothes grubby from tussling with the snake, Sophia approached a stall selling baked goods. A man cut her a stern look, eyed her cautiously, as he greeted her. "What would you like, young girl?"

Sophia lowered her benevolent emerald green eyes and pouted. "A loaf of bread, please, mister, but I have no money."

"I'm not a charity," the man replied, obviously not convinced by Sophia's plea. "Be gone."

Dash growled at the man as Sophia relaxed her drooping lips into an upturned smile and turned away. She needed food, Anne needed food, and Dash needed food as well. Sophia wandered farther down the market street until she came to another bakery store with several loaves of bread laid out on a small stand. She considered asking the man standing behind the wooden rack nicely for a loaf but dismissed the idea for fear of rejection. She waited until the man was busy serving a customer and then walked up to the rack, snatched a loaf, turned around quickly, and shoved the loaf down her dress, hoping he hadn't seen her. Her hopefulness quickly diminished when she heard the words, "Stop! Thief!"

Sophia ran, weaving her way through the gaps between the shoppers. A whistle sounded in the background followed by another shout: "Stop! Thief!" She knew the *Bobbies* were on her trail. She was at a full sprint and the shrill cry of the whistle soon diminished. Then she heard, up ahead, off to her right, another whistle. *The Bobbies are trying to flank me.* She cut a hard right, Dash matching her stride for stride, down a side alley between rows of houses. From the far side of the alley a high-collared trench-coated Bobby appeared blowing his whistle. She spun to retreat. Her exit, but found her way blocked by a second Bobby. Both ends of the alley guarded she scanned the sides. Adjoining houses created impenetrable walls. Each increasing beat of her heart seemed to pump out the beading sweat on her forehead.

Hearing a smacking noise she turned her attention to the Bobby at the far end of the alley, who was advancing slowly, slapping his baton against his large hand. "You know what we do with thieves?"

I'm trapped, she thought. Her heart was a riot. Dash began growling, glancing left and right at each Bobby in turn. A clunk sounded and, suddenly, the Bobby's roundish top hat tumbled forward. The Bobby spun around. Armed with a large stone Anne steadied her aim. He slammed his baton into his hand. "Right you, little brat…" The Bobby ran towards Anne, tripped, toppling forwards.

Sophia focused on Dash, the *object* the Bobby had tripped over. "Good girl," she said. Without a moment's hesitation, she seized the opportunity and ran around the fallen Bobby towards Anne with Dash in tow. All three sprinted down the street parallel to the main street, with the sound of the Bobbies in pursuit echoing from behind. A distant sound of a train's whistle caught Sophia's attention. She shouted, "That'll be our ticket out of here."

Down another alley, across a yard, then onto a wider street they raced. Whistles sounded close behind, very close. Sophia dared not look back. Up ahead in the distance, the freight train, passing slowly through the street crossings, squealed its whistle. "Quick!" Sophia yelled. "We can make this." Sophia accelerated, her knees pumping higher at the start of each long stride. Anne and Dash, fuelled by adrenalin, did likewise. A few feet out from an open freight cart Sophia turned towards Dash and extended her arms. Using the outstretched arms as a makeshift step, Dash instinctively leapt into the freight car. Sophia reached forward, grabbed the edge of the freight car's door, and in one swift movement swung her legs onto the floor of the wooden car. With one arm hooked on the cusp of the door, she turned and thrust her other arm towards Anne. Fatigued, Anne stretched out her hand, trying to catch Sophia's hand. But rather than closing, the distance between their outstretched fingers grew wider. With each passing moment Anne slipped farther away, her eyes portraying a battle between hope and defeat.

The Bobbies were closing on her. "Come on, Anne, you can do this!" Sophia shouted, extending her arm as far as possible from the freight car door. Anne dug deep, deeper than she ever had before. She used her remaining energy to make a few long desperate strides and swung her arm out toward Sophia's palm. Their hands connected. Sophia closed her grip and, grunting, swung her into the freight car just as Anne's legs gave out. The Bobbies stopped, doubled over with hands on their knees, gasping for breath, staring at Sophia and Anne. One, red faced, threw his hat onto the ground.

Sophia waved cheekily to the Bobbies. "Goodbye!" She turned to Anne. "We made it."

Lying on the floor with her clothes drenched in sweat, Anne heaved for breath. "We sure did."

Sophia pulled the loaf of bread from beneath her dress and broke into three equal parts, one for each of them. Dash wasted no time in gulping down the food. Anne picked her bread into smaller pieces and chewed each morsel as long as she could before swallowing.

Chapter 10 - The train

Anne sat between two ragged bales of hay and leaned against the firm shell of the freight car and felt the vibrations of the clickety-clack of the train's wheels riding the rails through her back. "How long until we get to London?"

"I'm not sure," Sophia replied, chewing her last mouthful of bread. "Probably an hour."

"The sooner the better," Anne said, rubbing across the tip of her scrunched up nose. "This carriage stinks."

The wooden floor of the freight car was stained with oblong dark spots and the strong ammonia smell left no doubt what had painted them. Sophia was reminded of her times cleaning the bathroom at the orphanage. A group of orphaned boys had stayed with them for a few weeks while awaiting transport to an all-boys orphanage. Around the base of the toilet in the privy, the floor was stained with similar dark spots made by the boys who, too young or too careless, had missed the mark when relieving themselves. One evening at dinner Sister Catherine told the boys in front of everyone, "*If you can't aim your doodle with accuracy, please sit before peeing.*" The boys' faces lit up like overripe red tomatoes. Sophia smiled in the train as she had at the dinner table that night when the boys virtually died of embarrassment. She turned to Anne. "Yeah, I think they normally have cattle in here."

Dash scurried over to Sophia and rested her head on Sophia's warm lap. Her brown eyes stared up towards Sophia with a pleading, pat me, gaze. Sophia responded by gently stroking the hair on the top of Dash's head. "Anne, do you remember your parents?"

Anne bit down on her bottom lip and said, "No. Well sort of." She pulled at some loose strands of hay. "Sometimes I get glimpses of memory."

"Sorry," Sophia said, sensing Anne's uneasiness. "I didn't mean to bring up hurtful memories."

"It's okay." She wound a strand of hay around her index finger until it formed a tightly-coiled band. "My middle name—Angela—is the same as my mum's." With her thumb, she spun the hay ring. "What's yours?"

"Oh, I don't have a middle name," Sophia shouted over the screeching of the train's steel wheels grinding on the tracks as the carriage veered around a sharp bend. "Well, none I know of."

After the noise subsided, Anne said, "I was with them when they died." She wiped a lonely tear from her eye. "Sometimes I have nightmares about the accident."

Sophia continued to stroke Dash, staying silent as Anne recounted the incident.

* * *

On a dark rainy night, late in the year 1866, four-year-old Anne sat in the back of a bumpy horse carriage with her mother Angela. Anne peered through the window at the passing two-story upmarket buildings nestled side by side and illuminated by flickers of white light cast by the full moon threading its rays between gaps in the wispy sheets of miserable clouds. The glass fogged with each breath she exhaled. "How much longer until we get there, Dad?" Anne shouted.

Her father, seated on the driver's bench of the carriage wearing a dark brown trench coat and broad brim hat to shelter him from a light drizzle, shouted his answer above the clopping of the horses' trot. "Not long now, princess."

Without warning, the carriage came to a sudden stop, throwing Anne and her mum off their seat. Anne heard the horses rearing as she reseated herself. "Are you hurt?" Angela asked, hugging the girl to her side.

"I don't think—" Before Anne could finish her sentence the carriage accelerated. The horses galloped madly as if fearful for their lives. "What is happening, Mum?"

Her mum grabbed her hand. "I'm not sure." Anne could hear her father shouting, "Whoooa… Calm down boys …" trying to regain control of the horses. His words were in vain, for the carriage rocked steeply to one side as the horses charged around a sharp bend.

"I'm scared," Anne said, squeezing her mother's hand with all her strength. The black veil of her mum's hat covered her face. Anne wondered if, behind the darkness of the veil, she would see fear in her eyes. Another sharp turn, and this time the carriage did not right itself. The pitch violently tossed Anne into the door of the carriage, which was now its floor. Momentum propelled the carriage off the wet cobblestone street, across a short strip of grass, then over the embankment at the edge of a river. A loud splash echoed through the chilly night air as the carriage plunged into the icy waters. Water rapidly filled the carriage. Anne, her focus blurred and movements labored, pushed on the door handle. No good, the pressure of the water was too great for her effort. She turned toward her mother, trembled at the sight of a stream of blood flowing steadily from a deep gash on her head.

"Mum!" Anne yelled. No response. She grabbed her mum around her torso. Using every ounce of her might, she propped her mum upright keeping her head above the rising water. The light faded as the carriage descended deeper into the depths of the river. Engulfed in darkness, Anne shivered in a mixture of cold and fear as water claimed her final air pocket. She closed her eyes, fully expecting to meet the grim reaper. A strange pressure gripped her arm. Her nerves, numb from the freezing water, could not identify the source. She moved through the smashed window of the carriage, dragged by an unknown force. Above her, she viewed the water's surface, so pretty, a wavy white layer of hazy light like a halo. Then her mind went dark, struggling to find oxygen.

Anne's lungs burned as she coughed out a spurt of water. A second later, the blurred vision of a clothed man, dripping wet and soaked to the bone, formed before her eyes. As her senses returned, she realized that the swaying motion she felt was his shaking her by the shoulders. She coughed again, expelling more water. She drew in a deep breath, filling her lungs. "My mum and dad: Are they okay?"

The stranger's lost blue eyes peered blankly into the distance. His mouth parted slightly as if he was going to say something, but he did not and instead his lips recoiled into a pained frown. He returned his gaze to her, and replied, "Come on. Let's get you some warm clothes." He offered his hand. Anne grabbed it and, with his help, rose. Her legs buckled, but his strength kept her from falling until they regained a shaky foundation. With his support, they sauntered together toward a gathering crowd. An elderly woman in the crowd passed the man a woolen blanket, which he draped over Anne.

Several men gathered along the side of the embankment staring into the waters that had swallowed the carriage. Anne scanned around searching frantically for her mum and dad. A few hundred yards up the road she could make out a small crowd congregating around a man lying in a dark recess of the bend. Her stomach churned as she fought to wrestle free of the notion that she was witnessing her father's final resting place.

* * *

Sophia whispered, "I'm so sorry, Anne."

Anne wiped her eyes with the back of her wrist and continued. "It wasn't long until the Bobbies arrived and took me to the local station. They were nice. The sergeant gave me warm milk, while one of the officers found me some clothes. Boy clothes, but they were warm and dry." Dash forsook Sophia's lap and headed for Anne, where she licked at the tears wetting Anne's cheeks. Masking her mourning, her lips curled into tiny smile. "The sergeant went on to explain that my mother had drowned in the carriage. They just couldn't get to her in time."

While Anne spoke, Sophia moved over to her, shoved the bale of hay to one side, and sat down beside her.

"My dad," Anne paused, taking in a deep breath, "died from being tossed off the carriage."

Sophia wrapped her arm around Anne's shoulders. Dash jumped between them both and nuzzled into her own resting spot.

"That night, the sergeant took me to the orphanage where I met you for the first time."

"I remember," Sophia said, tightening her hold on Anne. "You did not speak for way over a year. The sisters were beginning to think you were dumb."

Anne nodded, thinking back to the many creative ways Sophia attempted to get her to speak. The most notable effort was when Sophia suggested that cleaning her tongue with soap might work. They found out it didn't, and for her efforts the Sisters rewarded Sophia with cleaning duties for a month. "You eventually got me to speak," Anne said.

"Not me," Sophia corrected. "Jesus did."

"Well, you introduced me to Jesus. I remember you taking me by the hand and leading me to Jesus hanging on that huge crucifix in the church," Anne said, staring out into passing countryside as if reimaging the scene. "You started praying for me, for Jesus to come into to my life, to heal my hurt. I listened, and figured to myself, 'Hey, if this Jesus man can take away my pain, my loneliness, why not let him come into my life?'" Anne gazed directly into Sophia's watchful eyes. "Then the strangest thing happened. A warmth engulfed me. The feeling I use to have when my mother would cradle me or when my father would kiss me on the cheek goodnight. I felt safe." She took a moment to collect her thoughts. "I felt secure and no longer alone."

"Of course you didn't feel alone, silly. You had me!"

Anne gently slapped the side of Sophia's leg as she chuckled. "You know what I mean, Sophia."

Sophia tickled her under her ribs. "I do." They both laughed, for a moment allowing their worries to vanish in a chorus of joy.

After the laughter subsided, Anne asked in a more serious tone, "Sophia, did you steal that bread?"

"Don't worry. That is between me and the Big Guy to sort out."

Anne pursed her lips, drew in a deep breath through her nose, and let her tired eyes close. She slowly exhaled one long sigh. With Dash and Sophia by her side, she experienced a sense of contentment—Love.

Chapter 11 - Cistercians

Sophia gently nudged Anne. "Wake up, Anne. We are here. The train is stopping."

Anne's eyes opened and closed repeatedly in little jerks, clearly doing battle with the desire to stay asleep. "Already?" she replied, followed by a yawn.

After the train slowed to a walking pace, they leapt from the carriage and scrambled away from the railway to a nearby dirt track. They followed the trail to London Station. Across from the station entrance, Sophia cut her eyes down the long line of people waiting for tickets. She had no doubt they would be queuing for several minutes or more. On the platform, some relaxed on benches reading their morning newspaper while others stood casually waiting. One guy whistled a tune that didn't sound familiar to Sophia, though the uplifting melody warmed her heart. Nobody appeared to notice him or, if they did, they simply ignored his joyful song. New arrivals from an earlier train were leaving for town by foot. Near the station entrance, a man wearing a cap and overcoat stood by a knee-high stack of newspapers shouting, "Get your *Illustrated London News* here. Read all about the survivors of the Charge of the Light Brigade Reunion." A passing gentleman handed him several coins, took a newspaper, and continued into the station. The salesman waved a newspaper in the air, shouting, "The ripper has laid claim to another lady of the night. Read all about it! Get your news here."

"He seems like an educated chap," Anne said.

Sophia nodded. "He sure does."

Seeing their approach, the salesman stopped yelling and smiled. "Well then, what can I do for you two fine young ladies?"

"Sir, we were wondering if you knew the way to Hyde Park," Sophia said. She pondered how he had addressed them as "fine young ladies." Glancing over herself and Anne, she considered their disheveled hair, soiled clothes, and shabby appearance. A more apt description would have been *"abandoned orphan ragamuffins."*

"I sure do," he said, pointing to his left down the paved street. "Follow this road into Maida Vale. In the center of town, when you come to the first crossroad, take a left." He gestured to his left with a flick of his thumb to give them a visualization of the directions to take. "Follow that road and it will take you past Hyde Park."

"Okay," Sophia said, nodding. "Thank you, sir."

"Wait," the salesman said in a raised voice as Sophia turned to leave. "Here, take this." He reached into his pocket and pulled out a shiny red apple.

Sophia accepted the gift. "That is most kind of you, sir. Thank you."

As they walked away, Anne said, "He was a very nice man."

Sophia picked up a flattish stone from the rocky road they followed. "He sure was." With the rock's blade-like edge, she sliced the apple into halves. She gave half to Anne, broke her half in half again, kept half for herself and dropped the remaining portion on the ground. Dash sniffed and nudged the dropped piece. "Don't be fussy, Dash," Sophia said. A couple more sniffs and then Dash ate her share.

Sophia glanced at the sun hovering just above the rooftops of the buildings of London. "It'll be dark soon," she said, picking up the walking pace towards Hyde Park. She had overheard many a conversation amongst Sisters Mary, Catherine, and Margaret. Stories on how the streets were unsafe after dark, especially for girls. In the late hours of the night the Sisters would sit in front of the warmth of the open fireplace knitting and chatting amongst themselves. They swapped horrifying stories about a notorious killer notching up another victim as he preyed on the women of the night in London or how the Bobbies spoke every other week on how their efforts to apprehend the murderer was coming along.

They had no idea, of course, that Sophia was hiding in the shadows eavesdropping on their grown-up talk. Sister Catherine referred to the killer as a demon-possessed lost soul while Sister Mary was more reserved in her descriptions of the evil man's actions, using terms such "mentally unstable."

Anne pointed towards a painted crest, a shield within a shield on the stone sidewall of a building. "Look. I remember that symbol," she said, before gazing down the alley between the buildings that bore the emblem. "Yes, I'm sure the Cistercians' monastery is down there."

Sophia gazed down the dark alley, wide enough for only a single-file advance, that led between two three-story buildings. The constricted passage reminded Sophia of the Sisters' descriptions of the place the monstrous killer would finish off his victims, places nobody dared tread, where screams went unheard. She shuddered. "You sure? Looks kind of creepy."

Anne took a second look, glanced to the either side of the alley, rubbed her chin. "Yes, I'm sure." She scratched her temple. "Well, pretty sure."

Sophia advanced down the darkened alleyway dodging the splintered remains of several broken wooden crates.

"You okay, Sophia?" Anne asked.

"Yep, I'm fine," Sophia replied, steadying herself and pushing the thought of the murderer to the recesses of her mind. Two minutes down the alley, which seemed endless, they came to a large solid oak wood door with a bulky iron handle at shoulder height and a closed slot—a peep hole—slightly above their heads. The same shield-in-shield symbol at the end of the alley was painted on the door in black ink.

"You going to knock," Anne asked, nudging Sophia, "or just stand there?"

Truth was, Sophia felt uneasy. Many questions raced through her mind. *Why is this monastery down the end of this alley? What was Sister Mary doing coming to a place like this?* Finding no answers, Sophia rapped the heavy iron ring against the wood.

A moment later, Sophia jolted as the slit opened with a loud clunk and two warm brown eyes peered out through the peephole. In unison, Sophia, Anne, and Dash took a step backward. "Yes?" a male voice behind the door asked.

Sophia cleared her throat to ready her innocent persuasive voice. "Um, sir, we would like to read some books in your library."

"Oh, you would," the man said in an inquisitive voice, "would you?"

She hesitated, debating whether to run or stay, before coupling her hands behind her back, replying, "Yes, sir."

"And where do you dwell?"

"Saint Juliana of Pavilly Orphanage."

The eyes scanned Sophia up and down, then Anne, and finally Dash. At once, the peephole slammed shut, and the sound of several iron latches sliding echoed down the alley before the door swung open. A short balding man, slightly hunched over, and wearing a brown habit under a black scapular gestured them inside. "This way."

They followed the man who limped his way through the vast foyer. "It's so quiet in here," Anne said.

"We prefer a quiet existence," the man replied. He stopped before two bi-folding wooden doors twice the height of an average man. He grabbed the doors' two polished brass handles and took a few steps backwards to pull the massive doors open. They parted with a low-pitch creaking. He gestured into the opening. "The library is through here."

Anne and Sophia entered, followed by Dash. Sophia saw the man wink as Dash looked up at him. *Dog lover*, she thought.

Grand, magnificent, amazing. Sophia struggled to come to terms with the incredible sight of the library. Books wall-to-wall, floor-to-ceiling, placed on intricately carved shelves recessed into the massive walls that spanned three stories high on all four sides of the room. Ladders mounted on moveable platforms reached the heights of the bookcases. Various books, some of them open, lay on lecterns scattered around the vast room. In the center of the room, five feet in diameter, a wooden globe inscribed with the continents of earth eased rotating. A single curved oak beam that extended from the four wooden legs of the base to the top held the sphere in place.

"So many books," Sophia muttered, her eyes wide and gleaming like a child on Christmas morning.

Anne shrugged. "I know."

A nun, dusting the shelves, eyed them as she continued to work. "Where do we start?" Sophia said.

"Hmm…" Anne cut her eyes across shelves. "Do we try to find Esdras or Orders?"

"You're the expert when it comes to books," Sophia said. "So you tell me."

"The E's." Anne paced over to the bookcase wall closest to the entrance. "Let's start there." After finding where the A's started, Anne followed the flow to the B's and proceeded to the section of E's. "Up there, Sophia," she said, pointing towards the highest row of books, three stories up. "The ES's should start along the top row."

Sophia cut her eyes up eighteen shelves of books. "Right-o." She slid a nearby ladder over and proceeded to climb the wooden rungs.

"Be careful," Anne said, in a slightly raised voice. Sophia nodded and continued to climb. At the top, she scanned along the spines of the books to her right. *Esacar, Escape, Escapade, Esdor … Esdras.* She reached out, leaning and stretching as far as she could. From below Anne cried out, "Oh, do be careful, Sophia." The book remained at least half an arm's length away. "Anne, push me over," she shouted. Below, Anne shoved the ladder to the right. "That's brilliant, Anne." She reached out and grabbed the book titled *The Order of Esdras.* A sense of contentment caused her to smile as she hastily descended the ladder.

As Sophia stepped down from the last rung, a man's voice, powerful and commanding, said, "And what does a young girl like you want with *The Order of Esdras?*" She turned to see a man she guessed to be in his early fifties with short blond hair, dark brown eyes, and dressed in priest garb—a black frock with a white collar—standing before her reaching out towards the book she was holding.

"Well, you see—"

"Hand it over," the man interrupted.

Reluctantly, Sophia handed him the book.

"And what are your names?"

To Sophia's surprise, Anne responded instantly, almost as if under a spell. "I'm Anne, this is Sophia, and the dog is Dash."

"Ahh... I see... I shall not be rude. I am Father Gregor Mendel, but you two can call me Mendel. I never did like the name Gregor." He grinned. "Follow me, please."

Without questioning his request, Sophia and Anne followed Mendel. On the far side of the room, opposite the entrance, they stopped in front of the wall of books. Sophia presumed Mendel must have wanted to fetch a novel. Instead of taking a book, Mendel tilted one forward— a deep maroon leather-bound book *For the Sake of Man* by Suriel. "Stand back," he said. With a slow creaking sound, the wall of books moved forwards and then stopped with a thud. A moment later, the bookcase slid, grinding as if the wheels supporting the structure needed oiling, to the side revealing a secret passage, dark narrow, that led down a flight of steps. One meter inside, Mendel pulled a match from his pocket and lit an oil lantern strung on the stone wall by a thin piece of old rope hanging on a hook. He unhooked the lantern and proceeded down the stairs. "Follow."

The narrow alley Sophia travelled earlier seemed relatively normal compared to the descending staircase she now ventured. *Creepy* would be one word she could use to describe the descent, but the word would not describe the scene well enough. At the bottom of the stairs, Mendel opened a small battered wooden door that led into a wine cellar converted into an office space. Bookcases stacked with books filled the walls. Four gas lamps, one on each sidewall, provided a warm yellow flickering light, bright enough to read comfortably by without straining one's eyes. A large oak desk with inscriptions carved around the edges blocked the full view of a tall high-back oak chair with green leather providing a cushioned back and seat. Many papers and rolled-up scrolls secured by red wax seals covered the desk in an orderly fashion. The crest stamped into the wax appeared to be the same as the one on the door to the monastery. Three maple chairs with red leather cushioned seats were situated in front of the desk.

"Please, please, take a seat, young ladies," Mendel said, placing the book *The Order of Esdras* on the desk as he seated himself on the green padded chair. Sophia gestured to Anne to take a seat while she kept a watchful eye on Mendel before slumping onto a chair.

Chapter 12 - Prophecy

Sophia analyzed Mendel, trying to discern if he was *friend or foe*. The priest collar he wore and his general, rather open demeanor gave her comfort. Her inner voice said to trust him even as her conscious mind searched for reasons not to.

Mendel put on a pair of silver framed glasses with spherical lenses and then flipped open the *The Order of Esdras* towards the back. After turning a few pages to locate a particular passage, he cleared his throat, and said, "This book speaks of prophecy where a young girl will come looking for this book on a quest to find Jeremial. Is that young girl one of you?"

Sophia shuffled her feet and turned her gaze towards the bookshelves.

"The book goes on to say this young girl will exhibit abilities that go beyond the capabilities of a normal human. Do either of you have any such abilities?"

Anne said, "Once, quite a few years back, I fell down an embankment, broke my leg and So—" She stopped abruptly, reached down and began rubbing her shin. "Ouch," she whispered, turning her attention to Sophia. "Why did you kick me?" Sophia glared at her with one brow raised. Thereafter, Anne fell silent.

Mendel directed his focus towards Sophia. "So, *you* have these abilities?"

Sophia bit down on her bottom lip, ignored the question, and resumed scanning the books on the shelves. Many were topics related to spiritual warfare: angels, demons, myths, and legends.

"The prophecy says the girl is a descendent of angels," Mendel said, lowering his head so that his glasses slid down to the tip of his nose as he eyed Sophia over them, very carefully, before continuing. "There is a legend about a group of twelve angels led by one named Araton who gave up their wings, and became thereby somewhat mortal—to live amongst the humans. In that capacity, they had the ability to involve themselves more personally in human affairs. They are said to have had descendants."

"Nephilim?" Anne queried.

"No, the story, somewhat vague in areas, occurs after the great flood. This group of angels, holy angels, volunteered at the request of the highest authorities. They came to assist in the battle of evil in the world within the mortal realm at a time when sorcery, dark magic, and necromancy were rampant."

"I don't remember reading that in the Bible," Anne replied.

"Dear girl, not everything that happens in the world is in the Bible. That said, however, what you can be sure of is that what is in the Bible is factual—and without error. Some things are better kept secret. The enemy reads the Bible as well." He slid his glasses back up the ridge of his nose. "Know this: God does not sit idly by when the world is in times of distress. Evident by how God gave his only son, Jesus, when the world needed a savior. He cares for us and so do his angels." He directed his attention back to Sophia. "What do you know about your parents, Sophia?"

"Never met them." A wave of remorse washed over her—a feeling of losing something she held dearly, yet she, unlike Anne, never knew her parents to lose them, which caused the emotion to stir up a raging inner conflict. Her fingers rolled into clenched fists in an attempt to squelch the rising adrenalin increasing her heart rate. *Could I truly be a descendant of an angel?*

Mendel leant back in his chair, rubbing his chin while keeping his gaze fixed on Sophia.

"Tell me, Sophia, has anyone tried to harm you or those you love?"

A reflexive thought bubbled up: *Time to become the questioner.* She knew it was most likely to protect her from having to think about the death of her loved ones. She closed her eyes and felt the sadness, the awful grief, over losing the Sisters and Mr. Brumby almost hit her before she said, "Where did you get that book?"

"Sister Mary from your orphanage donated the book to our library several years ago. Interesting, is it not?"

Sophia nodded, admitting to herself that the situation raised questions to spark curiosity.

"Tell him what happened," Anne said, her droopy eyes pleading.

Can I trust him? Sophia thought. *What if he is one of the ones who wants to kill me? But then why would Sister Mary have given him the book, and why would Diniel tell me to search for the book?* After considering all of those questions, she decided it was time to put the facts on the table. "Sister Mary, Sister Catherine, and a friend named Mr. Brumby have died because of me."

Mendel nodded, lowered his eyes. "We heard about the fire at the orphanage."

Anne and Sophia spun around directing their attention on footsteps coming down the stairs.

"No need to be alarmed, girls. It's Michael. He will be joining us."

A young man in his late teens entered the room. Mendel greeted him and asked him to sit. Sophia looked him over. Handsome, shoulder-length hair, dark and straight, sapphire blue eyes, slender physique, and about six feet tall. Anne looked him over, too, and as she did her face lit up and her cheeks blushed a rosy red.

"Michael, meet Sophia and Anne."

"Pleased to make your acquaintance," he said, in a smooth, polite voice.

"Michael, who turned eighteen only days ago, is our newest White Monk."

"Oh," Anne said, "a monk," sounding a little disappointed.

Sophia rolled her eyes. Many a times Sophia had seen Anne falling for older teens or as she would tease Anne, having a crush on one fair-faced young man or another.

Mendel slammed the book shut. "Enough prophecy. Tell me, Sophia, what do you want with this book?"

"We figured the book might tell us where to find Jeremial."

"Uh huh. Well the book certainly will." He paused. "The thing is." Mendel reopened the book, this time to the front section that revealed a hidden compartment. The first several chapters were dummy pages, with a square section chiseled out to allow for storage. Mendel withdrew a bracelet from it with five silver charms equally spaced, one a small crucifix, the rest small discs, each inscribed with a different symbol—an earth, a star, a moon, and a sun. "How can I be sure you are the ones of which the prophecy speaks?"

"You mean the *one*?" Sophia replied.

"No, the *ones*," he said. "The prophecy says to give this bracelet to the travelling companion."

Anne's eyes widened as she bolted upright in her chair. "Me?"

"Yes, I believe the prophecy must be referring to you, Anne. I doubt it means Dash."

"There is also this." Mendel retrieved a tiny golden key from the compartment. "It is said this key will unlock the cross of the one of whom the prophecy speaks."

"The cross?" Sophia replied.

"Yes. May I take your necklace, Sophia?"

Sophia had forgotten she was even wearing the crucifix Sister Mary had given her, hidden under the neckline of her dress. She took the shiny silver cross in her palm and eyed it before handing it to Mendel.

Key in hand, he turned the crucifix over. Towards the top of the cross, nearly invisible to the naked eye, was a tiny slot glowing faintly white. As he inserted the key, the white glow suddenly surrounded the key and cross like an aura. Startled by the reaction, Mendel dropped the cross onto the desk.

Sophia gawked in amazement as the key turned by an invisible force and then vanished, seemingly consumed by the white light. She carefully retrieved the cross from the table, examined it for any change. Towards the side, she discovered the tiniest of clasps. She unhooked the metal latch. The cross opened to reveal a compartment inside containing a stack of several paper-thin flat silver crucifixes. "Hmm," she mumbled before flipping the crucifix over on her palm. Six crucifixes in total, nearly weightless but sturdy as pure silver, rested on her hand. A faint white glow surrounded each one. "What are they?" she asked.

Mendel leaned in for a closer look. "I don't know. That is something you will need to work out."

Sophia placed the crucifixes back inside the cross, closed it, and then put the necklace again around her neck, allowing the cross to dangle on the outside of her clothes.

Anne eyed the bracelet like a puppy eyeing a fresh bone. "Yes, you can take it," Mendel said. Without hesitation, Anne snatched up the charm bracelet. She had never had a piece of jewelry before. Her eyes went owl-like as she placed the gift around her wrist. "Wow, it's so pretty."

"What now?" Sophia asked.

"Now, you carry out the prophecy and go find Jeremial."

"Where is he?"

"Hermitage Castle on the border of Scotland. The journey will take you several days, which is why Michael is here."

Sophia glanced towards Michael. "And why?"

"The prophecy states that a newly dawned White Monk will accompany the chosen to The Order of Esdras to protect them on their journey."

"Protect us," Anne echoed, facing Michael. His lips curved slightly upwards, not quite into a full smile. Her cheeks blushed.

"What if we don't want protecting?" Sophia asked, arms crossed over her chest. The way she reckoned it, having Michael travelling with them would only add to her responsibility.

"You will not be responsible for me, Sophia," Michael said as if reading her thoughts. Her arms relaxed a little at his reply.

"Right," Mendel said. "For the journey you are going to need supplies." He looked the girls over, added, "And some new clothes. Tomorrow, I'll have Sister Bridget take you clothes shopping."

"Shopping," Anne said, her eyes widening even more.

Sophia cut her eyes at Anne, figuring the girl must be thinking all her Christmases had come at once.

"Michael, show the girls to the guest room. Then have Sister Bridget meet them there to show them to the bathroom and gather them some sleep wear. Can't have them sleeping in those dirty clothes."

Michael nodded, then stood and proceeded to lead the girls out of the room.

"Dinner is at seven," Mendel said as they left. "Have Sister Bridget bring the girls cleaned and dressed in something presentable."

Chapter 13 - Jack

The grandfather clock chimed six times in the Whitechapel home. Each medium-pitch clang reverberated through Jack's vertebrae as if they were part of the instrument making the sound. Time for him to leave the house and stalk his prey, something he acknowledged was wrong but did to sustain his life. That he had sold his soul to a devil in exchange for mortality was undeniable. Before each hunting expedition a haunting question echoed through his mind: *Did I make a mistake? What happens when my mortality finally comes to an end? Everybody dies. What then?*

He pushed the queries to the back of his mind as harrowing thoughts of Hell disturbed him to the point of mental collapse. The day he took his first life, he realized the gravity of the decision he had made. Catholics would spread tales of Heaven and Hell, at least to him they were nothing more than tales. He spent years convincing himself they were fables by gathering with others who did not believe. In the company of atheists, his anxieties waned and life was more comfortable. By mixing with those who shared his beliefs, he could sin without expecting ramifications or even taking responsibility for his actions. Yet at the same time, the taut strings of his conscience would tug on his heart. Strings he hardened to lessen the strain.

A typical English night awaited him outside: light drizzle, cold, damp, unforgiving for those who loitered in the elements. After slipping on his long dark gray overcoat and lifting the hood, he stepped over the threshold into the gathering darkness.

Distant coughs echoed down Whitechapel road. People walked through the depressed streets, some with umbrellas, others holding newspapers over their heads to shield themselves from the misty rain.

No laughter, no smiles, only a sense of dread and fear in this place. Where is the love, children laughing and playing, families walking together? Locked away in their houses, the vile weather keeping them inside. Only laborers dared the elements on their journeys to and from their workplace, not for any thrill but out of necessity to put food on the table. Poverty was no stranger to Whitechapel.

His black leather shoes provided reasonable protection from the puddled cobblestone road as he trudged to his destination. A three-hour walk lay before him. His arm would tire holding his black doctor's bag containing the instruments he required, not only to do the killing but also the dissecting. The walk would not be without pain. Constant pangs will shoot like sparks from his tumor into his nervous system reminding him why he would do what his conscience valiantly fought against.

Jack's conscience was what bothered him the most—bothered him more than the pain of the tumor. Why did his inner voice deplore his actions so much? *A moral law?* A law he was bound to by some unseen force, by a doctrine, but not one that he had been taught but rather one he had been bound to from birth? While he accepted the fact that he could break the law's rules, his conscience nagged him, without ceasing, never giving up, and only silenced through his deliberate efforts, pushing to the remote recesses of his mind the uncomfortable sensation of being held accountable to the laws written in his soul.

In the distance, he heard the familiar voice of preaching bellowing from Friends Burial Ground, a Christian Revival Society started by a fellow named William Booth. Jack had a disdain for Christians, a hatred he struggled to understand. It was as if something had infected him creating an angst for anything holy. To Jack, Jesus remained nothing more than a casual curse word he overheard people use. An invisible man long dead now nearly nineteen centuries and believed in by only the gullible. He couldn't deny that he noticed a twinkle in the eyes of Christians, however, a sparkle of hope, even those deep in poverty, a glimmer he longed for.

Dorset Street. The lonesome road surrounded by warrens of small dark streets containing the greatest suffering, filth, and danger. His hunting ground for the night awaited him. His chosen prey: women of the night. He tried to convince himself that ridding the world of those involved in sin would somehow mitigate his own act of evil. But deep in the cellar of his soul he recognized that murder, regardless of the victim, breached a commandment of God the preachers shouted through the streets. *Thou shalt not kill.*

In the darkness of the shadows, he opened his bag and retrieved a white cloth stained with the saliva of past victims. He doused the cotton with chloroform. Time to wait for his opportunity. The hours ticked by, but Jack had learned to be patient. One time he had rushed in to ambush a victim only to have a passerby interrupt the act. That night he was almost caught. Since then he took his time and awaited the faultless opportunity, like a fisherman waiting for his line to pull. He watched the night, waiting to execute the perfect crime.

A woman with long red gorgeous hair and no doubt returning from a trick came into view. She was wearing a heavy full-length dress and applied scarlet lipstick with a small circular pocket mirror as she walked the street. Opportunity, meet Jack. Her vision obscured, her senses directed to her own actions, the last time she would ever apply lipstick.

Slithering out from the shadows, he crept behind the unsuspecting victim and slapped the chloroform-soaked rag over her nose and mouth while dragging her into his den of shadows. Her beautiful brown eyes would bulge, he knew this, as she struggled in vain to gasp for air. The muffled sounds, hardly audible, would eventually cease.

Her body would go limp. She would then lose consciousness, never to awaken again. He whispered in her ear, "Shh, my darling. It will be over soon." Those were the very words his mother used to say to him when his father, in a gin-fueled rage, would beat them.

The instructions Mephis gave him this night was to remove a heart. The task was relatively simple for Jack, a trained surgeon. He knew just where to slice and which bones to saw through to make retrieval of the sought-after organ as quick and effortless as possible. The prey would not feel any pain, a fact that in some ways comforted him. He did not want to torture his victims. Life was all he sought, and the price to be paid for his life was the life of another.

Job done, he wrapped the bestilled heart in a white cotton sheath and placed it in his bag. He closed the victim's eyes and took one last look at her. He gritted his teeth, hating himself, and began the return journey to his dismal Whitechapel home.

Chapter 14 - Dinner

Sophia eyed Anne as the girl gazed at herself in the full-length dress mirror. The sparkle in her eyes was accentuated by the flowing pearl-white long-sleeved dress she was wearing. The thin silky fabric hugged her torso and flared just a little at her hipline downward to allow unencumbered movement. She twirled, letting the dress fan out.

"You look stunning," Sophia said.

"And so do you," Anne replied, taking in Sophia's outfit, identical to hers except it was a pale sky blue.

"You are both gorgeous," Sister Bridget said. "Now, come, we must attend dinner."

"Where did you get these dresses, Sister Bridget," Sophia asked.

Sister Bridget smiled warmly as her eyes seemingly gazed on a distant memory. "We were once young," Sister Bridget said with a little pant.

As Sophia and Anne entered the dining room, all those sitting rose from their chairs. Sophia froze for a moment, taken aback by the gallant gesture. Nobody had ever stood for her.

"Please, young ladies, take a seat," Mendel said.

Sister Bridget pulled back an empty seat for Sophia then another for Anne. Sophia's cheeks warmed as she realized that everyone seated around the twenty-seat table had eyes fixed on her. Mendel sat at one end of the table and Michael at the other. Sisters and monks occupied the rest of the seats. Every person had been served the same dish, a bowl of tomato soup and a small loaf of bread. A queue of candles equally spaced extended down the center of the table from one end to the other. The candles combined with gas lamps set in sconces around the sides of the room provided warm, tranquil lighting.

"Brother Michael, would you lead us in grace, please?"

Michael cupped his hands, bowed his head, and began to speak. "Father of us all, this gathered meal of your fruits is a sign of your unfailing love for us. Bless us and our food. Help us to give thanks each day. Through Jesus Christ our Lord. Amen!" In unison everyone said "Amen" creating a sensation of grace in harmony.

Just as they were about to partake of the soup, they heard the sound of footsteps, moving quickly, beyond the door. All eyes turned to the door, tracking the hasty approaching noise. The door swung open, slamming against the wall. A monk entered. Between great heaves of breath, he shouted, "Mendel, they are coming…!"

Mendel and Michael rose in unison. "Quick, Michael, take them through the escape tunnels," Mendel said. "We will stall them." The Sisters at the table began to pray while the monks scattered through different exits.

"Who's coming?" Sophia asked.

"I'll explain later," Michael responded. "For now, we must go. Follow me."

"Wait," Mendel interrupted. "Take this, Sophia." He handed her the book *The Order of Esdras*.

"Quickly," Michael said, his tone urgent. "We have no time." They scurried through the kitchen into a large storage room filled with various foodstuffs. The room reminded Sophia of small hedge maze. Floor-to-ceiling shelves formed walls of food. Narrow openings between them created corridors that led off in different directions.

Sophia struggled to keep track of the changes in direction and which way they had already been. At times, it seemed as though they were travelling in circles. "This way," Michael said as he walked into some shelves on a wall stocked with crates brimming with various vegetables. He was doing the impossible, walking through solid matter. Half his body passed through the wall. Sophia took a few steps backwards as Anne cowered behind her. "Don't be afraid," he said. "It is an illusion."

Sophia shuffled forwards within an arm's reach of the illusory wall. In position, she reached out and watched her trembling hand pass through the shelf, then the wall. It was an odd sensation. Her mind told her matter was there but her sense of touch proved otherwise. "Here goes nothing," she said, venturing through the fake wall and stepping foot in a room on the other side.

She heard Anne's voice cry out beyond the wall. "Are you okay, Sophia?"

"Yes," Sophia replied, "just step through."

An instant later, Anne leapt through the illusion.

Sophia first studied her reflection, a near perfect duplicate of herself, on the highly polished wooden floor, before turning her attention to the rest of the hidden room. Intricate golden patterns covered the pure pearly white walls. The ceiling was a masterpiece painting of Angels and Demons battling in the clouds using medieval weapons—swords, shields, bows, and arrows. Exquisite. As she scanned further around the room, it dawned on her what this space was: *a secret armory*. Several staffs were strung on one wall and dozens of books were shelved on another. The books did not seem normal, however, for they all had a faint white aura glowing about them.

Michael opened a large ornate mahogany chest that stood in the center of the room. From within, he retrieved two white leather jackets insulated with wool. "Here, put these on. It'll be cold on our journey."

Sophia slotted her arms through the sleeves of the jacket, felt a strange warmth immediately come over her, not a warmth created by the thick wool but an energy that charged the material. Michael took one of the books and a wooden staff. The staff appeared to be two thick vines, green and glossy, wound around each other and joined at the top to create a foundation for an ivory cross. At the far wall of the room, he placed the bottom of the staff into a round hole in the ground. A large clunk like that of a large heavy lock opening, echoed through the chamber. He knelt and then lifted a floorboard to reveal a length of short rope. On pulling the rope, a square section of the flooring lifted. "After you, young ladies."

Sophia peered down into the dark cavern the trapdoor exposed. A wooden ladder descended. Without much thought, Sophia clambered down.

"Wait," Anne said. "We forgot Dash."

"No, she will be waiting for us," Michael said. "Come, now, we must hurry."

The only light in the room vanished as Michael sealed the trapdoor above on his descent. Pitch-blackness surrounded them, but for the faint white glow of the book Michael was holding. "Stay still," Michael said, before adding, "fiat lux."

Sophia did not understand what the words meant, though the dialect sounded familiar, like Latin the Sisters would sometimes speak. After speaking, the top of Michael's staff, the crucifix, emitted a bright white light that illuminated the cavern.

"Cool," Anne said, gazing around the dusty cavern. "I hope there are no rats down here." She screwed up her nose. "I hate rats."

* * *

Mendel retook his position at the end of the table and awaited the intruders' entrance. Moments later the main doors burst open and several constables rushed in. The one in charge slapped his baton against his hand. "Where are the girls?"

Thrusting the chair backwards as he rose, Mendel shouted, "How dare you charge in here and interrupt a prayer session!" The Sisters, without showing the slightest disturbance, continued their praying.

The police officer, apparently unconvinced by the retort, narrowed his eyes like a snake. "We know they came in here! Witnesses saw them entering the alleyway."

"Do you see any girls other than our lovely Sisters?"

Methodically, the officer glared at each Sister in turn. "Hmm…" He paced around the table to within Mendel's personal space. "If we find them in here I'll have you arrested."

"Well you just do that," Mendel said, stomping his foot.

"Right men, search this place," the Bobby yelled. "Leave no stone unturned."

* * *

"Who are we running from, Michael," Sophia asked.

"The Bobbies, or do you call them police?"

"Oh," Sophia sighed. "I wouldn't have thought they would chase us this far over a loaf of stolen bread."

"They're not," Michael said, shaking his head and placing a hand on her shoulder.

Sophia gazed into Michael's calming eyes, her own brow drooping under the weight of curiosity. "Then … *what?*"

"You're wanted for questioning on suspicion of arson resulting in the deaths of Sister Mary and Sister Catherine."

Sophia shook her head, slowly, as her eyes watered. She felt a sharp sting erupt from her chest as if someone had hammered a nail through her throbbing heart. "But …"

"I know, Sophia," he said, letting his chin drop. His eyes conveyed full understanding. "You don't have to tell me."

Anne said, "I guess when we ran from the Bobbies in town it looked suspicious."

Michael nodded.

Sophia blotted her eyes with the sleeve of her dress. "Can't we just go to the Bobbies and tell them what happened?"

"And tell them … *what?*" Michael said.

"Hmm. We could tell them we were not there when the orphanage burnt down."

"And where are you going to say you were?"

"At Mr. Brumby's," she said.

"Yes," he said, "and where is he now?"

Sophia nodded. "I see."

"They are also looking to interview you regarding his death. You were seen running around with his dog."

"Oh, right. The situation doesn't look good."

"We are fugitives!" Anne said, a glint of excitement in her eyes. "On the run from the law!"

"Indeed," Michael said. "You are innocent fugitives."

"How do you *know* we are innocent?" Sophia asked.

"I doubt you would have come to *us* if you were guilty?"

"I see." Sophia drew in a deep breath and tried to make sense of the situation.

"We must keep moving." Michael nodded toward a passage, the only exit other than the trapdoor above that led out of the cavern. "They will not find us down here, but the longer we stay, the more difficult it will be to leave London." The granite walls narrowed, forcing them into a single file, as they proceeded. Michael, leading the way, swiped old uninhabited cobwebs with his staff.

"Where are the spiders?" Sophia asked.

"The weather is too cold for their food during this time of the year," Michael said, sweeping away a wall-to-wall cobweb blocking the way forward. They hide in dark crevices awaiting warmer weather."

Anne brushed strands of fallen web from her shoulders. "That's a relief."

At the end of the passage, a short ladder led up to the ceiling. Michael ascended the wooden rungs and pushed upwards on the ceiling. Nothing. He pushed a little harder, releasing a grunt as he did. A squealing noise, metal on metal, sounded as a slither of artificial light-streamed in. "We really need to increase the maintenance around here," he said. He strained and rammed the ceiling panel with all his might and, with a loud crash, the trapdoor flipped fully open. "Wait here a second." He scurried up the ladder and vanished through the opening.

"Where did he go?" Anne asked, peering into the light above.

"Probably to make sure it is safe for us to come up," Sophia said.

"He's so gallant," Anne said, blushing.

Sophia rolled her eyes.

Moments later, Michael shouted from above. "Okay, it is safe. Come on up."

Sophia gestured for Anne to go first. After the short ascent, Anne disappeared from sight.

Her turn. On climbing into the area above, the strong smell of livestock reached her. "A barn," she said, making the final step off the ladder onto a hay-covered floor.

"A stable," Michael responded, gathering three prepared leather haversacks. "Here, put these on." Sophia placed *The Book of Esdras* inside the haversack before slipping the carryall over her shoulders. Michel pointed to the far side of the stables. "This way." Around a corner, three magnificent horses stood before them, two charcoal and one pure white.

"Wow," Sophia said, her eyes blooming from buds to fully formed roses. "They are magnificent." A familiar bark interrupted her appreciation of the stallions. "Dash   ! You are here." She knelt and allowed Dash's tongue to give her a friendly hello across the side of her cheek. She stroked Dash who was all too eager to lap up the attention. She realized that part or her affection for Dash came from wanting to keep Mr. Brumby's memory alive.

Michael untied the horses. "The prophecy says that *the ones* can ride. I hope that is true."

"Yes, it is," Sophia said, rising onto her feet. "Sister Mary took us riding several times. A nearby farm handler donated his horses and time. He gave us and our orphan sisters lessons."

"Right." Michael mounted the white steed. "Hop on a horse."

Sophia climbed onto one of the charcoal horses. "What are their names?"

"The one you are riding is Solitaire, Anne's is Eclipse, and mine is Lancelot. Prize horses. All three are extremely well-conditioned and capable of a full day's travel at a decent pace."

Michael shouted: "Kneel." His horse Lancelot followed the instruction and bowed on its front legs. He then patted his leg and looked at Dash. "Come on, girl." Dash leapt up onto Lancelot and seated herself in front of Michael.

Sophia's eyebrows raised in surprise that Dash knew what to do. *Well-trained dog and horse.*

"Away we go!" Michael said as he led them out of the stables.

Chapter 15 - Revelations

The soft echoes of Sophia's horse's canter on the cobblestone road mixed with her companions' horses' clopping carved a sweet lullaby through the moist air. The odd stomp in a shallow puddle reflecting the flickering yellow light of gas-powered street lamps occasionally interrupted the harmony. "Where are we going?" Sophia asked.

"Regents Park." Michael pulled the reins to steer Lancelot's gallop. "It's not far from here and will be a safe place to spend the night."

"The park?" Sophia questioned. A cold chill cascaded down her spine, leaving a trail of goose bumps in its wake. "At night?" Harrowing thoughts of the ripper and Mephis flashed through her mind. "Safe?"

"Yes," Michael replied with a single nod. "The part we are going to is safe."

On entering the green flat pastures of Regents Park, Michael said, "Now we make our way to the Inner Circle."

With Solitaire at a steady trot, Sophia admired the lush gardens. Grander versions of the flowerbeds Sister Margaret cared for behind the orphanage, bursting with thousands of red roses with the occasional white rose scattered amongst them. "Angels amongst the plants," Sister Margaret would say, pointing to the white roses as the children gathered around. Then she would continue with elaborate stories about how angels truly are among us. Sophia would sit with mouth agape and eyes glued to Sister Margaret as she snuggled next to the other children and listened to the wondrous tales. Now, after what she had seen recently, Sophia wondered if the stories were more than mere fables. Moving on from the gardens Sophia eyed a lone white swan, wings at full stretch, gliding in to land on the still waters of a lake covered here and there with blankets of lilies. *Wouldn't it be wonderful to be able to fly?* she thought.

"We're here," Michael said as he pulled Lancelot to a halt on the edge of a paved road that appeared to arc in a large circle. "This is the Ring Road. The center of which is called the Inner Circle." He cut his eyes across the bushes and trees and then proceeded to follow a semi-concealed path, straight and narrow, through the trees towards the Inner Circle. He dismounted at the point at which the path connected with two other paths coming from the North and South creating a cross. Michael kicked away some leaves and debris in the center of the paths' intersection and uncovered a small circular indentation that could easily be mistaken for a defect in the stone. It was no defect, however, for when he placed the end of his staff into it, a striking cobalt glow illuminated for a brief moment at the point where the staff touched the ground. Sophia shrugged, thinking: *A bit of a nonevent.* After remounting Lancelot, Michael led them back through the trees to the Ring Road where they waited.

"What's going on?" Anne asked.

"I'm not sure," Sophia responded as she shifted around on Solitaire to relieve the discomfort of the saddle. Then all of the sudden, as if spooked, Solitaire jolted. The ground vibrated. In the distance, along a bend in Ring Road a section about one step in width sank into the ground ... followed by another behind it ... and then another, continuing towards them. Each section descending slightly less than the previous. Her troubled horse, swaying his head side to side, took two paces backwards. When the last section formed, she traced her eyes down the curved descended area, where part of the Ring Road use to be, and beheld a curved stairway providing a pathway down to an underground stone archway.

"This way," Michael said, leading the way, riding Lancelot down the stairs. Solitaire protested until Sophia prodded him with successive jabs of her heels. As they entered the archway, each step they had crossed ascended, sealing them beneath the earth.

Gas-powered torches spaced at regular intervals on either side of the stonewall passageway provided light. Sophia scrutinized her surroundings like a hawk stalking a rabbit. "What is this place?"

"A network of passages and safe havens spanning underground across England," Michael explained. "It's been in use for centuries."

As they moved ahead, torches lit as they approached, somehow sensing their presence. As they passed, the torches behind them extinguished. Sophia presumed their weight triggered them. She had once read about a self-lighting hallway. As people walked down the hall, the pressure of their weight squeezed open valves under the floor that allowed gas to pass through pipes. Before the gas reached the lamp, it created pressure on a levered flap that caused a bit of flint on the other end of a lever attached to the flap to strike, creating a spark, which lit the lamp. Only wealthy people had such devices.

Michael interrupted her recollection. "Some sections have been converted into the subway for trains."

"So everyone knows about the tunnels?"

"No. Very few in fact. A few workers stumbled across them when constructing the subway. Since then, colleagues have been busy sealing off sections they believe workers are liable to discover so we don't lose the entire network."

Next to a solitary wooden doorway perhaps six feet high in the side of the tunnel, the trio and Dash dismounted. The horses barely managed to duck under the alcove of the entrance. Inside the room, Michael secured the horses to an ageing timber trough set against the dusty stonewall. "These caverns are huge," Sophia said.

"Yes, large enough to hold a troupe of fifty men comfortably."

"Why?" she asked, staring at the ceiling.

"In times of war they were indispensable for moving army units. Or for reconnaissance."

Sophia eyed the rough-hewn ceiling. Several cavities suggested the mixture of stone and dirt had fallen. "The roof looks a little unstable."

"Yes, unfortunately, maintenance isn't carried out as often as needed, but we will be okay here for tonight."

"Shouldn't we keep moving?"

"It'll be cold and dark out tonight," Michael said as he propped himself into a seated position against the stone. "Not enough light to travel."

"Why don't we take the tunnels?"

"A little farther along, they end and we will have to go back up to the surface."

"I see," Sophia said as she and Anne sat cross-legged on the floor near Michael. "Ground's hard."

"Yes. I'm afraid the luxury of a soft bed will evade us tonight."

Anne positioned her haversack to use as a pillow. She lay down, staring upwards at the ceiling. "I don't mind. I'm used to sleeping on hard surfaces." She wiggled a little, seemingly in search of the optimally comfortable position. "Our mattresses at the orphanage are not much softer."

With his staff resting across his lap and his haversack to one side, Michael closed his eyes.

Sophia watched as his lips moved, but no words came out. She presumed he must be praying before seeking sleep.

"Sophia," Anne whispered.

"Yes."

"Do you think we will make it, you know, to the Order of Esdras?"

Sophia pondered the question for a moment, but an answer eluded her. She remembered Sister Mary telling her to see the cup as half full not half empty. "I'm sure we will."

"Rest now, Sophia," Michael said.

She shook her head. Adrenalin stilled fuelled her body masking her fatigue. "But I'm not tired."

"I am," Anne whispered.

"We have a long journey ahead of us," Michael said in a calm but commanding voice. "Rest."

Reaching into her haversack, Sophia withdrew the book *The Order of Esdras* and flipped the pages to the first readable section.

At the top of the page in bold print were the words ***1862 – A Father's Last Act***. The text read more like a work of fiction than a prophecy.

* * *

1862 - A Father's Last Act

This will be a simple task. No blood. No screams. A drop of poison to slowly sap away the life of the mother and the unborn. Battling his inner voice, Jack attempted to convince himself that this would be easier than the typical task Mephis asked him to do. Thus, systematically, he ascended the dustless grand marble staircase to the second floor of the stately house where his victims slept. Each step pleaded with him—yelled at him— to turn back. Each step was harder than the last to conquer. His eyes cut to the many valuables, paintings, artifacts, and silverware that he could effortlessly steal. Money, however, was of no value and no reward to Jack. No matter how much wealth he had, pounds and shillings would not extend his life. Only Mephis was able to accomplish that miraculous feat. Local currency was not something Mephis accepted in exchange for his services. No, Mephis wanted something considerably more personal. Jack understood the price—his very soul.

Peacefully, Sophia, his target, slept in the grand king-size bed next to her husband. Jack wondered what she might be dreaming. Something pleasant. Or maybe a nightmare. Whatever she was dreaming, it would be her last.

From the inside pocket of his weathered trench coat, he withdrew a small glass vial filled with a green translucent liquid. He opened the vial, hovered his hand over her mouth, and allowed a single drop to fall free onto her lips. The liquid, like a snake scurrying after prey, slid from her luscious red lip into the depths of her mouth. His job done. He slipped silently into the darkness.

Outside the bedroom, he waited patiently to ensure the deed was completed. First came the sounds of Sophia gagging, gasping for air. Next came her husband's frantic cry, "What's wrong?" Then Sophia's struggle for breath, so panicked, so vain, was silenced under her husband's shouting: "Sophia! What's going on? Sophia!" Jack sensed the anxiety, the vibrato of desperation dancing on the husband's vocal cords. A kind of sadness mixed with guilt enveloped Jack, for he knew the husband would soon lose not only his beloved wife but also the child in her womb. He quickly extinguished the sensation by justifying the callous act as a means to extend his own mortality. *Her or me.*

Scuttling through the bedroom door came the husband cradling his unconscious pregnant wife. Jack waited until the man neared the top of the marble staircase. There he made his move, stepping from the shadows wielding a dagger with a twisted blade. He plunged the sharp blade deep between the unsuspecting man's shoulder blades. A cry of pain echoed throughout the grand house, bouncing off every wall. Then came the unexpected: The husband spun. Sophia's legs hit Jack squarely in the head. The sudden blow caught him off-guard. Dazed, stumbling, he scrambled to balance himself but could not and tumbled over the balcony railing falling two stories down and landing on a wooden table, which collapsed under his weight. He heard the sound of glass breaking under him, *a glass bottle most likely*, felt shards of it slice into his skin. The pain, external rather than internal, was new to him and quite bearable. He lay still and listened to the husband frantically descending the stairs and then exiting through the front door.

No matter, he thought. *Soon enough the poison will finish the task, and the dagger will claim its prize.* He rose, pulled the glass fragments from his coat and flesh, cutting his hands in the process. Staring at his palms, he watched, in a transfixed state, the wounds weep droplets of blood as he battled his pangs of conscience over his actions. He was not seeing his own blood. He was seeing the ghostly blood of his victims, each drop reflecting their last facial expression before death claimed them, reminding him of his crime.

* * *

In a daze, Sophia closed the book. The reality behind the words hit her like an icy cold rainshower on a bitter windy day. Chilled, her body shivered. *My parents? Jack killed them.* Returning to where she left off she continued to read … how the husband carried his pregnant wife down the street, through the pouring rain, eventually arriving at his final destination, the foyer of St Thomas Hospital. Then, in almost a trance-like state of disbelief, she read about the birth—*her* birth.

* * *

1862 – The Birth

Smiles illuminated Angela, the nurses, and Dr. Gregory as the infant's cries filled the room. "It's a baby girl," Dr. Gregory announced.

"She is beautiful," Angela said.

"Well, she is going to need a mum," Dr. Gregory said as he passed the baby to Angela's waiting arms. "How about it Angela? We all know you and your husband have been trying for a child for some time. Are you inclined to adopt this orphan? Or at least to look after her until we can find a relative?"

Angela beamed a smile that cast the warmth of the sun rising on a cold winter's day as she cradled the baby. "We can certainly give her a better home than an orphanage."

"Okay, then it's settled," Dr. Gregory said. "I'll organize the paperwork."

The baby stopped crying, comforted by Angela's sweet embrace.

"One last thing," Dr. Gregory said. "What are you going to name her?"

Angela glanced at the bracelet on her mother's wrist. "We should probably call her Sophia, after her mother." She bit her bottom lip.

"But you know what? My husband and I have had our hearts set on the name Anne."

"Okay, then, Anne it is," Dr. Gregory said as he turned to leave the room.

* * *

Sophia slammed the book shut. What she read changed what she had previously presumed. Her heart raced for answers increasing her body temperature. "Are you okay, Sophia," Michael asked, one eye open, the other closed.

"I'll be fine," she assured him, wiping newly-formed beads of sweat from her forehead.

Dash scuttled over and lay her head on Sophia's lap. Sophia stroked the dog's side gently. The presence of Dash calmed her somewhat and allowed her to ponder what the revelations meant and how they would change things. A few minutes later, she returned reading where she had left off.

* * *

"Wait, doctor!" Eleanor said. She was performing her final routine examination of the mother. Stethoscope in hand she exclaimed, "I hear a faint heartbeat!"

"But that's impossible," Dr. Gregory said, spinning around. "She's dead."

"Not her, the mother, a second baby."

"Are you certain?" Dr. Gregory asked. "A twin."

"Yes, I am absolutely certain!"

"Okay, team," he ordered, "prepare for a caesarian."

Angela's eyebrows lifted above her widening eyes. *A second child.*

The nurses and Dr. Gregory worked at a frantic pace. His priority, without needing to worry about the health of the mother, was to save the baby—Anne's twin. Within a minute, he had the newborn out of the womb. "Another girl," he said, while proceeding to cut and tie the umbilical cord. "And a fighter at that. It's nothing short of a miracle that she is still alive." The baby neither smiled nor cried as Dr. Gregory wrapped her in a blanket and placed her on a little side table to be weighed. "So, Angela, can you take both children?"

Angela glanced at Anne, then at the second child, and with a vacant expression said, "I would love to, but—"

"I understand," Dr. Gregory interrupted. "Finances, right?"

"Yes, finances." She frowned. "I'm so sorry, Doctor."

"Don't be. Times are tough. Better to have one adopted than both raised by the state."

Angela gazed at Anne with lips battling between a smile and a frown. "Seems a shame to separate them."

"We'll keep her here for a couple of weeks." He wrote some notes on a chart. "If we can't find someone to adopt her, we'll hand her over to the state." Dr. Gregory turned his attention to Eleanor. "Write up an arm band for this little cherub. Name her," he glanced at the mother's bracelet, "Sophia."

"Actually, doctor," Angela said, gazing into Sophia's eyes, "if we cannot find someone to adopt her, I *will* take her."

* * *

Closing the book, Sophia stared at Anne. For a moment, her expression was blank. A second later, a warm smile brightened her pretty face. *Anne said her mum's name was Angela. Could she be my sister? How did I end up at the orphanage?* Sister Mary had explained to Sophia, when she asked at age seven, that "a large white stork flew in carrying you from the heavens, holding you in a blanket under its long yellow beak, and left you on the front doorstep of the orphanage early one morning." Eventually, after Sophia quizzed her about the stork, Sister Mary came clean and said she had made the part about the stork up but the rest was true.

How she had actually ended up on the doorstep nobody knew. Sophia rubbed her bloodshot eyes. Her adrenalin had been diminishing from the moment she sat down. Fatigue started to hit her hard. *I need to keep reading.* On returning to the book, however, confusion racked her mind as she searched for the pages she had just read. All she found where the text use to be were blank pages with a logo, in black, in the center consisting of two feathers crossed one over the other. Her hands trembled. *What is this? How can this be?* She turned page after page, scanning the transcript for any resemblance to what she had read. Nothing. Gone. The words on the remaining pages recalled what Mendel had said. She placed her haversack on the ground, lay back and let her weary head fall into the soft leather. She stared toward the ceiling and cradled the book like a stuffed teddy bear. Eventually, exhaustion got the better of her, and she drifted to sleep.

Chapter 16 - Willow Tree

Refreshed from a deep sleep, a question reverberated in Sophia's mind as she mounted her stately horse Solitaire: *Should I tell Anne?* The subject plagued her as she trailed Michael and Anne through the underground tunnel. Several scenes replayed in her mind: the sight of Mephis shouting, "Sophia, Sophia, Sophia. You're one of the last," followed by Sister Mary placing the silver cross around her neck and telling her that she needed to go, leave the orphanage, and not return. Only as an afterthought had Mary asked her to take Anne. Then there was the dream in which Diniel had told her to find Jeremial of The Order of Esdras and made no mention of Anne. Finally, she recalled the scene when Mendel referred to Anne as The One's companion and gave her the bracelet.

"Are you okay, Sophia?" Michael asked. "You are awfully quiet."

"Yes," she said, gazing towards Anne. "Just thinking."

"Anything I can help you with?"

"No," Sophia replied, shaking her head, pausing a moment before continuing. "I'm beginning to think some things are better left unsaid."

"Indeed they are," he agreed.

She switched her focus to Michael, straightened her posture and sat upright, stiff as a pole. "Why do you say that, Michael?"

"Sometimes knowledge can make us vulnerable or provide our enemies with information they may not have otherwise known."

"Oh," she said, her voice softened and shoulders relaxed as his words resonated with her own thoughts.

"I don't like secrets," Anne said. "I struggle to keep them."

Truly, Sophia thought, recalling how on more than one occasion over the years Anne had almost let slip the time she had healed her broken leg. The most recent being with Mendel. One time, after she had fallen off a swing in the playground, her knees grazed, holding back tears with a brave smile, she had let slip, "At least you won't have to heal me this time, Sophia." Sister Margaret overhearing had asked, "By what do you mean, Anne?" Before Anne could reply, Sophia interrupted, "Sometimes we play doctors and nurses," which was enough to satisfy Sister Margaret's incurable curiosity.

In the distance, the warm golden radiance of the early-morning sun peeked through the exit of the tunnel, growing brighter as they approached. Before leaving the passageway, they stopped and gazed in wonderment at the beauty of the landscape before them. Acres of multi-hued green pastures sparsely occupied with varied wildlife. Teams of horses in a plethora of colors grazed in harmony with the songbirds. The swallows fed on horse flies as rarely seen Cattle Egrets hunted insects stirred from their hiding in the grass. By the side of a slow-running creek, a herd of cows chewed on vibrant green grass. As Sophia left the tunnel she reckoned the change in scenery was like stepping into paradise. She had never seen, in person at least, anything as picturesque as the natural beauty around her. While the forest she frequented at the back of the orphanage was pleasing, there was an eerie sense of foreboding about it. Here, the immense openness gave a sense of freedom. She glanced behind her and saw that the exit to the tunnel had become virtually invisible, camouflaged by secluding oak trees.

Anne pointed to the cows. "Look! A manure factory!" She giggled. The sort of chuckle that causes others to laugh even if the joke is not funny.

"Now, Anne," Sophia replied in a mock-stern tone that reminded her of Sister Catherine. She smiled, then turned to Michael and asked, "Where are we headed?"

"To see an old friend of Mendel's who will aid us on our journey." He gave Lancelot a tender kiss with his heels, encouraging the stallion to a canter. In a louder voice, over the sound of the horses' hooves thumping the grassland, he shouted, "It's a full day's ride."

Across the fields they raced, the stiff wind splaying the girls' hair almost horizontal. A broad smile dawned on Sophia's face, the sensation of the ride—magical. In some moments, when all four of Solitaire's hooves left the ground, a breathtaking feeling of weightlessness, almost as if she was flying, swept through her body—thrilling.

A few hours later, in the shade of a copse of buoyant willow trees weeping beside a slow-running creek they dismounted. Sophia rubbed her bottom. "They should really make comfier saddles."

"You'll toughen up in time," Michael replied as he scouted the scrub.

"What you looking for?" Sophia asked with a hint of curiosity.

"A piece of wood to make a weapon," he said as he picked up a fallen branch as big around as his calf. "This will do."

"What can we do?"

"Collect some dead branches for a fire."

"Okay."

Under the willow, Michael withdrew a knife from his haversack and carved the branch into an oblong, six inches in length and one inch thick, with rounded ends. By the time he finished the girls had collected an armload each of assorted branches. Dash, as helpful as ever, lugged a stick between her jaws, tail wagging with pride.

Sophia dropped the make-do firewood. "How are we going to start the fire?" Sophia asked.

"I have some flint in my haversack," Michael said. He fetched it and within a few minutes had a healthy campfire going. Their morale lifted as the warmth from the golden flames touched their skin. "Can you keep this fire going, Sophia?" Michael asked as he rose.

Sophia nodded. "I sure can. Where are you going?"

"To hunt for some lunch."

"Great," Anne said. "I'm famished."

"You're always hungry, Anne," Sophia replied, though her stomach agreed with Anne.

"Would you like to join me on the hunt, Anne?"

She leapt to her feet. "Sure would."

Dash attempted to follow before Sophia called her back, tempting her by throwing a stick.

* * *

Anne and Michael shadowed the creek bed towards some low-lying grassy hills. "What are we hunting for?" she asked.

"Quiet now," Michael whispered. "We are close." Crouching, he continued forward, tenderly setting down each foot on the clayish creek bank. The soft dirt helped muffle his footsteps.

Anne gazed around trying to find what Michael was tracking. Then, in the distance, she spotted two large grey furry ears poking up in the grass. "There's a rabbit!" she shouted.

Michael laughed as the rabbit ran away. "Yes, Anne," he said, shaking his head. "That is what we are hunting."

"Oh." Her face turned a pale shade of red. "I think I scared it."

"Likely," he said, smiling. "No matter. We will find another." Before long, Michael sighted another pair of ears protruding above the long grass. He readied his aim and then with all his might launched the makeshift weapon. The chunk of wood spun through the air before clipping the tips of the rabbit's ears. "Missed," he whispered, screwing up his nose as the rabbit scuttled away.

"Can I have a go?" Anne asked.

Michael cut his eyes around, shrugged. "Can you throw?"

"I sure can. I'm darned good with rocks."

"Okay, then." He passed the weapon to Anne. "Give it your best shot."

Together they moved stealthily through the scrub, hunting for another target.

* * *

With a thin branch, Sophia stoked the fire and watched the small golden sparks take their brief flight, like dancing fireflies, before extinguishing. Dash, panting from fetching sticks, rested by her side. Ten throws and returns seemed about enough for her. After the last throw, Dash hesitated, then instead of running, walked to the stick and returned with the branch in her jaw as if to say "enough." Sophia rummaged through her haversack, withdrew *The Order of Esdras* and flipped through the pages. Her eyes widened as she came to a new story.

* * *

1862 The Nursery

Cold, wet, hungry, rain pelting his black trench coat, Jack trudged up the street one labored step after the other. The broad brim of his hat served as a gutter to pool the rain before releasing it to cascade over the side. He did not care. His mood was bleak after Mephis tore him apart over his failure. The newspaper headline, 'Miracle baby survives after father and mother die' told Mephis everything he needed to know. He did not even bother to read the story. Instead, Mephis used the paper, after rolling it up like a baton, to beat Jack until he crumpled to the floor writhing in pain. Then he threw the rolled-up paper at Jack and said two commanding words: *"Fix it."*

At such times Jack pondered why he even wanted to extend his miserable existence. A painting by Michelangelo he had once seen in the Sistine Chapel during a trip to Italy was seared in his memory *The Last Judgement*. The scene depicted in the fresco created within him a sense of profound dread. The image of naked people being cast off a boat in fear only to end up in the grip of a snake haunted him. He feared death. His motivation was to keep the grim reaper who he sensed stalked his shadow at arm's length.

While wiping his shoes on the straw mattress outside St Thomas Hospital's main entrance, Jack swept the rain off the front and sleeves of his coat. He removed his hat, gave it a quick flick, sending a wash of water to the ground. He gazed at the broad rim, allowing his vision to blur while thinking of the past. A decade had passed since the last time he had entered a hospital. Only the last time he was an acting highly-skilled senior surgeon who was there to save lives not take them.

He placed the hat back on his head, turned it slightly left and right until he found the comfortable sweet spot. He opened his coat to expose his doctor's garb underneath, along with a stethoscope dangling around his neck, and passed through the entrance.

Inside, he tipped his hat to the nurse behind the reception desk who acknowledged his presence with a smile. The cursory greeting assured him that the hospital staff did not personally know all the resident doctors on duty. He scanned the signs on the wall and located the one pointing to the maternity ward. His failed attempt two weeks earlier had brought him here to the very hallway he was now pacing towards the nursery. A single nurse on duty who was busy working at a desk was all that stood between him and a room full of baby cots. Jack glanced at the round dial of the fusee clock on the wall: 4:55 a.m. *On time*, he thought, the pre-dawn hush prior to breakfast. He had planned it this way so all he would have to contend with was a skeleton shift.

His eyes were fixated momentarily on the second hand of the clock, hypnotized by how the thin needle jerked with each passing instant, knowing that with each quiver he was one tick closer to death. He shook his head to clear his mind and then moved out of sight. Jack opened his black leather doctor's bag and retrieved a white cloth pre-laced with chloroform. He took a few silent steps to move into position. He placed one arm around the nurse's waist and pressed the other over her nose and mouth and let the chloroform do its work. A little struggle, a few muffled screams, and then she went limp. He released his grip, allowing the body to slip from his grasp to the shadows under the desk. She would awaken in due time. *No need to kill her.* He needed only to do what he had to. *I am not a monster.*

* * *

Sophia glanced away from the text and took a few deep breaths to help calm her restless stomach. The thought of Jack, her parents' murderer, being so close to her when she was a baby filled her with an urge to scream. Calmer, she continued reading, her curiosity getting the best of her anxiety.

$* * *$

Four sleeping babies now an arm's length away, he smiled, not at the little ones' peaceful beauty as a proud father would do but at his sense of imminent accomplishment. The news report had provided him with the names of his prey, Anne and Sophia. Mephis, in his haste, had presumed there was only one baby. Jack had avoided correcting him for fear of further punishment. On the end of each cot he read: Richard, James, Sophia, Sarah. No Anne. *Surely they haven't separated them*, Jack thought. His eyes narrowed as he reread the nametags. He returned to the nurse's desk and searched the drawer for the birth reports file. He scanned down the page until he found what he was looking for:

Sophia – In nursery awaiting adoption.

Anne – In the temporary custody of Nurse Angela who will proceed to adopt if no relative is found.

Angela. He cursed silently on the way back inside the nursery. On seeing the sleeping child Sophia, Jack was unable to quench a stirring sense of admiration. *So beautiful. So peaceful.* He longed to feel the peace he saw in Sophia's tranquil state. With gentle hands he lifted the infant swaddled in a woolen blanket from her cot. A fatherly instinct urged him to protect the defenseless child. Scared the sensation would manifest, he hastily placed her in a wicker carry basket. She stirred a little. Outside the nursery, he searched for the closest emergency exit. A short walk past a few nurses too busy with their chores to notice him passing by with the basketed baby in hand, he came to a one-way exit typically used only as a fire escape. A quick look around showed no one in sight. He made his departure.

The rain had given way to light snow. Jack stuck to the dark alleys and lonesome backstreets on his way to the place where he planned to dispose Sophia. He could not bring himself to kill an innocent child directly. Therefore, he devised a plan to prevent the harassment of his conscience. When he arrived at his destination, he began to execute that plan. Under the shelter of a wooden bridge that crossed a narrow stretch of river, he held the basket over the water. *All I have to do is set her afloat. As it drifts downstream, the basket will take on water and slowly sink, and the icy waters will claim her. Easy enough.* But it wasn't. His hands started to tremble, as the image of the child asleep in such a peaceful state stabbed deep into his core. *She is sinless.* He fought with his conscience, attempting to justify his task. *Her or me.* The selfish reason he had used to legitimize the killing of the child's mother did not convince him. The doctor in him, the one who had sworn a sacred oath and used to save lives instead of destroy them, was winning this debate. He propped himself up against the wingwall of the bridge and set the basket on the ground beside him.

After several minutes of contemplation, he formulated a new plan. He knew of an orphanage not far away, *Saint Juliana of Pavilly Orphanage.* Daylight breaking, he made haste. On approach to the orphanage, careful not to leave a trail, he stepped only in places the snow had spared. He set the child on the front doorstep, rapped loudly on the wood, and then quickly retreated out of sight and waited, before leaving, to ensure someone came to the door.

"Mephis needn't know," he mumbled as he made the long, tiresome journey back to his Whitechapel home. "How would he ever know if she lived or died?"

* * *

"He couldn't do it," Sophia murmured, taking a break from reading. "He couldn't bear to kill me." After a moment of contemplation, she resumed reading.

* * *

"Sophia's gone," Angela told Dr. Gregory. "We have found no trace of her, doctor. Should we call the police?"

"I'm not sure what we would tell them." Dr. Gregory rubbed his chin. "Sophia needed a home. Let's hope whoever took her provides her with one. The authorities have been looking for a reason to shut this hospital down. If we involve the police, this incident may give them just the excuse they need to do so."

Angela nodded. "If it's okay with you, Doctor, I'll do my own private searching."

"By all means, Angela. But, please, be careful. We wouldn't want you to put yourself in harm's way or get into any kind of trouble."

Four years later, Angela received a letter under the door of her home on a dark, rainy night with instructions on where to meet for information about Sophia. The letter was signed "Jack."

* * *

The text ended. Sophia closed the *The Order Of Esdras* and then reopened to where she had left off. As expected, the pages were blank. She sighed. *How does this help me? Why is the book telling me these things? And how?*

"We're back," Anne said, holding a rabbit by the ears. "Look what I caught."

Sophia's voice raised in pitch simultaneously with her eyebrows, said, "*You?*"

Michael took the rabbit from Anne. "She has quite a throwing arm."

Sophia nodded, thinking back to the incident with the Bobbies in town. "That she does."

Michael took out his knife and began preparing their lunch.

"That's gross," Anne said, watching Michael skin the rabbit.

"Gross, yes," Sophia said, "but it will make quite the meal."

Chapter 17 - Stowe House

Shades of color, each just a bit dimmer than the previous, saturated the soft rolling hills as the sun dropped slowly below the horizon. Up ahead, appearing in the hazy distance, the large stately buildings that form Stowe House came into view. Sophia looked up at an impressive stone statue of a man on a horse set atop a massive stone pillar. As they cantered past the structure towards the house, a drove of quite vocal goats made a wailing bleat as they fled into the surrounding trees.

While securing her horse, Sophia tried without success to calculate the size of the house, which spanned some distance in both directions away from the central structure. "This place is enormous," she said.

"Yes, a lavish temple of delights," Michael said. He pointed to various facades as he led them towards the front door. "Several state rooms, each with its own stories and individual design wrapped in mythology and political themes, make up the bulk of the sanctuary." At the entrance, Michael tugged three times in rapid succession on a rope suspended from a discolored bronze bell. The chimes, sounding deeper than Sophia expected, boomed between the monumental pillars supporting the front portico—so loud that Anne covered her ears.

After a short wait, the rightmost of the auburn-color oak doors swung inwards, squealing as the hinges groaned under the weight. "Richard? I was expecting the butler to greet us," Michael said, extending his arm.

"I've been watching your approach from the upstairs study," Richard replied, shaking Michael's hand. "By George, it is good to see you. Last time, you were a tiny tot, coming up hardly to my waist level, and now you are taller than I." He gestured them inside, said, "Well, don't just stand there, come on in so you can introduce me to your companions. But, do be a good chap and leave that mutt outside."

Dash moaned, circled a few times, and then lay down and curled her body into a resting position.

Through an arched opening on the side of the foyer, they entered a sitting room. The extravagance of the interior astounded Sophia. A concert grand piano glistened under the gentle light filtering through the soft white cotton curtains over the grand bay window. The ornate fireplace, large enough to camp inside, crackled as flames devoured freshly cut logs, distributing comforting warmth throughout the space. The walls hung a series of portraits of people in exuberant poses showing off their best possible facets clad in flamboyant clothes, the cost of any article of which could feed Sophia's orphanage family for a year. As she lowered herself into the fine white leather cushion of the sofa between Michael and Anne, Sophia imagined herself sitting on a cloud—so supple and such a welcome relief from Solitaire's rather unforgiving saddle. Richard took a seat opposite them in a leather chair. He was an older fellow, mid-to-late fifties, with a face most women would not bother to take a second look at, capped with a bald crown walled by short receding hair. The buttons on his black dress coat strained to hold back a bulging belly suggesting not only that he ate well but had a tooth for sweets.

"Jolly good show, let me guess," Richard said while pointing. "Sophia is the one in the middle and Anne on the end."

"Right you are, Richard," Michael replied.

"Well of course, I am. But I did have fifty-fifty odds."

Sophia leant forward, eyebrows hovering low above her narrow eyes. "But how did you know our names?"

"Carrier pigeon, my dear girl. Arrived two hours ago from Mendel." He crossed his legs and scratched newly-formed stubble on his chin. "My, we are the suspicious one, aren't we?"

"Maybe," Sophia replied, sinking back into the plush leather.

From inside his coat Richard pulled out a cigar. "Mind if I smoke?"

"Yes," Sophia said. "That stuff will kill you, they say."

"Are we a scientist, too, Sophia?"

"No," she said, letting her voice fall just a bit. "It just makes sense. Breathing in smoke couldn't really be good for you, could it?"

"I suppose not," Richard said as he lit the end of the cigar.

"Why did you ask if you were going to smoke anyway?"

"Manners, my dear." He coughed plumes of smoke while pulling the cigar away from his lips. "Something you seem to be lacking."

Michael interrupted. "Richard, old friend, Mendel said you could help us on our journey."

"I could. But how do I know this feisty girl is *The One*?" His cold brown eyes glared at Sophia. "Can you do any tricks?"

"Tricks?" She threw her head back and eyed him. "What do you mean tricks?"

"I don't know. Levitate an object. Part a sea. What can you do?"

"Noth—ing," she said, turning her head from hard left to hard right.

Richard leant into the back of the recliner and took a deep drag of his cigar. Seconds later, he exhaled, creating rings of smoke. "I see."

"Convinced?" Michael said.

"Right you are, young Michael. She is a curious one." He licked his fingers, pinched the end of his cigar a couple of times to snuff the embers, and then stored the roll of tobacco back under his coat. "Let's not just sit around here," he said. "We have things to discuss in a more private location."

They all rose with Richard who, taking long swift strides, led the way. Apart from a well-polished suit of knights armor standing alone on the back wall of the first room they entered the space was empty. Rectangular marks on the floor, especially close to the walls, told Sophia furniture had been removed. "Have you been robbed?" she asked.

"No, I'm afraid not," Richard said. "Well, not in so many words. Times have not been very fortunate to us, requiring us to sell off assets to pay down debt."

After passing through several more doorways adjoining the staterooms, they came to a large empty room, circular, like a temple. A series of arched niches in the walls, separated by sixteen ornamented stone columns, held various objects of art. Above each one was a gas-powered glass lamp hung from the ceiling of an alcove two feet deep that projected inwards where the top of the columns met. The marble-tiled floor reflected the ornate domed ceiling. Several bands above the alcove lined the curvature of the room each with its own decorative pattern. The pattern of the first band alternated between a shield symbol and a face with a long nose and eyes set eerily close together. At a rough count, Sophia calculated 24 faces and shields. The next higher band consisted of etchings of people in the stone, dressed old-style as if from biblical times and various animals—a lamb, a cow, a lion. Embedded in the marble floor in the center of the room was a brownish square tile with a solid bronze circle inside.

Richard positioned himself on the decorated spot. "Michael, be a good chap and close the door we came through."

As Michael closed the door, the square Richard was standing on sank about two inches into the floor with a clunk. Sophia's cross necklace vibrated between her breasts as her body jittered from the quaking movement of the floor. She watched the second hand on a wooden clock mounted above the door tick five times before the tremors stopped.

"Right, there we are." With a thump, as Richard stepped away, the marble square tile snapped flush with the floor. "Grab the door, Michael."

Michael touched the handle and took three unhurried steps backward as the door swung open. "How is that possible?" Sophia asked as she gazed down the marble staircase beyond.

"Stowe House has many secrets, my dear," Richard said, as he began the descent. "The room rotates."

"But how?" Sophia asked.

"Let's call it English ingenuity."

At the base of the stairs, Richard jostled a key back and forth in the bronze keyhole. He mumbled something under his breath, which Sophia could not quite catch, several times, presumably from frustration. "Ahh, there we go," he said. "Blasted door, stubborn as my wife."

Richard kicked a few books strewn on the floor to the side as he entered the room. "Careful you don't trip."

Inside Sophia carefully stepped around little heaps of books scattered across the floor. Books, books, everywhere books. On shelves, across tables, stacked in piles. Hardly a square foot in the chamber that did not have a book. After navigating through mounds of books, Richard took a seat behind a round wooden table, surrounded by six handmade maple wood chairs. Sophia circled the table. The back of each chair had a protruding carved face. In pairs, male and female, two of the faces had no eyes, two no ears, and two no mouths. *Odd*, Sophia thought.

"Take a seat," Richard said, shuffling through the books spread across the table. "Ahh. Here it is." He pulled toward him a large book twice as high and wide as an ordinary book with the gold-gilded title *Angels* on front. "Right, Sophia, I'm going to ask you a couple of questions. This will go much quicker if you answer them honestly."

"I wouldn't do otherwise," she said, nodding while crossing her fingers under the desk, an old superstitious trick she had learnt to allow her to tell a white lie. Some secrets she was determined never to reveal, Anne's heritage being one of them.

Richard stopped flipping through the book when he came to a picture of a male holding a glowing silver-white sword about to strike what looked like the shadow of a person. The angle he faced and the position of the sword hid his identity. On his back was a bow, but no quiver, which Sophia thought strange. Halfway up his forearm, framed in a yellowish glow, he wore an armlet. Around his waist, an elaborate belt with peculiar inscriptions held up a pair of ordinary-looking white trousers.

"Who's the man?" Sophia asked.

"No idea," Richard replied. "Not important." With his finger, he scanned down the page. "Did your parents exhibit any powers, Sophia?"

"I never knew them. They are dead."

"Oh. Hmm. Well, in that case, do you know whether when they died their bodies disintegrated?"

"Disintegrated?" *A strange question.* She took a moment to think back to what she had read in *The Order of Esdras*, and recalled nothing to indicate that they disintegrated. "Not that I'm aware of."

"They must not have carried the gene. Mendel expected as much."

"Gene?"

"Yes. Mendel works in the area. It is said our bodies contain an elaborate system of genes. They make our bodies unique. There is a specific gene that Mendel calls the 'Angelic Gene' which descendants of the twelve angels may carry. When they die, their bodies rather than merely eroding like the rest of us in decomposition simply disintegrate, immediately on death, to dust."

"Oh. Then why didn't my parents…" she swallowed an unpleasant taste of fear "disintegrate?"

"Sometimes the gene skips a generation, or two. Genetics. Funny thing. They say that is why I am bald and my father is not, but his father is. Skipped right over him. Lucky bastard."

"Sir, mind the language in front of the ladies," Michael said.

"Yes, indeed," he said, tipping his head. "Please accept my apology."

Sophia nodded. She had heard much worse over the years. "Is there any way to check me for the gene?" she asked.

"No, not physically. I don't have the equipment." He continued to read. "You will nevertheless know sooner or later when you will exhibit powers not of this earth." Anne caught his eye. "I suspect, from Anne's expression, that you already have. However, all things considered, and with what Mendel said in his note, there is little doubting you are descended from angel-human conception many generations ago."

"So, I'm an angel."

"No, no dear. Only God ordains angels," Richard said. "Angels are created beings as such. You carry the Angelic Gene." Richard continued flipping through pages.

"Oh." Her eyebrows melted in a puddle of disappointment. "How then do I have powers?"

"You needn't be an angel to have powers. The gene gives you an edge to tap into spiritual gifts that elude us humble gents."

"But if I die, I disintegrate?"

"Well, your body does." He quickly scanned over a paragraph. "Your soul? Well, there seems to be some contention on what happens to a soul inside a body carrying the Angelic Gene when terminated. Nobody seems to know. You may stand the Last Judgement like the rest of us mere mortals."

"That's comforting," she replied. In her mind, she was more concerned for Anne than herself. A new question arose in her thoughts: *Does she have the Angelic Gene?*

"Ah ha," Richard said, "this is what I was looking for." He brought the book up close to his face and scanned the text. "Be a good girl and place your hand on the center of the table."

Chapter 18 - The Test

Sophia placed her hand palm down fingers together on the center of the table.

Richard removed a feathered quill from an ink well and hovered it over her hand. Sophia asked, "Are you going to write on my hand?" With a swift movement, he raised his hand, and then stabbed the quill down forcefully through the center of her hand. Anne screamed and covered her eyes. Sophia's face turned snow white as if the new wound had provided a drain for the blood to flow from her agonized expression. Her lungs screamed for the air she exhaled in a shocked gasp. She jerked her arm in an attempt to free herself. The quill impaling her hand stuck in the wood prevented her trembling hand from escaping.

"Are you mad?" Michael shouted, leaping off of his seat. He grabbed the feathered end of the quill and reefed upward freeing Sophia's hand. A trail of blood streaked across the table as Sophia retracted her hand. She cupped her wound and, oddly, the pain subsided rapidly.

"Pass your hand here, dear girl," Richard said. "Don't be afraid. I'll not stab you again."

"You had better not," Michael said, glaring at Richard.

She extended her quivering hand towards Richard. He spat on a handkerchief and proceeded to wipe the blood away covering her skin. No wound, her hand had thoroughly healed. "See there, Sophia, you do have tricks."

"You have a terrible way of testing things," Michael said.

"Don't be too hard on me, young chap," he said, with a nod. "I had to be sure."

"And what if she hadn't healed? Then what?"

"Hmm," Richard said, rubbing his chin. "I didn't contemplate that outcome."

Anne, peeking between the fingers covering her eyes, asked, "Is it safe to look?"

"Yes, it is," Richard replied.

"So what now?" Michael asked.

"Well, let's see." He returned reading through the paragraphs, skipping some, studying others intently. "Another test."

Sophia shifted back in her chair. Anne covered her eyes, "Not another one."

Richard laughed. "No fear. This one does not involve blood."

Anne, removing her palms covering her eyes, said, "That's a relief."

"Hmm. Let me think," Richard said, leaving the table. He approached a bookshelf and removed a small ceramic pot. Back on his chair, he tipped the container and allowed four tiny metallic silver spheres to roll onto the center of the table.

"What are they?" Sophia asked.

"They are called 'ball bearings,' an ingenious little invention by Jules Suriray. Quite a bright chap." He focused on Sophia. "I want you to try to move them."

Sophia reached out and pushed the ball bearings with her fingertips so that they rolled towards Richard. "No," he said. "Not with your hands; with your *mind*."

"My *mind?*"

"Yes. Concentrate on them and force them to move with your mind."

"Wow," Anne said. "If you can do this, you'll be able to cheat at marbles."

Sophia shook her head, once dismissing Anne's idea (although she found it somewhat intriguing) and a second time demonstrating doubt about her ability to accomplish the task. "Move them with my mind?"

"You can do it," Richard said. "Concentrate now."

She studied the bearings. Round, small silver balls, no larger than her pinky fingernail. *Impossible,* she thought. The words *move, move, move* echoed through her mind. Her teeth clenched from a mix of frustration and concentration. Her eyes narrowed, presuming a tighter focus would help the task. Nothing. "This is stupid," she mumbled.

"Think of where you want the balls to go," Richard said. "Be specific in your thoughts. Imagine your hand reaching out and pushing them."

Her head started to ache from the intense concentration. An image came to her. She saw an invisible hand, a projection of her own, reach out and flick one of the balls with her fingertips just as she had done with her physical hand. It moved. Not far, but it rolled a short distance. The response broke her attention.

Richards's eyebrows raised. "Ah, there you go."

"Wow," Anne said. "That is so weird."

"It's tiring," Sophia said, rubbing her temples.

"Yes. I can imagine it would be, but will get easier the more you practice," Richard said. "Now try again."

Sophia returned her focus to the balls and this time her mind visualized them in a new way. They broke down into many miniscule particles—thousands and thousands of them—combined in the shape of the sphere. The air around them appeared as tiny atom particles that formed one giant mesh in which the balls existed. Next, the tabletop appeared as one mass of atoms, swarming like miniscule bees. No longer seeing things as solid objects but as so many parts of a greater object, her thoughts honed in on the atoms she wanted to control. Intently, she focused on the spheres. They began to roll, slowly at first, in unison, in a circle each chasing each other. Michael's eyes widened as their speed increased to the point at which they appeared to be a solid silver ring.

Then the unthinkable. With her mind, she lifted them from the table, creating different patterns by moving them at incredible speeds. First a figure eight, then a more complex configuration of four circles joined together and after that an astonishing representation of a cylinder. To complete the picture the balls moved at velocities faster than light, leaving solid trails. All of a sudden, the balls stopped and fell back to the table, each bouncing several times before rolling to a halt. Sophia collapsed forward. Her head struck the wooden tabletop with a solid thump.

Michael reached over. "Sophia!" Anne jumped out of her chair and stood beside her. Richard, his eyes like slits, just peered intently at Sophia.

Moments later, Sophia lifted her head, touched her fingertips to her red forehead, straining as if her skull weighed a ton. Drops of blood dripped from her nose. She rubbed her brow in an effort to ease the throbbing not only in her head but in her mind.

Richard tossed his handkerchief towards her. "Wipe your nostrils, dear." She did so, clearing away all signs of blood. "Impressive," Richard added. "I think that will do for today. You require further practice my dear, and you'll be able to do that on your journey. Your next destination should be to visit Reverend Robinson of Fuller Church in Northampshire. I'll send him a message by pigeon post to let him know you're coming. The side trip will not take you far off your path to Hermitage Castle."

"Why?" Sophia said, shaking her head, trying to dispel the heavy grogginess that had come over her.

"You'll find out when you get to Fuller Church."

Chapter 19 - Remembrance

Jack knelt on weeds and decaying flowers in front of a weathered stone tombstone in the small graveyard at the back of St Anne's Church in Whitechapel. Once a year he came to this place and allowed his mind to wander off to thoughts of his only brother. Today, however, he had broken his routine and come earlier, months earlier, than he normally did. The reason for breaching his regular schedule started when Mephis assigned him a new task—the task of fixing a failed job that had haunted him daily. Unfinished business. Here, he hoped to be able to find some peace, some reasoning, some justification to comfort him for what lay ahead. He pulled a cloth from his doctor's bag and wiped the dirt and grit from the letters chiseled in the stone that spelled his brother's name—Elidin—as his mind was awash in scenes from his past.

* * *

"I'm so blessed to have such a brother, Jack, a surgeon like you who is able to help me," Elidin said, lying shirtless on the examination table in Jack's office. "The money I make from carpentry, while enough to feed me, is hardly enough to pay for medical treatment."

"Where does it hurt?" Jack asked.

"Slightly above my stomach, there to the right. There appears to be hard patch."

Jack pressed on his brother's abdomen with both his hands exploring the area of discomfort. Elidin winced as Jack's hand pressed down on a section just above his navel. "What do you think?" Elidin asked. "Am I going to die?"

"Surely not," Jack replied. "We should be able to fix this."

The next day, Jack had opened his brother up to investigate the extent of the internal growth. What he found knotted his gut—a large tumorous growth, a contorted mass of hardened cells, extending from his stomach up into the thoracic cavity, in some places leaching onto his right lung, contaminating the healthy tissue. Amputating the mass would require removing a large part of his brother's stomach and liver and—killing him. He closed the incision, powerless to do anything.

Elidin, sitting on the chair next to his brother's desk, gazed at the blank emotionless expression on Jack's face. The appearance told Elidin all he needed to know, but he awaited the words, in earnest, to be sure.

"I'm sorry, Elidin," Jack said. "There is nothing I can do."

"How long do I have?" he asked.

"A month," Jack replied. "Perhaps two … at best."

Elidin's eyes welled with sadness. He blinked, sending the last tear he would ever shed cascading down his cheek. "I'll be okay," he said. "Just means I'll be heading to heaven sooner than I thought I would be."

"Right," Jack said, his eyes narrow, tongue touching his lip.

Over the next few weeks, Elidin, a devout Catholic who had given his life to Christ in his teenage years, spent many hours at St Anne's Church, donating his time, using his carpentry skills to help with jobs that required undertaking. He negotiated with the priest to be buried in the cemetery out back. His last will and testament left all his earthly belongings to the church. Not that he had much to give, but it made sense, for he had no family of his own and his brother was in no need of money.

Late one afternoon, Jack asked, "How can you believe in a God who allows you to die from such a terrible affliction?"

"I discovered a long time ago," Elidin said, clearing his throat, "that a life with God is better than a life without." With a glitter of joy in his eye, he added, "Regardless of circumstance."

An hour later, he passed away.

* * *

"All a life with God got you was an early funeral," Jack whispered, before moistening the cloth with his spittle and then wiping the grooves of the letter n, the final letter.

Jack had never understood why his brother listened to the street preachers who inevitably led him into the church. He had no use for their prattles. Life was unkind. He knew enough about Charles Darwin's evolutionary concepts, which had spread so quickly through the medical and scientific community, to know the world did not need a God. As a surgeon, he had witnessed his fair share of people dying from all sorts of ailments—those who believed in God and those who did not. Mother Nature seemed quite fickle when it came to who lived and who died. Though he had to admit that people of faith appeared to suffer less in their dying, finding some strange kind of peace he did not understand. That alone, however, was hardly enough to substantiate their claims of an Almighty Creator. Where is God when those who place their faith in him are suffering and dying of illness? Jack had never seen him. Some surgeons believed in God, and a few even believed in miracles. Jack wrote them off as isolated events or early misdiagnosis.

His brother had told him that the church priests and parishioners would pray for him. What good did it do him? He died. What bothered

Jack the most was that his brother did not seem to care he was dying and in fact showed no fear of death.

Finished cleaning the grooves, Jack put his cloth away. He whispered, "Maybe if I wasn't cursed with the fear of death, I wouldn't have to kill."

He gathered up the dead flowers and left.

Chapter 20 - Church

As a guest of Stowe House, the night passed more quickly than Sophia desired. Richard provided them with an elaborate dinner, consisting of sumptuous foods unfamiliar to Sophia, such as caviar, a word she had never heard. Richard explained that they were a rare delicacy—fish eggs. For dessert the kitchen staff baked an Apple pie. The rich taste lingered on her lips and the alluring scent loitered, in her nostrils. Then there were the sleeping quarters. She and Anne shared a stately room all their own with a king-size bed fitted with silk sheets that made rising in the morning to the sound of a rooster's cock-a-doodle-do no easy task. The soft, gentle feather mattress provided such a delightful and unfamiliar comfort that enticed her to a longer stay.

Breakfast was another feast. Tangy smoked bacon and eggs accompanied with something Richard referred to as French toast. *Greasy* toast was more like it, Sophia thought, but it tasted wonderful, buttery. She wondered if such food was healthy. From the looks of Richard it might not be. She excused this gorge, though, sensing meals ahead may be scarce. Well-fed and well-rested, they were ready to travel to Fuller Church to meet with Reverend Robinson.

Sophia wondered what awaited them at their next destination. She was no stranger to church. Every Sunday, without fail, Sister Mary would take the children of Saint Juliana of Pavilly Orphanage to the quaint Catholic parish nearby. The building was as simple in design as a kid's hand-drawn sketch of a triangle on top of a square with a rectangle for the door. The only remarkable feature was the crucifix above the peak of the triangular roof. Father Bendington, the church's priest, administered the service as though it were a mini-theatrical production. He and various members of the congregation assumed the role of biblical characters and saints and acted out the stories, like moral plays from the Middle Ages. Father B. was quite the entertainer. He referred to himself as "Shakespeare of the Church." While Sophia read the Bible on a daily basis, watching the Bible performed, acted out, in the context of current events helped her to understand how the Bible was indeed God's word. A feather-light sensation fluttered through her stomach as she remembered the laughter and tears experienced during the plays with her orphanage family. She missed them, missed Sister Mary and Sister Catherine.

"Whoa…," Michael said, pulling Lancelot to a halt on the outskirts of Kettering, a small town in Northamphshire.

"What's up, Michael?" Sophia asked, curious as to Michael's sudden stop.

"I sense someone might be following us," he replied, scanning their surroundings. Seeing no one, he said, "Hmm… Might be my imagination. Let's keep moving."

Outside of Fuller Church, an impressive chapel much larger than Father B.'s church, they secured their horses and then proceeded inside.

"You can't bring that dog in here," shouted the voice of a man sitting on a pew to their left.

"Dash," Michael said, pointing to the entrance, "outside." With a whimper, Dash, tail between her legs, begrudgingly left.

"Gee, so many places are anti-dog," Anne said.

"Don't be too hard on them, Anne," Sophia replied. "Somehow I doubt the Sisters would have allowed Dash inside the orphanage."

From the waist-high platform of the pulpit at the back of the church, a man standing behind the lectern said, "Ahh. You must be the three about whom I was awoken in the early hours of the morning by the cooing of a carrier pigeon."

"Reverend Robinson, I presume," Michael said.

The man stepped forward, extended his arm. "Yes. And you must be Michael."

While shaking his hand, Michael proceeded to introduce Sophia and Anne. Sophia felt a warmth coming from the reverend. She sensed he was a man of God. He spoke clearly, conveying each word with a gentle smile. His glistening eyes inspired trust. "Come, come," Reverend Robinson said, as he stepped down from the pulpit and led them towards a side exit of the church.

Outside, in the alley next to the church, a two-horse open carriage awaited. "Impressive." The wagon had two facing bench seats, leather-cushioned with high backs, that accommodated six passengers. The driver had a matching cushion bench seat.

"I'm not getting on that," Anne said.

Her words triggered Sophia's memory of hearing Anne relive the agonizing carriage accident that claimed her adoptive parents' lives. Though on occasion Anne did take horse-drawn cart rides with the Sisters, it was always a challenge getting her onboard. "It'll be fine, Anne," Sophia assured her, clutching Anne's sweaty palm. "You can sit with me in the back."

"No," Anne said, pulling her hand away. "I'm not getting on."

Reverend Robinson knelt on one knee in front of Anne and took her hand, "Would you give me the honor of your company upfront with the horses?"

Anne gazed at the front seat and then stared into Reverend Robinson's comforting eyes. She smiled and accepted the invitation. Michael stuck two fingers between his lips and blew out a piercing whistle blast. Within seconds, Dash, tongue hanging out, tail wagging, came charging around the corner of the church towards them.

Sophia climbed up into the back of the carriage and seated herself with Michael by her side and Dash at her feet. "Where are we going?" she asked.

Reverend Robinson replied, "To the River Ise." He gave the reins a short whip and the horses commenced a trot. "The river is not far from here, about ten minutes."

Inside the back of the cart, under the seat in front of her, Sophia noticed three large white cloth towels. *Wonder what they are for?* she thought with a quick shrug of her shoulders.

As they approached the river, the sound of a choir of male and female voices echoed ghost-like across the rolling landscape sun-kissed gold by the afternoon sun. The cart pulled to a slow stop behind some trees separating them from the river. Michael reached down and picked up the towels. "You going swimming?" Sophia asked.

"Not me," Michael replied, grinning. Sophia's curiosity rose a notch.

"Down by the riverside," the words sung by the choir could be clearly heard as they ventured through the trees. On the riverbank, forming a queue that extended from the top of the bank to water's edge, stood eight men about two feet apart, bare-footed and dressed in pure white pants and shirts. To their left, a corridor-width away, stood eight women also bare-footed and wearing pure white full-length dresses. Below them in the water were two men waist-deep in the river. They continued to sing, "Jesus will lead you, to the waters of love, to the waters of life." When the song seemed to finish, they repeated the verse with a variation of the same theme creating a continuous, lively, spirit-filled rhythm.

Reverend Robinson continued down the riverbank through the aisle between the men and woman into the clear water and stopped between the two men waist-deep in the water. There he turned to face Sophia and Anne holding a black leather-bound Bible in his hands. He nodded, seemingly indicating he was ready.

"Anne, Sophia, I'll need to take your coats and haversacks," Michael said.

"Why?" Sophia asked.

"Your baptism, if you want to."

Sophia had not given her baptism much thought for some years. Sister Mary had once told her, "When you feel the time is right in your own heart, then you will be baptized." The sweet refrains of the music, the kindly man of God, where they were: everything seemed perfect. Her heart thumped a resounding *yes*. The time had come. She handed her coat to Michael. Anne followed suit. Sophia took Anne's hand and, together, smiling, they walked with a slight skip in their pace down towards Reverend Robinson. Sophia dipped her toe in the cold water and shivered. She closed her eyes and said a short prayer, "Jesus, please warm my body in the icy water." Then she ventured forth, undeterred by the cold.

Sophia stood between the man on the left and Reverend Robinson, while Anne took her position between Reverend Robinson and the man on the right.

Reverend Robinson spoke: "Anne and Sophia, in keeping with the example of Jesus, you have presented yourself this day that you might receive the sacrament of baptism. Baptism is not itself the door to salvation, but rather is an outward sign of the new birth God has wrought in your heart. It proclaims to all the world that you have taken Christ Jesus as the Lord of your lives, and it is your purpose always to obey Him. In order we may know you understand the significance of the step you are taking, I ask you these questions: Do you believe in God the Father, the Son, and the Holy Spirit? That Jesus Christ the Son suffered in your place on the cross and died but rose again? And he now sits at the Father's right hand until he returns to judge all people at the last day? And do you believe in the Holy Scriptures as the inspired Word of God? That by the grace of God every person has the ability and responsibility to choose between right and wrong, and that those who repent of their sin and believe in the Lord Jesus Christ are justified by faith?"

Anne and Sophia replied in unison, "I do."

"Do you intend by this act to testify to all the world that you are a Christian and will be a loyal follower of Christ?"

"I do."

Each man placed a hand under his charge's lower back and a hand under her shoulders. Then, synchronized and with arms crossed shoulder-to-shoulder, Anne and Sophia allowed themselves to fall backwards.

Reverend Robinson said, "Anne, Sophia, I baptize you in the name of the Father, and of the Son, and of the Holy Spirit. Amen."

As Sophia's head broke the water, she radiated a smile, closing her eyes moments before the water engulfed her. Then, as if time had slowed, she experienced the sensation of passing through a doorway and into another place—a realm of complete peace and harmony where there was no pain, suffering, grief, or sadness, just an overwhelming sense of contentment. In that moment of immersion, the Holy Spirit in his purest form of love, joy, peace, patience, kindness, faithfulness, and gentleness held her. She did not want to leave. The man holding her raised her up. And as she came from under the water, all the darkness and pain of the world hit her full-force like a massive sledge hammer battering her stomach. The force overwhelmed her body. She gasped. At the same time, though, her body and soul revitalized to be a disciple of God, to walk in newness of life. She glanced at Anne, who was beaming a smile, exhibiting a radiance of delight Sophia had never seen in her before.

The men and women on the riverbank cheered and clapped as they rose out of the water and onto the bank. Michael passed each girl a towel. Even though she should be freezing, Sophia was not. Her soul burned with the white fire of the Holy Spirit, warming her. She used the towel to dry her hair and clothes.

After Reverend Robinson dried himself, he prayed a blessing over Sophia and Anne. "Lord, Heavenly Father, grant these two souls, who have withstood and will endure the darkness of this world, your heavenly light to protect and fill them with the courage and strength they require to do your will. Grant them the right to return to you when their journey is over. In the name of the Jesus Christ. Amen."

"Thank you, Reverend," Sophia said, beaming graciously.

"And no more stealing, Sophia," Reverend Robinson said with a gentle smile and a stern tone.

She wondered how he knew, but decided not to ask and instead only nodded.

"We will walk back to the church," Michael said, "to give the girls a chance to dry off in the afternoon sun."

"Very well," Reverend Robinson said. "I'll eagerly await your company. I'll give you a place to rest for the night, warmer than sleeping outside. I would have carried out the baptism in the baptismal pool at the church, but in his note Richard said that Mendel insisted that you girls be baptized in the river." He headed off towards the horse and cart.

Sophia gazed around. "Hey, where did all the other people go?"

Michael looked at her with one eyebrow raised, said, "What people?"

"The choir of men and women dressed in white who were singing … standing on the river's edge."

"There was no one else here, but the Reverend, Anne, and I," he replied.

"But…" She thought of debating it further, but realized that Michael had no reason to lie. *Who were they?*

"I saw them, too," Anne said.

"Really?" Michael added, rubbing his chin. "How strange."

"There was also a man in a dark trench coat hiding amongst the trees," Anne said.

Sophia turned and surveyed the trees. "Whereabouts?"

"Up there," Anne said pointing. "He's gone now. I only saw him briefly just before the baptism."

Squinting, Sophia scouted back and forth across the trees.

"Yes," Michael said. "I have been sensing a presence of a dark soul. We best be on our guard."

Jack, Sophia thought. *Could it be him?*

Chapter 21 - Anne

Under an oil-lit lamp, Anne sat on the step to the rear entrance to Fuller Church stroking Dash. Sophia and Michael had retired for the night in the house next door. Anne thought about the heavy waves of events over the last few days. Each wave carried a flood of mixed emotions that pulled her down like a whirlpool—trying to drown her. The baptism helped to provide a life jacket, keeping her afloat, but she still experienced a sense of longing—of purpose.

Everything seemed to be about Sophia. Sure, she was her companion, but what was that, exactly? *An accessory?* Even during dinner, which Reverend Robinson prepared, all the questions were directed at Sophia. How did you feel after the baptism, Sophia? How are you finding the journey so far, Sophia? How are you holding up under the pressure, Sophia? *Nobody asked me anything. Did they even notice that I was baptized too?* Michael and Sophia appeared to have a relationship with each other that she didn't share, and that one really hurt because she fancied Michael. Even though there was a five-year age gap, she would get older, and then there would be a glimmer of hope they could be together. At least that is what she dreamed.

It was more likely he would be with Sophia, she thought, *the prettier and smarter one.* Age thirteen was somewhat a curse. Her body wanted to be a woman, but her age restricted her actions. She picked up a fallen twig and sketched a smiley face in the soil. She smiled. *Everything will work out. I have to trust in God.* Though she believed in Jesus—after all he had healed her pain—she struggled with doubts. *Maybe I'm kidding myself,* she thought. *Why would God let my parents die? Why would God let the Sisters die?* Hard questions she struggled to find answers to. Truth was, she couldn't. Using the point of the twig, she changed the smile to a frown. *Perhaps it's time for me to go my own way.*

"Hello, young lady," a voice called from the night.

Dash sprang to her feet. Out from the darkness stepped a man whom Anne recognized as the man in the trees during the baptismal ceremony. "Hello?" she said.

"You must be Anne," he said, standing a few feet away. "I'm Jack."

Dash started to growl. "Dash, behave yourself," Anne said, patting the dog's head. "I'm sorry, Mister, she is normally playful with strangers."

"Oh, that's okay, and, please, call me Jack."

"What do you want, Jack?"

"Nothing, just to say hello."

"How do you know my name?"

"I had an encounter with your mother."

"Angela?"

"No. Your real mother."

Anne snapped the twig in two, rose to her feet, narrowed her eyes. "What do you mean, my *real* mother?"

"Oh, didn't they tell you, Anne, that you were adopted?"

"Adopted?" she replied, the word weighing her brow down.

Dash started barking.

In the distance, Anne heard Sophia call out, "Anne, are you okay?"

Anne called back in Sophia's direction, "Yes, I'm fine." When she returned her attention to Jack, he was gone. *Strange man,* she thought.

The question of her adoption plagued her. *Could that be true? Why would he say such a thing? I need to know.* She ventured into the darkness in search of Jack. Dash followed. "Go back, girl," she shouted. Dash whimpered before retreating. "Where could he have gone?" she mumbled, walking along the side of the church to the main street.

She noticed him standing on the other side of the road, a shadowy figure, and then he turned and ran into a narrow alleyway. *Perhaps I should get Sophia and Michael,* she deliberated. *No, I can do this. I can show them I'm capable of doing things.* She pursued him. The buildings either side of the alley blocked the white moon glow and the glimmering light from the gas-powered street lamps. Her visibility into the darkness shortened to hardly more than arm's length.

She jolted. Her heart skipped a beat and she exhaled a short scream as the sound of a crate toppling over filled her ears. A black scavenging cat ran past her leg. *What am I doing?* She turned to head back …. But without warning a forceful hand slapped a white cotton cloth over her nose and mouth as a strong arm hooked her around the chest. A sweet smell filled her nostrils. She panicked, struggling with all her might, but the grip was too strong. The night sounds around her became faint— distorted. The distant streetlight blurred. She heard a whisper, "Shh, my darling. It will be over soon." The more she resisted, the deeper she breathed, the faster her vision faded. Her world faded into a mist of haziness. She fell into unconsciousness.

* * *

"What is it, Dash?" Sophia said as Dash tugged on her dress. "Michael," she shouted, "I think something is wrong!"

Michael ran in from an adjacent room. "What is Dash doing in here?"

"She darted in and began pulling at my dress, between barks."

"I think she wants us to follow her somewhere," Michael said. "Where is Anne?"

"She was outside with Dash."

"Wait here," Michael said, sprinting out of the room. Moments later, he returned with his staff. "Show us the way, Dash."

Head down, sniffing the ground, Dash led the way. The back of Sophia's head throbbed with each beat of her quickening heart. Her stomach churned as if a mini-tornado had touched down. *I shouldn't have left her alone.* At the side of the street, Dash paused, let out a short growl, then continued, sniffing her way across the paved road— stopping at the entrance of the alley. Michael peered into the darkness. "One sec'," he said. He raised his staff and said, "Fiat lux." Within a second, the top of his staff began to glow. Using his staff to illuminate the way, he proceeded. A little farther down the alley, Sophia came to a sudden halt. She slapped her chest as if trying to beat life into her stilled heart. A message scrawled in dripping red liquid on the side of the building read:

IF YOU WANT ANNE, COME TO THE COUGHTON CROSS

She bent over, elbows jutting hard into her gut, and gasped. "No... This is all my fault." She placed her palms on her sweaty forehead, partially covering her pained eyes. "I promised her we would be fine, that nothing would separate us." Her stomach heaved, propelling half-digested food onto the ground. "Tell me that isn't Anne's blood, Michael."

He shook his head, shrugged. "I'm not sure, Sophia." He stepped over and placed his strong arm around her. "I'm sorry."

She wiped her mouth on her sleeve. "Where is Coughton Cross?"

"It's an ancient mark stone in the southwest corner of the Forest of Arden," he said, analyzing the ground. "It's about 40 miles from here."

"What are you looking at, Michael?"

"Drag marks of feet," he said. "They go this way." He ventured farther down the alleyway.

Sophia froze. "What is that?" she said, pointing to something in the corner, black and furry, lying in a pool of blood.

Michael strode towards the object. "A dead cat. Its throat has been slit." He sighed and continued following the drag trail until it stopped where the alley opened onto a grassy field. Michael scanned around while speaking. "Horse waste," he recommenced searching, added, "flattened grass, in the shape of horse hooves. Several of them. He must have tied up his horse here. There are more tracks leading off into the distance, a canter width apart." He pointed northwest. "Leading towards the Forest of Arden."

"We must follow," Sophia said, "and get her back."

"It'll be a trap, Sophia," he said, shaking his head. "But, well … we have no other choice."

Chapter 22 - Bait

His task—setting the trap with Anne as bait—complete, Jack mounted his steed. He wiped the cold sweat off his forehead, wishing it was as easy to wipe away his guilt. With a kick of his heels, he bought his steed to a gallop, heading towards Birmingham.

A few miles on, Jack lurched forward, hunched over, and hugged the horse's neck. A searing sting, as if someone were tugging on his intestines, shot through his lower abdomen. The tumor made its presence known, a constant reminder of why he carried out the evil deeds for Mephis. Over the past weeks, since discovering Sophia was alive, Mephis had been holding back on providing the healing Jack required. He accepted the punishment because, after all, thirteen years ago he had his chance to ensure that Sophia would never be a problem … but failed. Each day the physical pain had become more intense and was now at moments excruciating. *Hopefully now*, he thought, *after succeeding at this task, Mephis will relieve my agony.*

The mission, which began when Mephis sensed a surge of White Energy at Stowe House, sounded simple enough to Jack. Mephis had instructed him to abduct Anne and place her and a transparent crystal sphere, glowing red from a ball inside shaped like a furry orange, in a clearing in the Forest of Arden. Jack had not expected, however, the explosion of red energy that occurred shortly after he placed the sphere in the scrub on the forest floor. It was not harmful to him or Anne but had turned a circular region of the forest into a burnt-out wasteland. He guessed that was simply part of what needed to be done to execute Mephis's dark magic. Tracking Anne's whereabouts was another matter, but had proved easy enough. The very day Mephis located her at Stowe House, Jack, after visiting his brother's grave, set out on horseback, cantering as fast as the stallion could take him. Before long, the mount became fatigued, requiring him to find a replacement. Stealing horses was simple enough for Jack.

At Stowe House, he waited out the night and then followed the trio to Kettering, stalking them from a distance, awaiting his opportunity. He realized why Mephis told him to abduct Anne. Using her as bait was a simple, safe way to lure Sophia into Mephis's snare.

At Birmingham, Jack trotted towards a pub near the local railway station, doing his best to ignore the reverberation through his spine of the six chimes echoing form the bell tower at the top of St Philip's Cathedral. Each booming dong brewed anger and hate as thoughts of God crossed his mind. Why, he pondered, would a loving God abandon him and allow the affliction of the disease that tormented his body—the same disease that killed his brother? For only one reason: He doesn't exist.

He dismounted the horse and entered the pub, not bothering to secure the steed. Inside only a handful of patrons gathered around the bar, most disheveled, still here from the night before drowning the reality of their sorrowful existence with booze. Only one woman was in the joint, a broad in her twenties, not fair of face and of rough vintage, but attractive enough to arouse sexual thoughts in Jack. He wondered why a woman would be here. A bit rough around the edges, she didn't strike him as a hooker come searching for a trick. *Must have her own demons she is running from*, he thought, watching her knock back shots of liquor.

He slid onto a seat at the bar. "What will it be?" a barman asked, wiping down the counter with a sodden rag.

"A tankard of your best," Jack said, slamming a coin on the counter. Moments later, the barman replaced the money with a mug. Jack gulped down the beer, screwing his nose at the bitter tang. He tolerated the taste only because it would dull his pain—emotional as well as physical (and maybe more the former than the latter).

A few drinks later the woman shouted, "Get your hands off me, brute!" Jack glanced over and saw her empty a mug in the man's face. *Unwanted grope*, Jack thought.

The man with beer in his beard was burly in size, not someone you would want to meet alone in a dark alley. He rose from his chair with a red face and flexing muscles. He snatched a bottle off the counter and swatted it backhanded into the side of her head. She folded to the ground with a thud. Not finished, the man stomped on her hand with the heel of his boot. "Bitch!" he yelled and staggered out of the pub.

Nobody but the barman tended to the woman who lay on the ground in a pool of her own blood. At the woman's side, the barman yelled, "Any doctors in here?"

A man sitting close to Jack said, "Hey, ain't you a doctor? That looks like something a doctor would carry."

Jack glanced at his bag. The man was right, of course, but he was not there to be a good Samaritan but to drink away his pain.

"This man is a doctor," the man shouted.

The barman stared at Jack. "Don't just sit there, man. Come and help the lady."

Jack put his mug down, grabbed his bag, and headed for the woman. On his knees, he wiped the blood from her face to assess the damage. Relatively unscarred. A majority of the blood flowed from a small gash above her right brow, which appeared to have taken the brunt of the impact. A piece of glass protruded from her eye. "She's going to lose that eye," Jack said, removing the fragment. He then bandaged her eye with gauze from his doctor's bag. *Odd* he thought, using the contents of the bag for something other than murder. Over the years, the purpose of his bag had changed from saving life to taking it. After dressing the eye, he turned his attention to her fingers, which were twisted and snapped in several places. "What's her name? Jack asked.

"Kate," the barman said. "She's a regular: Kate Kibble."

"She'll have crooked fingers for the rest of her life, but she should be able to move them," Jack said as he set and splinted the broken bones.

The police arrived. After giving up trying to take any comprehensible statements from the drunken patrons aside from Jack who gave the best description of the assailant he could, they picked Kate up and said they would take her to the nearby hospital.

Not wanting to attract any more attention than he already had, Jack left. He strode to the station to await a train to London. Time to go home to Whitechapel. A train ticket was his personal reward to himself for a task well done. *Give me a chance to rest*, he thought. Horse riding, the constant movement, only magnified his physical discomfort.

A poster tacked up on the wall next to the ticket window drew his attention. WANTED it read. Under that were sketches of Anne and Sophia, and under their names FOR MURDER. The drawings were quite detailed and made it obvious to Jack that the fugitives were blood relatives. *Perhaps because I know they are*, he thought. The resemblance was striking. Similar cheek bones and jaw lines and though the black-and-white sketches did not show their eye and hair color, he knew them to be the alike. *Sisters, near twins at that.* A memory from nine years ago came back to him of that night he slipped the note under the door of Angela's house. That night Anne should have died in the accident he had orchestrated. His attempt to clean up at least one mistake. That was an error he did not want Mephis to discover for fear of the consequences. He could not fathom how Anne and Sophia had managed to end up together as a result. A remarkable coincidence or the work of another power? Maybe that Diniel fellow Memphis had mentioned had something to do with the happenstance. Jack did not know, but the question irked him. Today he felt fortunate to have failed in erasing Anne. She provided the perfect bait to atone for both of his slipups.

Chapter 23 - Forest of Arden

Sophia gazed to the east and admired the glowing orange horizon. *The sun would soon rise*, she thought. Her horse Solitaire had championed the several hours of darkness trotting through the long thick grass covering the overgrown trails as if he knew Anne's life was at risk. Every time she caught sight of Anne's horse Eclipse without a rider lashed by a short piece of rope to Lancelot, a lump formed in her throat.

She feared they moved somewhat slower than Jack, giving him at least a few hours' lead—possibly more. "We are nearly there," Michael said, "just a few hundred yards from Coughton Cross. We'll secure the horses here and travel the rest of the way by foot." He dismounted and proceeded to tie Lancelot to a nearby tree. Sophia followed suit.

Michael led the way as they traversed the narrow dirt trail between the trees in single file with Dash at the rear. A short walk later, they entered the clearing where the Mark Stone lay. Michael rushed over to the stone, crouched down, and began scanning the ground. "Two sets of horse trails, one leading here from the south and the other leading away in a northerly direction," he said, continuing to scout the tracks. He pointed into the dense forest. "They went that way on foot but only one returned."

The pre-dawn sounds of various species of birds chirping their morning harmonies washed through the trees as they ventured into the forest. A little way in, the singing stopped. Vibrant trees gave way to the charred and twisted remnants of once majestic oaks. Other than the sounds of the scorched undergrowth cracking beneath their feet, the forest was silent. "This is creepy," Sophia said, eyeing the trees and wondering if they or something else was watching her. Great cobwebs began appearing spanning between the branches, sparse at first but becoming denser the farther they travelled. Then Sophia halted, trembling, the sight before her was unimaginable. A spider's web ten times her height spanned across a clearing. The silk threads, thick as rope, formed an intricate web of jagged circles condensing to a center point. Anne, wrapped in a silk-like cocoon two stories above the ground in the heart of the web, stared at Sophia. The chilling sight sent shivers down Sophia's spine.

Anne's head barely peeked over her web sheath. She shouted, "Behind you, look out!"

Sophia and Michael spun around to see a large black spider scrutinizing them with each of its many eyes of various sizes. Without warning, sticky web blasted from between its fangs, channeled from its spinnerets. It connected first with Sophia and then with Michael. Dash scampered off into the trees.

The spider reeled in the thread attached to Sophia. She fell to her rear, dug her heels and hands into the undergrowth attempting to halt her advance. Mini trenches formed beneath her palms and feet as the spider dragged her towards its waiting fangs, which secreted a greenish fluid. Her muscles burned as she fought with every ounce of her strength to win the tug of war for her very life. She was losing. One of the spider's eight long barbed legs reached out to grasp her. She let out a shriek loud enough to startle birds a mile away to flight. The limb descended then latched onto her, and effortlessly hauled her in. With two forelegs, the spider rolled her as if she was a rag doll, while wrapping her with silk thread streaking from spinnerets—securing its meal. Cocooned, she wriggled with all her strength in an attempt to break free. Helpless, she watched as the spider turned its focus on Michael.

On his feet, Michael leaned back and stiffened himself against the pull of the spider's tow. He readied his staff between his hands. The spider stretched out a leg. With a quick wrist flick, he deflected the limb to the side. Using the other foreleg, the spider swiped towards Michael. He ducked in time for the leg to sweep over his head. Rearing, fangs raised, the spider lurched. Michael dived forwards, rolled onto his back, holding his staff upright. As the spider overshot, Michael thrust his staff into its underbelly. Black, acidic, liquid oozed from around the puncture wound. The great arachnid sprang upwards using all eight of its legs. The thread holding Michael snapped leaving him on the ground, free. Michael rolled to his feet, and then fled for the shield of a nearby tree. He spied the spider in among the treetops near some web sacs. Nine egg sacs exploded, nearly simultaneously, in a white puff. Newborn spiders emerged, each as long as his forearm. In rapid succession, they rappelled by thread to the ground.

Drenched in her own sweat, her arms barely able to move an inch, Sophia continued struggling to free herself. No matter how much she squirmed the threads held her tight. The more she struggled, the tighter the cocoon seemed to become.

In an organized fashion, the baby spiders lined up in a straight line facing Michael. Once in position they scuttled towards him. He stepped from the trees holding his staff firmly between his hands. From out of nowhere, a silver crossbow bolt whistled through the air and hit one of the baby spiders with such force that it threw the oversized creature into a tumble until it rolled to a stop, facing the sky, legs curled inward—dead. A couple of seconds later, another spider suffered the same fate, followed by a third. Michael cut his eyes to the source of the whizzing bolts. Reverend Robinson, crossbow in hand, valiantly fixed his aim on another of the creatures. The remaining clutter of six spiders scattered, seemingly confused by the events. Michael charged. He raised his staff, targeted a straggler, and with a swift strike struck the arachnid. The black orbed abdomen of the spider exploded in a jet of dark ooze. Two spiders charged towards Reverend Robinson. He reloaded his crossbow in time to halt the first attacker before it even left the ground. The second leapt into the air, fangs out, towards the Reverend's face as he finished loading a bolt. Armed, he aimed. The spider inches from him, he fired, the quarrel hitting its mark and sending the impaled creature scuttling to the ground.

Meanwhile, the remaining three arachnids focused their attention on Michael. The first one leapt towards his chest. He sent the spider flying with a great looping swing of the staff. The other two prepared to leap. Michael readied his staff. Together they launched. He swung the staff, deflecting one with a swift hacking blow that slammed the spider into the ground. The other landed on his shoulder, sinking its large fangs deep into the left side of his neck. He reached over with his right hand, grabbed the spider and squeezed, crushing its life away and then throwing its carcass to the ground. Blood seeped from two puncture wounds on the side of his neck.

Sophia stopped struggling to free herself from the constraint that she imagined must be like wearing a strait jacket. A flushing sense of relief cascaded through her body as Reverend Robinson hovered above her. "I'll get you out, Sophia," he said. He swiped a silver dagger from a sheath under his left trouser leg and sliced through the striated strands of the cocoon.

Michael, his face contorted with pain, turned a shade of blue as he clutched the side of his throbbing neck. He staggered towards them, each step clumsier and slower than the previous. A body length away, he collapsed to the ground.

Her arms free, Sophia wriggled out of the cocoon and scrambled over to Michael. As if by instinct, she placed her hands over the side of his neck and closed her eyes. As expected, the white light radiated from her hands into the side of Michael's neck. Several seconds later, the white glow faded. Sophia removed her hands—the wound was gone. Michael's eyes slowly opened. "I thought I was on my way to the afterlife," he said, rubbing the side of his neck.

"Not while I'm around," Sophia replied, helping him to his feet.

"We have a bigger problem," Reverend Robinson said, pointing.

The giant spider, seemingly recovered from the earlier wound, lowered from the trees by a thread.

"Not again," Sophia said. "Let's split up."

The Reverend reloaded his crossbow. "I'll draw the loathsome beast towards me. Try to flank it."

Michael darted left, Sophia right. The spider stalked Sophia and shot a line of sticky silk towards her. This time, Sophia anticipated the move and easily dodged the attack.

Reverend Robinson fired. The bolt cruised through the air and landed in the larger of the spider's right eyes. When the arachnid spun towards the Reverend, Michael seized the opportunity to sprint, leap onto the beast's back, and plunge his staff deep into the unarmored abdomen. Black ooze gushed out of the wound as he withdrew his weapon. Wasting no time, Michael sprang forward and whomped the spider with tremendous force. The blow crushed the spider's thorax, instantly putting the creature down. "Team work," Michael said, leaping off his conquest. The spider squirmed from muscle memory, nothing more, before rolling onto its back with its legs curled inward in a death pose. Several seconds later, the dead arachnid began to dissolve into a dark charcoal-colored mist before disintegrating in a single puff.

"Hey!" Anne shouted. "Don't forget me!"

Michael retrieved the knife from his haversack. "Cut her down," he said, facing Sophia.

She took the knife, raced over to the web and climbed up the sticky mesh. "I'll have you out in a sec'," she said, cutting through the sac imprisoning Anne.

"I'm sorry," Anne said.

"For what?" Sophia said, as she helped Anne down from the web.

"Running off. I thought I could do something and be someone important."

"You are plenty important, especially to me."

"How so?"

"You are like my *sister*," Sophia said, contemplating whether she should tell Anne what she knew.

"Really?"

Sophia pulled her close and hugged her tightly. "Yes, *really*."

Dash, fresh from her hiding place in the trees, came scurrying over.

"Guess you're not one for spiders," Sophia said. Dash turned her head side to side as if to say, "Who, me? I was here the whole time."

Michael turned to Reverend Robinson. "Your timing was impeccable. How did you know where we would be?"

"It's the strangest thing. A dream, a man, Dan, Dun," he scratched his chin, "Diniel, I think, told me you might need my help. So I tracked you."

At the sound of that name, Sophia's eyebrows raised, but she did not say anything.

"Right," Michael said. "Well, we owe you and this Diniel fellow abundant
gratitude."

"What about the man who took you, Anne?" Sophia said. "Do you know where he went?"

"No, sorry. He took off running after the spider attacked."

Sophia turned to Michael. "What now?"

"We continue on our way to Hermitage Castle." Michael turned and faced Reverend Robinson. "Will you be joining us?"

"No, I would love to. I must say I have enjoyed the action. But I do have a church to run. It's my calling."

Michael nodded before turning to Anne. "Did the man who abducted you give a name?"

"Jack," she said.

Sophia gritted her teeth to stem the gruesome chill running down her spine. The name came as no surprise. Although, the thought of him being that close to Anne made her cringe. An anger fuelled a fiery passion inside her. *Jack's back. It's going to be either him or me.*

"Should we pursue Jack?" Sophia asked.

"Hmm. I doubt he was behind the giant spider. That appeared to be the work of a sorcerer," Michael replied. "Jack is likely to be his servant. Let's head back to the Coughton Cross and make a decision there."

Chapter 24 - Birmingham

At Coughton Cross, Sophia watched Michael study the fresher of the two horse trails galloping off in a northerly direction. "Fresh enough to track," he said.

"We should pursue Jack," Sophia replied, a wave of anger tensioning her jaw.

"And if we catch him, Sophia, then what?"

Kill him was her first thought, but her conscience echoed, *but what would that make me? A murderer? I would be no better than Jack.* She recalled a conversation she had at nine years old with Sister Mary.

* * *

Sophia huddled with Anne in the adoption room at the orphanage, her right cheek continuing to swell and forcing her eye closed. She wept, droplets of trauma reflecting the man who hit her, the man who was going to adopt her. For the first time in her life, Sophia felt discarded, worthless, not wanted. She reconciled the strike as punishment for stomping on his foot. *Maybe I deserved to be whacked*, she thought. At the same time, anger and hate brewed within her a strong desire to rear back and sock the man right in the nose—retaliate.

Sister Mary crouched in front of her then and gently pulled Sophia's hand away from the side of her face where it was hiding her bruise. "Well, that is going to be some shiner," she said.

"I don't want to go with him," Sophia stuttered, between heaving sobs. "Please, Sister, don't make me go."

"You're not going anywhere, child. Don't you worry."

"But the man, won't he come back?"

"No."

"I hate him."

"Don't be like that," Sister Mary replied, blotting the tears from Sophia's cheeks with a cotton handkerchief. "Hate will rot your tender, joyful heart and then you'll be no better than he is. Let God deal with him."

* * *

"Sophia," Michael said, "are you with us?"

"Oh, yes, sorry, I drifted off into a memory," she said. Even though she had healed from the event physically, there was still a scar on her heart. Her right eye had remained sealed shut for days due to the swelling. *Funny* she thought, *I healed Anne's broken leg four years later, but back then I couldn't even heal my own bruised face. Not that I tried.*

"Do you want to follow him?" Michael asked.

"No, let God deal with *him*," she said.

Michael nodded. "We'll head to Birmingham, St Philips Cathedral. It's not far. We can rest there before the next leg of our journey."

On their horses, cantering towards Birmingham, Sophia's eyes cut to a series of passenger cars to her right. A black engine puffing steam far enough ahead in the distance to look like a toy train set headed towards London.

Shortly afterwards, the bell spire of St Philip's Cathedral towering above the houses glistened in the rising sun. They slowed to a trot as they entered the streets. People, oblivious to anything but their individual tasks, went about their morning business. Some headed to work by foot, horse, or carriage. Others flipped the sign of their storefront from *closed* to *open* preparing for the day's trade. Sophia noticed an occasional person glaring in their direction, in some cases even pointing towards them. She was not sure why, but figured it was perhaps because they did not look like the regular town folk. Two teenage girls on horses accompanied by a young White Monk with a dog. *I would probably point, too*, she thought.

A man in his mid-forties, slim, with short brown hair and dressed in a black shirt with a clerical collar and black trousers ran out to greet Michael as they approached Saint Philip's Cathedral. "Brother Michael, come quick! Leave the horses. My men will take care of them."

Michael dismounted. "Quickly, girls, do as Father Roman says."

Father Roman led them through the cathedral's main hall into a rear doorway that opened into a short hallway that ended at the entrance to a small library. He flung the door open and once they were in locked it behind them. "My men saw your arrival in Birmingham. No doubt others did as well," Roman said as he tilted a book with the number seven on the spine in among a shelf of other identical books. He pulled on the bookshelf, and, like a door, it swung open. "Through here."

After entering a confined dim lit passage lighted by a single oil lamp, Roman pulled the shelf closed behind them. At the other end of the corridor, he unlocked a sturdy wooden door with one of a dozen or so identical-looking steel keys dangling off an iron ring on his belt. Once inside the room, Sophia took a quick look around. Four beds, two on each side of the area facing inwards, with a timber oak-hinged box at the foot of each. On the wall above the head of each bed was a polished wooden crucifix.

Roman said, "*Wanted* posters of Sophia and Anne are pinned up in the post office, train station, pubs, and other places around town. WANTED FOR MURDER. The likeness of the artist's rendering is quite remarkable."

"Really?" Sophia said, somewhat curious as to what she might look like in a portrait.

"People will have recognized you," Roman said.

"That would explain why some people were staring at us," Sophia said.

"Is there a reward?" Anne asked.

"Yes, and a sizeable one at that," Father Roman said. "Most likely by now someone has contacted the local Bobbies. Fear not: You'll be safe in here. But, I must ask, why have you come here?"

"We are in need of rest and food, Brother Roman," Michael said.

"I presumed as much. That we can certainly supply. You may remain here till morning. The Bobbies will be here soon. I best be available to greet them when they arrive."

"Thank you, kindly," Michael said, with a gentle bow of his head. "We will leave before sunrise."

Father Roman left as each of them, including Dash, took a seat on a bed.

"Dash, on the floor," Michael said. She whimpered before finding a place to curl on the ground.

"I'm beat," Sophia said, lying back on her bed.

"Yes," Michael agreed. "We can all do with some rest."

Ten minutes later, a knock on the door roused Sophia from her slumber with a jerk. A young nun entered the room holding a plate of food: freshly baked bread, cheese, chicken, and various fruits. The nun placed the tray on the vacant bed. "I hope this food will be suitable," she said.

"Absolutely," Anne said, drawing in a deep breath. "The bread smells … amazing."

"I'll come back shortly with some refreshments."

"Thank you," Michael said, bowing his head toward the Sister.

They gathered around the bed. Michael said grace and immediately after the Amen they began attacking the food. Dash scooted between each of them, tempting them to give her food. None of them could resist Dash's studied expression of pity—*feed me, please, please, feed me, I am but a poor dog, who can't do for herself.* During the meal, the nun returned with three cups, a bowl, and two jugs, one of water and another of grape juice. She placed the bowl on the floor, and then filled it with water. Dash drank.

"I think my stomach is going to explode," Anne said, returning to her bed, where she lay on her back, hand on her stomach. "I've eaten too much."

"Me, too," Sophia said. "But I think I'll have one more chicken leg."

The meal finished, they retired to their beds. Sophia wondered as she lay on her back staring at the plain white ceiling how Anne was handling the recent events. She wanted to ask her, but at the same time did not think dragging up memories of her ordeal with Jack would be wise. At the end of the day, she figured, Anne would talk to her about it freely when she was ready to do so. Her vision blurred as she let fatigue, once again, take her into sleep.

* * *

Sophia gazed out over the vast waters of a lake, reflecting an ominous sky bruised with dark clouds. Violent winds troubled the water's surface, creating toppling white horses in the caps of waves among the many swells. The icy water lapped at her toes, causing them to curl.

"Troubled?" she heard a voice ask.

"You're in my thoughts again, Diniel," she replied, continuing to stare across the unsettled waters.

"Actually, I'm in your dream," he said.

She turned to him. He tipped the brim of his white hat downwards in a courtly gesture of greeting. "Why are you here, Diniel?"

"I was about to ask you why you *want* me here?"

"Questions," she said.

"Fire away, but be quick," he said, glancing towards the sky. "I have a little time."

"Why are you helping me?"

"I have my reasons," he replied, shuffling his feet.

"Anne is my sister, right?"

"Without a doubt."

"Should I tell her?"

"That is for you to decide."

A bolt of forked lightning fired from the sky and pierced the center of the lake. Sophia jerked, startled by the following crack that turned into a rolling rumble, trembling the stones under her feet.

"I don't think that was part of my dream," she said, turning her focus to the lake.

"My time is up, I'm afraid."

She turned her attention back to Diniel, but he had vanished.

The water lapping on her toes warmed, and steam begin rising from the surface of the lake. She took two steps backwards as the water turned into a deep red, overcome by flaming molten lava. Intense heat forced her to retreat up the bank. In the middle of the lake of fire, a whirlpool with a dark center formed. Soon after, Mephis wearing his shrouded cloak masking his face rose from the swirling pool. He pointed towards her. A streak of red energy shot from the tip of his finger in her direction so fast that she hadn't a chance to move. The ray struck her in the chest, wrapped around her, and shook her forwards and backwards while squeezing tightly, sucking away her breath. She struggled to breathe. All went dark to the words, "Wake up, Sophia, wake up."

She awoke to see Michael, his hands on her shoulders, shaking her gently back and forth to bring her out of her sleep. "We have to go," he said.

After grabbing her haversack, she followed Michael out of the only other door in the room. "Why are we going this way?" she asked as they proceeded down a narrow stone passage.

"The church is surrounded by Bobbies, so we will be taking the sewers."

"That sounds unpleasant," Sophia said, screwing up her nose.

"That is what I said," Anne added.

They passed through several food pantry rooms before finishing in a dead end. The only exit was a trapdoor set in a wooden floorboard.

Michael lifted the trapdoor exposing a short rusty ladder. "You first, Sophia," he said.

"Right," Sophia replied. She climbed down a few rungs and jumped the rest of the way. "It's dark down here."

"We'll use my staff for light," Michael replied. "Your turn, Anne."

After Anne descended, Michael passed Dash down the opening to Sophia below before climbing down. A couple of rungs down, he closed the trapdoor before sliding down the ladder. While holding his staff at arm's length he said, "Fiat lux," the familiar words he would say before his staff provided light. The top of his staff glowed a pure white, illuminating their environment.

"What language are those words in?" Sophia asked.

"Latin, in English it would be 'let there be light.'"

"Is it some kind of spell?"

"No, not at all. The words are an instruction the staff understands. Instead of pressing a switch to turn on the staff's light you say a voice command."

"Voice command," she mumbled, thinking: *Next thing you know, the things will probably start talking back.*

The sewer consisted of a corridor, not much taller than Michael, split down the middle by a dug out section, about four feet across, filled with water carrying the sewage from neighboring buildings. Pipes at regular intervals connected with the main channel by smaller trenches flowing in from the side walls. Drips, making a distinct plop sound as they landed in puddles, occasionally fell from the arched ceiling of moss-covered bricks.

"What are those squealing, scurrying noises?" Anne asked.

"Rats," Sophia replied.

"Not giant ones, I hope," Anne said as she shuddered.

Michael glanced at a piece of paper he held. "This way, I believe," he said, pointing.

"How do you know?" Sophia asked.

"This map," he said, showing the paper to Sophia. "Father Roman provided a quick sketch for our escape."

"Neat," she replied, studying the map. A single line mostly straight but for a few ninety-degree turns plotted a path between outer lines she presumed represented the sewer walls. The words Aston Hall, with a rough drawing of a horse, marked the end of the line. *Crude but effective*, she thought.

Chapter 25 - Powers

"I'm sorry, Master," Jack said, on his knees in the basement of his Whitechapel home, awaiting the next strike. Apologizing was the best rebuttal he could conceive of. Not that Mephis comprehended the word sorry. Once again, Mephis informed him physically and verbally that he had failed his task to eliminate Sophia. He pondered how they could have escaped, but his mind failed to visualize any conceivable way.

Mephis wiped a spot of blood from the red ruby set in his golden ring. A moment before, in the course of smacking Jack's left cheek with the back of his hand, the sharp-edged jewel sliced through Jack's skin leaving behind a tattered red trail. "How hard can it possibly be to eliminate one girl?" Mephis said, circling around Jack. "I don't ask for much, Jack, in exchange for your life, and yet you continually disappoint me."

"To be fair, you tried to kill Sophia once yourself and failed," Jack replied.

"Silence!" Mephis shouted, drawing back his hand as if to strike again.

Jack held up his hands, palms out, cowering, in front of his face anticipating another assault. He struggled with mixed feelings over the failure. Part of him felt somewhat relieved that Sophia and Anne had not died, especially directly or indirectly by his hands. The other part of him, which longed for healing to cheat death, regretted the situation. The pain from the several slaps across the face Mephis had administered was nothing compared to the jagged glass stabbing sensations he experienced every other minute from his gut. Each movement was like being forced to walk barefooted on a street laced with broken glass and gnarled metal, always wondering if the next shard would slash the tender flesh.

"You are lucky you are no good to me dead," Mephis said as he placed his palm on Jack's forehead. Red energy circled his hand building to a large sphere. Jack's body convulsed, shaking back and forth, as two streaks of energy beamed from the ball of energy into his eyes.

Seconds later, Mephis raised his hand. Jack crumpled onto the ground. A sense of euphoria ran through Jack's body as the internal pain dissipated. His tumors retreated, not gone but reduced in size. For now, forgetting the world around him, he curled up on the floor and enjoyed the moment of respite.

"See, Jack," Mephis said. "I am a fair man." He slipped into the chair behind his desk. "While you were gone, Jack, I discovered the location of an item that will help achieve my goals. We leave as soon as you manage to pick yourself up off the floor."

* * *

Three hours later, they arrived by horse on the outer edge of West Norwood Cemetery. "Where now, Master?" Jack asked.

"The catacombs, Jack, the catacombs," Mephis said, dismounting.

After a short walk, they came upon a weathered iron gate barring the entrance to a rectangular stone tomb. Behind the rusty bars, a set of stone stairs led underground. Mephis gave the gate a jerk and then a shove, which did little more than stir up some surrounding dust. He placed his index finger on the keyhole attached to the gate, and a moment later a bright red flash illuminated around the locking mechanism followed by a distinctive clunk. When he pushed the gate again, it opened, yelping like a dog after someone trod on its tail. "Come now, Jack, this should be fun."

Jack trailed Mephis down the narrow stone steps into a square room below. The area had an altar in the middle and a door on the far side. Ceramic pots and jugs of various sizes were scattered throughout the space. Mephis raised his right palm into the air and shouted, "Adustrum." A torch on the far wall began to burn providing much better light than the ambient light seeping down from the top of the stairs. "Grab the torch," Mephis said.

"Yes, Master," Jack replied. He scuttled over to the burning torch, which was resting in an iron holder allowing for easy removal or replacement with fresh torches. Taking it was a simple process.

"Open this door, Jack," Mephis said.

"Why are *you* not opening it, Master?"

"In case it's trapped," he replied, shaking his head. "I'm no fool."

A foot from the door, Jack performed a visual search for any sign of trip wires that may trigger some sort of booby trap. Everything appeared to be in order. He took a deep breath of air, held it, and pulled the door open. Surprisingly, the door opened with little effort. Dust appeared to be the only thing disturbed by it.

"On you go, Jack. I'll follow right behind."

The torch Jack held cast a yellow glow, vibrant and flickering, that cast long shadows that danced about the corridor. Along the walls in coffin-size recesses, like bunks, up to three high in some areas, lay human remains. Some were covered with rotting rags, some naked but for jewelry around their necks or rings on their skeletal fingers. The sounds of perpetual moans, some distant, others as close as the remains he passed, haunted him. He knew they must be in his head, his imagination, like the ringing in his ears he occasionally experienced—though in this case it wasn't ringing but whimpers of the dead.

Jack's foot sank an inch into the stone floor. A click sounded. *A trap trigger*, Jack thought. He attempted to retreat. Too late. Darts spat out of small holes in all four walls piercing his sides. Sharp, stinging pains, like wasp stings, radiated from each impact point but quickly faded. He pulled each thin wooden dart out of his flesh by its feathered tail. "You are lucky," Mephis said, "the poison on those darts wore away a century ago. Not even my healing power would have saved you from that."

Jack nodded, quelling a rising desire to retaliate. He hated Mephis and his smug attitude. At times, he wanted to knife him but knew that would be a death sentence for himself.

"Do be more careful," Mephis added, giving Jack a slight push in the back to keep him moving. "Not all the traps will be as forgiving."

A short time later, the corridor expanded into a square room, large enough to comfortably accommodate twenty people. The same coffin-like recesses were set in the left and right walls, stacking up to four high, most empty except for a few containing skeletal human remains. Some of the alcoves contained jars and pots. On the far wall, opposite the entry, a floor-to-ceiling mural lent an added depth to the space. Jack's brow raised as he scanned the artwork. A man dressed in a shrouded maroon cloak stood under a starry full-moon sky at the center of a ring of stone archways. *Like Stonehenge*, he thought. Red beams of energy circled through the stones creating a crisscrossed pattern like flower petals. Surrounding the circle of arches an army had gathered. It was no regular army, but a battalion of the undead. On the frontline, naked skeletons carried nothing more than a sword and a shield, raised, as if they were cheering. Farther back, men and woman partly clothed with their flesh rotting, wielded rocks and sticks.

"Impressive, isn't it, Jack?" Mephis said. "An army of undead. Corpses animated to life by souls of the Underworld."

Thoughts of the painting *The Last Judgment* resurfaced in Jack's consciousness roiling a queasy sensation in his stomach. The notion that one day his soul would rise into a rotting corpse turned his mouth dry with trepidation.

Chapter 26 - The Sewers

The underground tunnels all started to look alike to Sophia. Passages connecting on the left and right, cross-junctions and intersections formed a maze-like network. If not for the map Father Roman had given Michael to navigate, they would certainly be lost. A distant rumbling drew her attention. "What's that noise, Michael?"

Michael gazed in the direction of the sound. A second later, his eyebrows arched under eyes wide open with urgency, he said, "We have to get out of here *now*. Quick, this way." He led them down the main tunnel to the nearest available exit ladder. The rumbling sound increased with every passing second. Whatever the noise was, it was coming their way. Michael climbed the rungs, lifted the hatch above then dropped back down. "Up you go, Anne, quick now." Anne wasted no time making her escape.

"Won't we get caught up there, Michael?" Sophia asked.

"Better that than the alternative," he replied. "Your turn."

The deep rumbling sound was like nothing Sophia had ever heard before. The walls of the sewerage system began to shake. She could not see anything, but every fiber of her being told her to run and run *fast*. She stepped onto the rusty ladder, looked over her shoulder—still nothing. Skipping every second rung, she ascended. Up top, she reached back down into the sewer entrance, taking Dash from Michael's arms and lifting her to safety. Michael gazed to the right. His face drained of all color leaving the flesh a ghostly white. He cut his eyes back to Sophia and winked … and in that blink of an eye, he was gone. Her heart racing, she stared at the torrent of water gushing through the tunnel below.

"What happened?" Anne asked.

"Michael, he's... he's..." She paused. Her heart stuttered with each word. "He's gone." Dazed, confused, she slumped down onto her bottom.

"Hey you, get away from there!" a male voice shouted.

The words reverberated around Sophia's head but did not register. Her mind was a haze of survival thoughts for Michael. *Could he survive that? Is he dead? Drowned?* Seconds later, the middle-aged bearded man hovered over her. "It's dangerous to play near the sewers, girl."

She did not respond, lost in a fog of questions, retreating from reality.

"Hey, are you okay?" the man asked.

"Sophia," Anne said, crouching beside her.

Michael. He can't be gone, Sophia thought. The image of his single wink before he was violently swept away kept flashing in her mind—blinking on and off.

Anne shook Sophia by the shoulders. "Sophia!" she yelled.

"What's wrong with her?" the man asked.

"Umm..." Anne gazed around twirling her hair between her fingers. "Her favorite doll fell down the sewer."

"Oh, the man said. Well, from the sound of it, the sewers are being flooded, which means the doll is likely to be carried out to Edgbaston Reservoir. It used to be called Rotton Park Reservoir."

"Really?" Anne replied, her eyes wide.

"Sophia, you hear that? Your Michael doll maybe washed out to the reservoir."

Those words lifted the fog in her mind. A spark of warmth flamed up in her heart. The notion that Michael may be alive fuelled her with renewed hope. She shook her head, attempting to further clear her thoughts. Moments later, she turned to the man, "What direction is the reservoir, sir?"

The man pointed down the road. "Three blocks down this street, take a right, followed by a left at the first junction, and several blocks later you'll come to the side of the reservoir. You can't miss it."

Sophia rose. "Thank you, sir."

"Are you sure you're okay, young lady?" the man asked. "You look awfully pale."

"I'll be fine," Sophia replied, taking Anne's hand. "Let's go."

Following the gentleman's directions, they jogged through the streets until they came to the side of the vast reservoir. Sophia shielded her eyes from the afternoon sun as she peered across the water. Nothing. Her stomach felt heavier as each second past. She continued scanning for any sign of Michael. Over near a walled area of the reservoir, she spied a wooden rowboat with two Bobbies on board. *What are they doing?* One of the Bobbies reached over the side of the boat and appeared to be shuffling around in the water. She could not see what he was doing because the side of the boat blocked her view. The boat began to roll and the Bobby nearly lost his balance and ended up in the drink but for the fast actions of the second Bobby, who steadied the boat by outstretching his arms across the sides and used his body as a ballast to calm the rocking. Once recovered from his near fall, he dragged a body into the vessel. *Michael?* Her impression was confirmed when she saw his staff and haversack pulled into the boat. *Is he alive?*

"We need to get closer," Sophia said, cutting her eyes across the sides of the reservoir. "Come, let's go this way." She followed the water's edge, alternating her gaze between the rowboat and scouting a path across the bank. Soon she came to a canal blocking the way forward. The rowboat entered its own waterway on the opposite side of the reservoir and disappeared from view.

"Where are they taking him?" Anne asked.

Two possibilities came to her mind. A jail cell if he was alive, a morgue if he was dead. "I'm not sure, but we will find out," she replied. What disturbed her most was how the Bobbies were on the scene so fast. It was as if they had been waiting for Michael to be flushed out of the sewers—or, more likely, waiting for her and Anne to be flushed out of it. In other words, they had intentionally flooded the sewers to flush them out. The idea brought a wave of nausea. An image of the drawing of the two of them, the likeness of which Father Roman said was "quite remarkable," flashed in her mind with the words WANTED – DEAD OR ALIVE under them. Seemed the Bobbies, in actuality, did not care which way.

The chime of the bell tower of St Philip's Cathedral sounded. Sophia counted them. Five in total. "We should go back to Father Roman," she said.

"Good idea," Anne agreed. "He will know what to do. But how do we find our way back there?"

Sophia pointed into the distance. "The bell tower, it's a landmark that should be visible from nearly everywhere in Birmingham. We'll stick to the back streets where possible to avoid the Bobbies."

"Okay," Anne replied.

The streets were teeming with people heading home from a day of work. Some trudged along as if they had been lugging around heavy weights. Others were more upbeat in their step, seemingly wanting to get home as fast as possible. Sophia avoided eye contact with people as much as possible, and the passer byers seemed content to ignore the girls. The occasional person smiled and waved, or merely nodded politely. Sophia returned their gesture of goodwill with a warm smile, but quickly turned away to reduce the chance of being recognized from the posters Father Roman told them were hung about the city.

A block from the cathedral she encountered two Bobbies. The first, mounted on a horse, appeared to be patrolling around the outskirts of the church. The second Bobby approached on foot from around the corner ahead of them. She grabbed Anne's arm and moved swiftly into an alley, followed by Dash. "Quick, behind here," Sophia said, pointing to a high stack of wooden crates. Together, they crouched down. The echo of the Bobbies boots on the stone pathway grew louder until coming to a stop an arm's length away. Sophia, Anne, and Dash alike held their breath. After a couple of seconds, the footsteps restarted, fading with each stride. Sophia whispered, "That was close."

"How are we going to get to the church with so many Bobbies around?" Anne asked.

"I'm not sure." The idea of walking through the front door of St Philip's seemed unlikely. Bobbies would surely be stationed there. She leant back against the wall of the alley and looked to the sky. An idea came to her. "We wait, till Mass. It is a big cathedral. There will be many people. We can split up and blend in with the crowd."

"Good idea," Anne said. "I think that might just work."

195

"We'll need to move around to the front," Sophia said, rising from behind the crates.

"What about Dash?"

"Hmm," Sophia said, looking at Dash. "Dash, go to Father Roman." Dash tilted her head side to side as if trying to understand what Sophia was saying as she repeated the command: "Go to Father Roman." She barked once and then turned and dashed off.

They took an alley away from the cathedral, cut through some back streets to appear opposite the entrance to the church behind the closest house. As expected, Bobbies patrolled around the entrance and circled the perimeter of the church grounds.

Chapter 27 - Hidden

"Stand back, Jack," Mephis said, retreating from the mural.

Jack, facing the painted wall, took a few steps backwards towards the entrance. "Why?"

"Well, we can search for the right button to press, the hidden lever, or some other concealed way of opening the secret door to this room. Or we can simply do it the easy way," Mephis said, raising his right hand. A small spark began to dance on his palm, which quickly transformed into a sphere of fire about the size of a baseball. He wound up and launched the blazing orb towards the mural.

Jack covered his eyes and retreated a few additional steps as the sphere exploded in a blinding white flash on impact with the center of the wall. The room vibrated. Dust and flying debris filled the air. Some minutes passed before visibility was restored revealing a jagged hole that would serve as a make-shift doorway leading into a hallway beyond the mural.

"There we are, Jack," Mephis said, venturing into the opening, "not the most subtle of methods but effective."

"Right you are, Master," Jack said, following.

Solid marble walls formed the short hallway that opened into a cramped room. Jack scanned the area. An altar, very similar to the one Mephis used in the Whitechapel basement, occupied one corner. Several vials and glass jars were scattered across its surface. Each jar appeared to contain a different animal fetus in some sort of dark brown preserving liquid. Less than a body width away, on a single wooden bed pushed up against a sidewall lay the skeletal remains of a human holding a staff. "He's been dead for some time," Jack said.

"Yes," Mephis replied. "John Dee has."

"Do you know him?"

"You could say we have run into each other a time or two in the past."

Mephis systematically cracked off John Dee's skeletal fingers that were curled around the staff. Each snapped like a thin branch of a long-dead tree. He held the staff in the air as if it were a trophy showing off its long ivory shaft attached to a small jade hand palming a crystal sphere the size of a walnut. "This will do," he said, pacing towards a vacant span of the wall. The crystal sphere on the staff's hand turned pale blue and then white mist gathered around the top like clouds in a morning sky. Mephis tapped the sphere against the wall. A little rumble occurred as a section of the wall slid to one side revealing an alcove. Inside a single closed book rested on top of a wooden lectern.

Jack shifted and peered over Mephis' shoulder for a closer inspection. The book's jacket was of some sort of fleshy black leather, but oddly the cracks in the skin were oozing little droplets of dark-red liquid— like blood—as if the book were bleeding. "John's book?" Jack asked.

"No, no," Mephis replied, shaking his head. "John hid it away to keep it from the likes of me."

"I see, Master." The hairs on his back stood at attention as a chilling thought slithered under his skin. *Why would someone go to such lengths to keep the book away from Mephis? This can't be good.* On closer examination, the title of the book came into view: *The Book Of The Dead.* The subtitle towards the bottom read: *A Necromancer's Guide.* "Necromancy?" Jack mumbled.

"Yes, Jack," Mephis bellowed as he took the book. He laughed a sinister shrill, dark and evil. "Sorcery is sport, but necromancy," his eyes widened and he touched the tip of his tongue to his upper lip, "well, that is war: It allows me to raise an army of the dead."

Chapter 28 - Betrayed

The moon perched low in the starry night sky. "Shouldn't be long now," Sophia said. "Mass is shortly after dusk."

"Do you think Michael is still alive?" Anne asked.

She shuddered at the thought, then whispered, "I hope so." In just a few days' time, Michael had become like an older brother—a long-lost brother she had never met. He had helped rescue Anne, putting his own life on the line. *Better yet*, Sophia thought, *he had put himself at mortal risk from the moment he accompanied them on their quest to find Jeremial.* Sophia was certain that Michael had known that the sewers were being flooded. But selflessly, instead of saving himself, he ensured that both Anne, she, and even Dash were safe.

"I do miss him," Anne said.

"Me, too, Anne." Sophia frowned. "Me, too."

Muffled voices from all directions grew louder by the minute as people arrived, some on foot, others on horseback, and a few in carriages. The entrance to the cathedral soon bustled with families young and old dressed in their evening attire.

"Anne, you go first. Leave your haversack here, behind that crate. We'll come back for them. Once inside, head for the rear door that Father Roman took us through."

"Okay," Anne said, as she stood up and sauntered across the street and blended with a large family as they entered the front door of the church.

Sophia placed her haversack on top of Anne's and then scouted the various families. In turnabout for an orphan, she *chose* a family whose children were of various ages, a few around her age. Within moments, keeping her head down, she walked on the outskirts of the family. Perfect: They seemed oblivious to her presence. With so many people hurrying to make their way into the church, the Bobbies seemed less concerned with identifying suspects as with keeping order and directing traffic. If they were looking, Sophia presumed they must have been looking for two girls and possibly a dog walking together.

Her plan worked. Inside the cathedral, with nary a Bobby in sight, she raced to the rear doorway without taking too much care in making a stealthy exit. On entering, a nun approached her. "Quickly, this way," she said. Sophia followed the Sister through a back corridor that ended at the base of the stairway leading up the bell tower. "Anne is waiting up there," the Sister said. "Father Roman will come soon."

"Thank you," Sophia said. The narrow stairs wound their way up the tower. Her breathing became labored as she navigated the steep staircase. At the top, under the large-domed bell, Anne greeted her with a warm smile and heartfelt hug.

"What now?" Anne asked.

"We wait for Father Roman. He'll probably not be able to get away until after Mass."

Anne gazed at the large bell. "I hope it doesn't ring while were in here, it'll be loud."

"Sure will," Sophia replied as she slid down against the wall and sat with arms hugging her knees.

"Sophia?" Anne said, taking a seat next to Sophia. "Could I have been adopted?"

"Why would you ask such a thing?"

"Jack," Anne said, absently scratching the floor with her fingernails. "He said I was adopted. It's why I pursued him. I wanted to find out more."

"What else did he say?"

"Some other things as we were on the way into the woods after I woke up. He seemed rather convincing."

"What sort of 'other things'?" Sophia asked, eyebrows raised, curious. *How much does Anne know?*

"He said Angela was not my birth mother." She paused before adding, "How did he know my mother's name?"

Approaching footsteps echoed up the stairs. Sophia and Anne leapt to their feet, hoping … "Ah," Sophia said, seeing first Father Roman's head. "Thank God." Both girls sighed in relief.

"Thank the good Lord you girls are alive," Father Roman said, climbing the last step. He swiped sweat from his forehead with a handkerchief and took a deep breath. "When the Bobbies said they were going to flood the sewers, I feared the worse."

"We made it out," Sophia said. "But … Michael…" She paused thinking how best to word it. "The raging waters carried him into the reservoir. That's where the Bobbies dragged him into a boat. He didn't appear to be moving."

Father Roman's expression turned suddenly to dread.

"He may be alive," Sophia continued. "I'm sorry." She shook her head. "I really don't know."

"Where did the Bobbies take him?" Father Roman asked.

"I'm not sure. After they pulled him from the water, we lost sight of him. That is when we decided to come here."

"I see." He scratched his eyebrow. "Come, the bell will sound shortly and we best not be here when it does."

A little ways down the stairs, Father Roman opened a door that led onto the roof of the cathedral. After a short stroll across the roof, they entered a small rectangular building. Sophia's eyes cut around the room. A painting of Jesus dominated the far wall. Sophia recognized the image as a variation of the Transfiguration of Jesus, which she had seen in a book Sister Mary once shared with her. The charismatic eyes of Jesus almost looked alive, as if they were peering into the room and staring directly at you no matter where you were in the room. In the mural, two men in worshipful poses were on either side of Jesus while three other men, looking a tad more sheepish, gathered on the ground before him. There were four chairs set round a long oak table situated on a tattered brown rug.

"Take a seat," Father Roman said.

"What is this room?" Sophia asked as she slipped into a chair.

"A place I come to think and pray."

"I like the painting," Anne said.

Father Roman glanced towards the larger-than-life mural. "Yes, it is a masterpiece. It is a representation of when Jesus went up the mountain with three of his apostles. Once there Jesus began to glow with a stunning white energy and the prophets Elijah and Moses appeared with a voice that boomed from the sky, 'This is my son, whom I love. Listen to him!'"

Sophia added, "The bridge between heaven and earth."

"Oh you know about the painting, Sophia?" Father Roman asked.

"Only what I read in a book some time ago."

"I see. You are quite knowledgeable for such a young girl, dear."

Sophia smiled at the generous comment. No one had ever called her "knowledgeable" before.

"You say Bobbies took away Michael?"

"Yes."

"I will investigate. There are only few places they would have taken him. Please wait here until I return." He left the room.

Moments later a scratching sound came from the door. Sophia pushed open the entrance and, as she expected, in ran Dash. Anne strode over and stroked the little creature, who returned her affection with a wag of the tail and sloppy kiss.

Sophia walked over to the painting for a closer look at the intricate details. Studying the canvas, she fantasized about being able to paint as well as the person who had created this artwork. *Such awesome talent*, she thought. Each strand of grass was a deliberate stroke in a particular direction. Up close, the blades of grass looked like blurred lines. A few steps back and all the strokes combined to create the picturesque landscape of the image. *Incredible.* Sophia spun around in response to a rather forceful rapping on the door. *Who is that? Father Roman would not knock. Or would he?*

Anne pushed the door ajar, and almost lost her footing as the door suddenly swung wide open. Sophia gaped, her mouth opening wide to release a gasp of air in response to the shocking sight. Six Bobbies charged in. She froze. Nothing to do, nowhere to run, she submitted to their strength as they lashed her hands behind her back with twine. A tear of surrender fell from her eye. Anne struggled and fought with a Bobby who was struggling to secure her hands. Sophia said, "Don't struggle, Anne, we'll be okay." With those words, Anne gave up the fight.

The Bobbies led them outside of the room. Father Roman, head down, avoided eye contact with Sophia. She gazed directly at him, shouted angrily, "Traitor!"

Father Roman caught her stare and replied, "It is for the best." He closed his eyes and nodded. Sophia interpreted his body language as saying he was sorry and at the same time asking for forgiveness. She shook her head, squinting, muffling her rage. She was not having a bar of it.

People on the street outside the church gathered to witness the commotion as Bobbies loaded Anne and Sophia, like criminals, into the back of an enclosed carriage. Sophia tried to calm Anne as they practically carried her in. The fear in Anne's eyes reminded Sophia of how Anne's mother had died in the back of the carriage. She imagined the harrowing thoughts that must be racing through Anne's mind. Having her hands tied behind her back no doubt added to Anne's anxiety. "We'll be okay, Anne," Sophia said.

Anne nodded limply, unconvinced.

The two Bobbies who had loaded the girls into the carriage sat opposite them. Anne started to hyperventilate, taking short quick breaths, and was at the crest of a full-blown panic attack. Her face was a patchwork of bleak shades of pale blue and red. One of the Bobbies whose nametag identified him as John, in an attempt to calm Anne, said, "You'll be all right. Take a few deep breaths." Anne deliberately took long several deep breaths, and the color on her cheeks evened. The Bobby's words appeared to have helped.

The sound of a whip cracking preceded a sudden jerk in the carriage as the horses began a canter. Sophia gazed out the window at the gas lamps lighting the street. "Where are you taking us?" she asked.

"The watchhouse, until morning," John replied.

"What happens in the morning?"

"You'll be transferred by train to London."

London. Back to where this nightmare began, she thought.

Several minutes later, through the window of the carriage, the watchhouse came into view. A bland building with iron-barred windows and a single iron door manned by a solitary Bobby. Quite small for a jail, Sophia contemplated, just large enough to keep prisoners until they were transported to more secure, permanent facilities.

The Bobbies escorted them inside and down a narrow hallway. They passed two empty barred cells before coming to the third and final hold. At that point, Sophia's rage ebbed and a wash of relief curled her lips into a little smile, for there on the other side of the bars stood Michael.

"It's good to see you girls," he said.

"Likewise," Sophia said, turning sideways and jutting her hips out just enough to reach between the bars and take his hand in a gentle grip. The Bobby used his keys to open the cell. A heavy clunk and then a grating sound as he slid the gate across the gritted floor.

"In you go, girls, and don't give me any trouble," the Bobby said. "I don't want to have to use this baton. But I will," he added once they were in the cell. He untied their hands, left the cell, and secured the gate.

"How did they catch you?" Michael said.

"Father Roman gave us up. The traitor."

"Traitor? Easy, now. Somehow I don't think that would be so."

"He led the Bobbies right to us."

"He sure did," Anne said, as if that part of the account were in dispute. "Not a nice man," she added. "He deceived us."

"I wouldn't think that of Father Roman."

"Then maybe you don't know him as well as you thought you did," Sophia said.

"Perhaps," Michael said, his brow ruffled, as he seemed to be sifting the possibility.

The two Bobbies who had escorted Sophia and Anne traded paperwork with the Bobby on duty. On his way out, John said to the Bobby on duty, "By yourself tonight, Jim?"

"Yes, night shift is a dreary, lonely job. But it should be a quiet night," he said, nodding his head toward Sophia, Michael, and Anne. "Only these three kiddies to watch over."

"Right. Well, we will be off. Good night."

"Night," Jim replied as he took a seat on a chair at the end of the hallway.

"What do we do now, Michael?" Sophia asked.

"Not much we can do but wait."

The cell was bare but for a slop bucket in a corner, which exuberated a foul odor, and four wooden bunks, two on either side of the room. Anne climbed up onto the top bunk and let her legs dangle over the side. Sophia slipped into the bunk underneath, lay down, and crossed her arms over her chest.

Michael took a seat on the lower bunk opposite. "If only I could have made it out a second sooner…. I'm sorry, girls, for letting you down."

"Don't be," Sophia said. The nasty provocation of anger kindled in her gut. Not at Michael, but at Father Roman. She struggled to comprehend why he had traded them to the Bobbies.

"Who wants to play Spot?" Michael asked.

Sophia laughed. "You want to play a game while locked away?"

"Can you think of anything better to do to pass the time?"

"I'll play," Anne said.

"All right, me, too," Sophia added. The idea snuffed her anger—for the time being. Her lips struggled not to smirk.

"Okay. I'll go first," Michael said. "One spot, two spot, three spot four. I spot a something blocking the hall."

"Bar," Anne yelled.

"Too easy," Sophia said.

"You're right," Michael said.

"Okay, my turn," Anne said, clapping her hands. "Let me think." She gazed around the room. "One spot, two spot, three spot four. I spot a something on the floor."

Sophia scanned the room. *Not much in here.* "Bucket," she said.

"Oh drat," Anne said.

"My turn now," Sophia said. "One spot, two spot, three spot four. I spot a something watching us all."

"Guard," Michael said.

"Nope," Sophia replied, shaking her head.

Anne shouted, "A Bobby!"

"Nope."

"Hmm," Michael said, cutting his eyes across the prison cell.

"There is nothing else in here, Sophia," Anne said. "You are cheating."

Hearing the familiar unlocking clunk followed by the grating sound of the sliding gate, their attention turned to the front of the cell.

"Right, you lot, time to go," the Bobby Jim said.

"What do you mean?" Michael replied.

"I'm letting you out."

"But, why?"

"Oh," he said, eyes cut upward, "let's just say that some of us trust Father Roman more than the state."

Sophia's heart fluttered at the same time as nausea churned her gut. She experienced at once a sense of relief and a feeling of guilt for judging Father Roman's actions.

"I knew Father Roman wasn't a bad guy," Anne said as she leapt from the top bunk.

I wish I had, Sophia thought, or could fib about it, at least.

"Your steeds are awaiting you outside, along with your dog."

"What about the guard outside?" Michael asked.

"He'll be off duty by now. We don't station a guard outside at night unless the prisoners are considered extremely dangerous."

"But how will you explain our escape?"

"Well, for *that*," the Bobby said, pacing to the end of the corridor and retrieved Michael's belongings. He returned and then passed Michael his staff and haversack. "I'll need you to whack me. Be a decent chap and do it quickly and convincingly."

"Whack you?" Michael said. "Ah, I see." He raised his staff, said, "I'm sorry to have to do this, truly I am." The Bobby nodded and closed his eyes before the impact knocked him to the floor.

"That's gotta hurt," Sophia said.

"Hopefully not *too* much," Michael replied. "Time to get out of here."

Outside their horses and Dash were waiting just as Jim said they would be.

"Our haversacks," Sophia said. "I stuffed them behind some crates near St Philip's Cathedral."

"We'll get by without them," Michael said.

"But *The Book of Esdras*," Sophia said, her tone rising, "is in my haversack."

Michael scratched his chin while staring at the moon.

Chapter 29 - Raised

The gravedigger should be the only man on duty, Jack thought as he peered through the glass window of a shack tucked away in a corner of the cemetery. Inside, seated at a small table reading a newspaper in the glow of a gas lantern, was his target—an elderly gentleman with a long silvery beard and a lazy eye. A cup of steaming tea rested next to him. Jack licked his lips, imagining the scent of the beverage, his favorite. He paced back behind a tree, picked up a small rock the size of a penny, and threw it at the shack's window. It was not strong enough to shatter the glass but did make a distinctive pinging sound.

A moment later the door to the shack opened, and the old man whispered. "Anyone there?" Lantern in hand, he stepped out onto the door landing.

The man's patrol—a clockwise pace around the shack—seemed obvious to Jack from the moment he stepped out the door. Jack waited until the man, whose right leg was seemingly unable to bend at the knee, hobbled past his hiding spot. Then, with chloroform-soaked cloth in hand, Jack took two quick strides out from the darkness, clamped his hand around the old man's mouth and nose, and hooked his other arm around the man's chest. The old man struggled, thrashing about like a fly in a spider's web, but his strength was no match for Jack. An easy takedown—easier in fact than many of the nightwalking dames he took down. As the man drifted into unconsciousness, Jack lowered him to a sitting position against the back wall of the shack. He took the man's lantern and went in the shack. Inside, he slipped into the chair, picked up the cup of tea and waved it just under his nose, breathing in the fresh scent before touching the cup to his lips. The warm minty liquid washed over his tongue. He closed his eyes, savoring the taste. Several minutes passed as he took his time consuming the tea, knowing he had a large job ahead of him. *My time to rest*, he thought. Before leaving, he fetched the gravedigger's shovel.

Shovel in hand, Jack paced through Kensal Green Cemetery under the night sky. The moon peeked between clouds occasionally providing glimmers of ambient light. Jack, however, preferred the moon to stay hidden, making his stealthy task easier. Within minutes, he arrived back to where he secured his horse earlier in the night. He laid the shovel on the ground and untied a rolled-up rug from the side of his horse. He unrolled the old straw-matted rug next to the grave and picked up his shovel. With a downward thrust, he plunged the spade into the freshly-placed soil. The steel blade descended a few inches. Using his foot, and positioning his weight, he forced the blade down the rest of its extent. His back already ached just a little, and he knew it would be no easy task to move the six feet of dirt covering the coffin containing the corpse Mephis instructed him to retrieve. "No more than a week dead," Mephis had said. "That is the age of the cadaver I require."

After several minutes of digging, Jack leant on his shovel to catch his breath. He listened to the night, still but for the occasional "who-o-o who-o-o" of an owl. A night ideally suited to his task so long as the rain stayed away. He wiped sweat from his brow to prevent the salty fluid from stinging his tired eyes.

Two hours later, the shovel's blade struck the hard wooden surface of a coffin. *A little more and I'm done,* he thought. A few minutes later, he pried opened the lid of the casket. Immediately, he covered his nose to prevent any more of the foul concentrated smell tainting his senses. The foul stench aggrieved his eyes, causing them to well with cleansing tears. He leapt from the six-foot hole, keeled over, and gagged, dry heaving. Then, another forceful retch, this one relieving him of the remnants of his supper. After gaining his composure, he returned to the hole.

The trapped stench had dissipated somewhat into the night air. He took his first look at the corpse. A woman. Decomposition had begun, and maggots were busy feeding on the side of her neck. Her face was gray and emaciated. Dark voids either side of her nose stared outwards from where her eyes used to be. He wondered if they had gone as part of her death or if insects had already made a meal of them, or perhaps some perverse mortuary attendant had wanted a souvenir. Strangely, he found the corpse beautiful in a way. The woman's long blond hair flowed down over her shoulders and splayed by her sides. Her figure still had an appealing allure. Even though her arms and legs had the same gray emaciated look as her face. Maybe the attraction was the long red tight fitting dress she wore. He was not sure.

With little effort, he lifted the thirty-pound corpse from the coffin and placed it on the rug. He rolled the rug around the corpse as if rolling tobacco in paper. Once secure, he tied a short piece of rope around the center and then slung his improvised body bag over the back of his horse. "Back to shoveling," he mumbled. Filling the grave took half the time and effort as the digging. His crime concealed, he led his horse the short walk back to the shack. After returning the shovel, he mounted his steed and commenced the one-hour journey to his Whitechapel home. Light rain had begun to fall, but he didn't mind it. The fresh droplets cooled and refreshed him. Helped lessen the tainted stench clinging to his clothes.

With the makeshift body bag over his shoulder, Jack plodded down the stairs into the basement. "Nearly there," he mumbled.

"You're back," Mephis said. "And you have the corpse."

"Yes, Master," Jack replied, unrolling the rug on the floor to reveal the cadaver.

Mephis held his newly acquired staff in one hand and the *Book Of The Dead* in the other and began chanting, "Excito mortuus." The sphere on the top of the staff filled with a red mist and began spinning madly like a mini tornado. In a louder voice, Mephis shouted some additional words he read from the *Book Of The Dead*, in a dialect Jack did not understand. The room started to shake as a vertical red crack formed, like a lightning bolt, and floated above the body.

The split grew in width. Then a black hand appeared at the edge of the crack, as if someone were reaching through from somewhere on the other side. The hand was no ordinary hand but appeared rather as a black shadow, with no depth, like a translucent phantom. A moment later, a head appeared, also as a shadow, followed by a complete body wafting through the crack. A shadow of a man now stood before Jack. It was no mere reflection; it was standing in the room, an entity like a black ghost.

"What is it, Master?" Jack asked.

"Oddly enough, they are called Shadows. Souls condemned to the Underworld. Some people refer to them as demons or evil spirits."

"But I thought you were raising the dead?"

"No, Jack," Mephis corrected, shaking his head. "I am creating a rift between our dimension and the Underworld to enable Shadows to come forth. With no physical form, however, Shadows cannot interact in our dimension, our world, the world they once lived in as humans before death."

The red energized crack vanished leaving the Shadow bobbing a bit, peering around the room. A cold chill, familiar to Jack, ran down his spine, only this one was somewhat colder than normal, almost freezing and causing his body to shudder involuntarily. He had experienced some creepy things, but this somehow bothered him more. The idea that souls exist in the Underworld, or what he presumed was Hell, made the Last Judgement and his eternal destination all that more real. If demons and a devil exist, then so must….

After pacing up and down the room, the Shadow floated into the corpse and vanished. Mephis began to chant additional words he read from the *Book Of The Dead*. A short time later, the eye sockets of the corpse glowed a deep blood red as the body wriggled slightly. Mephis stopped chanting. "See, Jack, there is a place for necromancy. Not only can it allow rifts, gateways, to form between the Underworld and Earth, but it also enables a Shadow to animate a corpse."

Jack took a few steps backwards, away from the body. *No wonder John Dee wanted to hide that book,* he thought. He jolted as the corpse sprang into a sitting position. Then the body's head turned side to side making the horrible creaking sound of bone rubbing on bone.

"What do we call it, Master?" Jack asked.

Mephis rubbed his chin. "Interesting question. I haven't thought of a name."

The corpse's mouth opened as if it were trying to speak, but no sound came out. A moment later, it rose from the floor, stumbling forward at first, before balancing itself into a stiff walk.

"How long will it last, Master? Will not the body rot?"

"The Shadow inside will slow the decay. But, yes, the vessel is temporary."

"What is the point then, Master?"

"A temporary army is better than no army, Jack."

"Will the Shadow return to the Underworld?"

"Ultimately, when the vessel becomes uninhabitable the Shadow will return to the Underworld or slip into the Spiritual Realm."

"Spiritual Realm, Master?"

"Yes. It is a place where Shadows in various forms feed off the negative energy created in our realm, Jack. Much easier for them to move into from the Underworld. To come here they need the assistance of someone like myself."

"I see, Master." Jack paused for a moment, before asking, "Will I end up in the Underworld, as a Shadow, when I die?"

"That's not going to be up to me, Jack," Mephis said, before vomiting forth an evil laugh.

"Who, then?" Jack asked.

"Your creator, Jack, who else?"

Chapter 30 - Thor's Cave

"There shouldn't be many Bobbies around now, Michael," Sophia said, mounting Solitaire. She desperately wanted—*needed*—the book *The Order of Esdras*. On her most recent attempts to read the book, nothing additional had appeared, but she held out hope that words would appear that would help her in some way. Help her make sense of who she was and what she was about.

"Right," Michael agreed. "Let's try to retrieve your haversacks."

Using the bell tower of St Philip's Cathedral as a landmark, they headed off. The streets were still and silent but for the occasional sound of a cat scavenging. "No sign of Bobbies," Sophia said, a block away from the Cathedral.

"The streets are quiet," Michael noted. "In some ways *too* quiet."

Across from the church, Sophia dismounted her horse. "The haversacks should be behind these crates." She pulled the stack of crates aside, rummaged around the hiding spot. "Hmm. I'm sure this is where I left them." After a little more searching, she said, "Ah, here they are." She passed Anne's haversack to her then proceeded to check inside hers. "The book is still within mine."

"Good," Michael said. "Let's not tarry. Sooner or later, the Bobbies will be on a mission to recapture the escaped convicts."

Back on her horse, Sophia followed Michael's lead as they trotted through the backstreets of Birmingham. "Where are we going?"

"A cave north of here, Thor's cave, about a four-hour ride if we keep up a reasonable pace. We can rest there until mid-morning before the next leg of our journey."

The ride through the quiet streets of Birmingham afforded Sophia time to appreciate what Father Roman had accomplished. When he realized Michael was in custody at the watchhouse, he most likely figured there would be little point in orchestrating an escape while Bobbies continued to search the streets for them. Instead, he devised a plan whereby they would be captured. Father Roman knew that once all three fugitives were in custody, the Bobby patrols would be called off. So he organized his man on the inside to facilitate an escape. A little remorse lingered over having judged Father Roman so harshly. *One day,* she thought, *perhaps I'll have the chance to thank him.*

Approximately four hours later, after a long trek, Michael pointed into the distance. "See those mountains. They call the place White Peak. The cave we seek is in that range."

Under the moonlight, Sophia could make out the vague outline of jagged peaks on the horizon. "Not much farther, then. How are you holding up, Anne?"

"I'm tired, but okay," she replied.

From the base of the mountain, they trotted up a narrow path that weaved its course up the steep mountainside. A short distance from the limestone crag, the cave's entrance, they secured their horses and continued the rest of the way on foot.

"This cave is huge," Sophia said, stepping through he arched entrance spanning six times her height and nearly twice again that height in width. "Why is this place called 'Thor's Cave'?"

"No one knows. The name has been passed down through the generations. Some say the cave is linked to the Norse god Thor. But they are likely fables," Michael said. "Find yourselves a comfortable place to rest. I'll go hunt us some food and bring back firewood."

Anne faced Michael. "I'll come with you."

"No, Anne," he said, kindly, "from the looks of those bags under your eyes, you need to rest."

"Come sit over here with me," Sophia said, finding a soft spot on the limestone floor covered with stone dust.

Michael left the cave. Sophia wondered if any animals inhabited the cave deeper in, hiding in the darkness, lying in wait or seeking refuge from predators. She wished she had a lantern to supplement the white ambient glow cast by the moonlight. Anne lay down with her head in Sophia's lap. Sophia gently stroked her hair. "I love you, Sophia," Anne said. "You are truly like a sister to me."

"And you are to me," Sophia replied, smiling, knowing the truth in the statement. She considered telling Anne about her mother, but it didn't seem the right time to do so. Anne seemed content to rest. Sophia closed her eyes and rested the back of her head against the cool, smooth limestone wall.

What seemed like moments later, Michael returned with a bundle of sticks of various sizes and a dead snake slung over his shoulders, its head and tail nearly scraping the ground.

"You were quick," Sophia said.

"I've been gone about an hour. Took a while to catch us some dinner," Michael said, dropping the sticks he carried.

"We're eating snake?" Sophia said, realizing she must have dozed off earlier.

"Yep, they taste quite pleasant cooked," he said. He laid the snake out across the floor.

Anne, still sleeping with her head on Sophia's lap, stirred a little. Sophia resumed stroking her hair to calm her. Sister Mary used to do that to both of them to help them get off to sleep on nights when thundering storms were about.

Michael built a fire with the wood, and within a few minutes the campfire was aglow with warmth. Using his knife, he slit down the center of the snake. With his fingers, he dug into the cut and pulled out the snake's guts and then began drawing off the snake's skin, like rolling a long sock off a person's leg. The snake stripped, Michael laid a stick across the top of the fire, propped up on either side by two sticks lashed together in a Y formation. He wound the snake's body around the makeshift rotisserie, occasionally rotating the stick to ensure even cooking.

"Smells good," Sophia said.

"Not long now and the snake will be cooked," Michael replied, stoking the fire with a branch.

"Thanks for everything you're doing, Michael, risking your life and everything. We were beside ourselves with fear after you were washed away."

He smiled, glanced towards Sophia. "You girls are family now."

Sophia experienced a warm tingling sensation flurrying throughout her body. She believed Michael's words. Since starting their journey, she had gained a sister and a brother, Michael. She smiled: *Family*. At the same time, she also carried great pangs of grief over the loss of the Sisters and her orphanage family. She knew once things settled down, if they ever did, she would have to face that devastating loss.

"Here you go," Michael said, passing her a strip of roasted snake meat. She gave Anne a nudge and waited for her to lift off her lap before accepting Michael's offer.

Sophia took a small bite of the snake as Anne received her own piece from Michael. To her surprise, the meat tasted good, a bit like chicken. Dash wolfed down her portion and seemed quite fond of the dish, fond enough to beg a second helping.

Anne chewed on the snake meat. "This is yummy," she said, the words just barely intelligible from behind the mouthful of food. Sophia thought about telling her not to talk with her mouth full but let the idea go. She smiled thinking back on how Sister Margaret used to say, "You'll catch a fly talking and eating at the same time. Keep your mouth closed." In hindsight, Sophia wondered if there was any truth to the statement. The saying did work, though. The girls always responded by closing their mouths. The fear of swallowing a fly was one powerful motivator.

"We'll leave around lunch time tomorrow," Michael said, finding a position to make his bed for the night. "That will give us and our faithful horses a much-needed rest."

"They are holding up well," Sophia said.

"Indeed. Better than I thought they would. I suspect your powers are helping them along."

"How so?"

"Hard to explain. Have you noticed the faint white light surrounding them?"

"Now and then," she replied. "But I've seen that faint white aurora around a few things in my life, so I didn't think much of it." Until now, she had never considered that the white glow around the horses might be in someway an effect of her powers. She also wondered if the aura surrounding Eclipse meant that Anne, too, had *abilities*.

"It is odd," Michael replied. "Your horse and Anne's horse both glow a faint white while you are riding them at certain times. The glow around my horse Lancelot only appears when I am riding in close proximity to you or Anne. When I do, Lancelot seems to become refreshed."

"Oh," Sophia said. She wondered whether Michael was becoming suspicious about Anne. *Maybe he knows that we are sisters, but isn't telling me for the same reason I don't want to tell him.* She did consider it possible, if not likely, that Jack has or will tell Mephis at some point, which rendered her motive for not sharing it meaningless.

"Are you doing something to my horse, Sophia?" Anne asked.

"Not consciously," Sophia said.

"Well, whatever, or *whoever*, is doing it," Michael interrupted, "it is helping us." He placed his haversack under his head as a pillow and closed his eyes. "Time to get some sleep."

Anne laid her head back in Sophia's lap. "This is comfy."

Sophia stroked her hair, allowing a sense of contentment to curl her lips into a tender smile. "Sleep well." She closed her eyes and rested her head against the limestone wall. Even sitting upright, all things considered, she was comfy and relaxed enough to drift off to sleep.

Chapter 31 - Created

Jack, sitting on a cushioned sofa in the lounge room of his Whitechapel home in front of the blazing fireplace, pondered Mephis's statement: "Your creator, Jack, who else?"

My creator? The statement challenged his conviction on Darwin's theory of natural selection. He had a basic understanding of the theory, which many intellectuals and men of science considered a mortal blow to theistic religion, while others dismissed it as unscientific speculation that required as much faith and assumption as the religions it presumed to render extinct. The theory holds that organisms are produced that survive on limited resources. Over time, these organisms struggle to acquire what they need to sustain their life. Competition breaks out between the organisms, and in some instances specific creatures or entire species die. Individual entities within groups vary with particular traits, and some qualities are passed down to offspring. Variations in the beings give more advantages to some over others. The gist of the theory is the better-adapted entities are more likely to survive and reproduce. Those species whose individuals have best adapted survive while others less adaptive become extinct. This process occurred over eons of time, billions of years. A typical picture used to describe the process shows a picture of a chimpanzee, transitioning into an ape, and then into a human. The theory impressed Jack as both logical and elegant. To the religious community, of course, and the Bible-thumpers such a claim was abject heresy. *But why*, Jack questioned, *would Mephis say my future destiny would be up to my creator?*

He stirred on his chair, uncomfortable with the questions. He pondered the possibility that both Darwin and Mephis were correct. Could God have used an approach similar to Darwin's theory to create life? The longer he thought about it, the more plausible it seemed—

especially given everything he knew as a surgeon about the intricacies of the human body and the evidence of exquisite design. On deeper reflection, he also considered, albeit reluctantly, the prospect that Darwin might be wrong. What he came to realize finally, which bothered him the most, was something that he had never considered—that Darwin's theory does not exclude the likelihood of a creator. All this time he had perceived Darwin's theory as providing clear evidence to demonstrate that God was not necessary in the creation of man. That was true to him, but at the same time, the theory did not show that God did not create man using natural selection as a means of creative delivery. In a way, evolution, the system itself, showed a process of intelligence. He began to sweat, heavily, under his arms and between his legs, as a feeling of being duped swept over him.

All this time he had been willing to do anything, literally anything, to cling to life, to the only existence he believed he had. Now he had to consider that if a god created him, a god would certainly have the power to extend his life after death in one form or another. He thought back to how Christians seemed to face death without anxiety, earnestly expecting that the true life began on the other side of human death. He recalled stories about the resurrection of Christ and a Bible verse he had so often heard the street preachers rant: "I am the way, the truth, and the life: no man cometh unto the Father, but by me."

Jack rose, paced towards the fire, grabbed a log, and placed it on the smoldering coals. Back in his seat, he watched the flames lick and lap at the new piece of wood—fuel for the hungry blaze. A disturbing image flooded his mind—a vivid image of him gnashing his teeth and weeping, surrounded in all directions by ravenous flames. He shook his head as if to clear the disturbing image, mumbled, "Pesky Christians, filling my mind with such horrid images."

Every time he closed his eyes, a different dark, disturbing image would form. On his last attempt to rest, he dreamt of being surrounded by Shadows. The evil creatures clawed at his naked body, ripping ugly gashes in his flesh. From the wounds, red energy, not blood, flowed. The Shadows bit into the source of the energy and gorged themselves on the steady streams as he squealed in pain. He compared the creatures to vampires, mythical humanoid beings that feed on human blood by night. The noticeable difference was that these Shadow beings were not after blood but rather some kind of red energy spilling out of him, generated, no doubt, by his evil deeds.

Jack dared not close his eyes for fear of yet another horrifying image. Instead, he gazed at the flames of the burning fire. After a while, tears welled in his eyes from staring at the hot fire and from a spring of long-quenched emotions oozing like miasma to the surface of his consciousness. He blinked to clear the fluid buildup. For a moment, he considered finding a Bible to read but then realized there wasn't one in the house. The Bible bothered Mephis, enough for him to destroy the two copies Jack had in the house. Jack had flipped through the book once or twice but never actually read much of it. Now, sitting in front of the fire, Jack questioned why the Bible bothered Mephis so much. At the time, Jack did not believe God or any god existed so the book that believers referred to as an account of *God's word* was unimportant to him. It was little more to him than Aesop's fables—a book written about a fictional character by men. He thought back to a scene a year before he diagnosed his brother's tumor.

* * *

"One second," Jack yelled, in response to the rapping on his door. He finished pouring his cup of tea before proceeding to the front door.

"Elidin," Jack said, "I wasn't expecting to see you today. You're looking well."

"I bought you a gift," his brother replied.

"Oh, well, do come in then." Jack led Elidin into the kitchen. "Take a seat. I'm pouring myself a cupper. Care to join me?"

"Please," Elidin said.

A minute later, Jack handed Elidin a cup of tea and sat down across the dining table from him.

From under his coat, Elidin produced a package wrapped in plain brown paper. "Here you go, Jack," Elidin said, passing the gift to his brother.

"What's the occasion? It's not my birthday."

Elidin laughed. "No occasion, and although you have been known to forget my birthday, I never forget yours."

"Right you are," Jack replied. He pulled the paper off the gift. "A novel," he said, seeing the brown leather back of a book.

"Not a novel," Elidin said. "And not just a book."

Jack turned the book over. An image on the front, framed in an oval decorative border, depicted a waist-up illustration of Jesus holding a staff and a scroll. Above his head were the words: *Search the scriptures*. Underneath, still inside the oval, were the words: *Thy word is truth*. Jack opened to the first page and read the title: *The Holy Bible*. "Well," he said, sighing, "a Charles Dickens novel would make a better story, but thanks all the same."

Elidin smiled. "You never know, Jack. The stories may surprise you."

"Maybe," he replied, shrugging. He placed the Bible on the table and then gave it a little shove off to the side as if it were a pie he had just discovered he didn't have a taste for.

"Does the Bible bother you, Jack?"

"Bother me? No," he replied, taking a sip of his tea. "I do have a copy. The one Mum gave me. The same edition that she gave you."

"Oh," Elidin said, his eyebrows raising. "I'm surprised you still have it."

"Well, it's around here somewhere. If memory serves, I think it's in the depths of one of my clothes drawers." He paused as he glanced at the gift. "So, why a Bible?"

"Fair enough question," Elidin replied. "A friend of mine lost his wife and son in a terrible horse accident." He paused before continuing. "Four weeks later he took his own life."

"Tragic," Jack said, cocked his head. "But what pray tell does that have to do with me?"

"In the back of the Bible, you'll find a note. Have a read sometime."

Jack furrowed his eyebrows. "I will."

* * *

"I never did read the note," Jack mumbled. Thinking back, he recalled taking the note from the Bible and placing it with his collection of letters. A sudden urge to read the note came over him.

Chapter 32 - The Note

"Where can that note be?" Jack muttered, tipping out a third box of assorted papers onto his bed. He went through each piece of paper scattered about, most of them letters from his patients thanking him for his caring service in the healing arts. He began collecting them back when he first became a doctor. During a patient's treatment, he would ask them to write him a letter when they had fully recovered. In one way, he asked the question to instill hope within them that they would in fact recover. Some patients he discerned never would, but planting a seed of hope lifted their spirits as well as their family members'.

"It's not here," he said, pushing the papers aside to clear a place to sit on the side of his bed. Head in hands, he tried to recall where he had put that note. Three wooden boxes were set on the floor, which used to hold his many letters. He stood over the third box and a yellow-tinged leaf of paper wedged in the depths of the container caught his eye. He knelt down and took a closer look. Sure enough, there it was, stuffed down near the bottom of the box. He sat down and began reading.

Dear Jack,

I hope this letter finds you well.

Well the letter did find me, Elidin, but it didn't find me well.

Somehow I doubt you will read this letter on the day I give you the Bible. But I am hopeful that one day in the near future you will find in your heart a desire to read my message.

You knew me well, Elidin.

I anticipate on the day I give you a Bible as a gift you will ask me why. Instead of entering into a debate, I figured that a written response, which you could read at your leisure, and more than once if necessary, may be a better guide.

You once asked me why I believe in Christianity and I failed to respond at the time.

I figured you were delusional, another mark conned by the wild-eyed street preachers.

I've thought about my reasons for some time and prepared the following reply.

Here we go. Conversion speech a-coming.

When you accept Jesus' teachings and apply the knowledge to your life, your life becomes better.

Right. So says you.

A time came in my life when I asked myself why I wouldn't want to follow these teachings. There is no downside. Christianity fills me with joy, gives me strength and hope during the tough times, and provides a solid foundation to build on. I could go on to explain how God makes me feel, but it's not something I can truly express in words. When you have Jesus in your life, you just … know.

Yes. I would have debated this. Having an imaginary friend is like a placebo. I know all about the benefits of filling people with false hope. I used to do it all the time to make my patients feel better, even those whom I knew would die.

Do I have doubts? Of course I do. Without doubts, I wouldn't need faith. My doubts allow me to question. Those questions lead to answers, which in turn strengthen my faith.

At times when I'm feeling doubtful, I think back to Jesus' disciple Peter, who walked side by side with Jesus and witnessed him performing sign and wonders, miracles. When Peter's faith was challenged at Jesus' crucifixion, he had enough doubt to deny that he even knew Jesus. Not once, but three times.

Only after Peter witnessed Jesus' return from the dead was his faith strong like a rock, strong enough, sure enough to lay the foundations for the Church of Christianity. Jesus said to Thomas, "Thomas, because you have seen Me, you have believed. Blessed are those who have not seen and yet have believed."

Well now, if God appeared in front of me, perhaps then I, too, would have faith.

Day in and day out, I feel truly blessed to have my trust in Christ.

I have no quibble or qualm with that, if it makes you feel better.

Can I physically prove that God exists? No. I doubt man ever will be able to do so scientifically. To me, that is like asking a fish swimming in a fish bowl to prove the existence of the ocean. Again, proof eliminates the need for faith, which is what God requires of us.

You are probably thinking that my doubts show a lack of belief. However, let me suggest to you that if God wanted to he could demonstrate his power and have <u>everyone</u> believe in him. If He did, though, He would take away a person's freewill to love God for whom He is instead of for what He can do.

When you see a wealthy old gentleman and his beautiful young wife who met him after he made his fortune, do you not wonder whether she married him for his wealth and the life he could afford her or for who he is?

Interesting analogy, brother.

If God shows us his power before we come to love him, He could change why we love Him. I love God for the life He bestowed on me and the grace He shows me. Whenever I doubt, I smile and thank God he gave me the freedom to choose to love him.

But you died. Where was your God then?

Faith, Jack: We don't think we need it when the sun is shining. When the sun goes down and darkness surrounds us, faith can provide a guiding light to help us navigate the unknown. My friend who committed suicide after losing his family didn't have faith. The lights turned off around him. He became stranded all alone in the darkness. Out of fear, he took his life rather than deal with the unknown.

A chill ran from the nape of Jack's neck down through all four extremities as he read the last paragraph. *Surrounded by darkness. With no visible way out.* That is how he had considered his situation. Although, oddly, the fear of death was what had stopped him from taking his own life to end his suffering. He blamed that on the painting *The Last Judgement.*

I hope you find faith, Jack. We never know when the day may come when we will require the gracious gift.

Jack realized that day had already come … and gone. He did not have faith. Memories of how hope helped his patients came flooding back to him. He gave them hope. Now though, he realized, there was nobody to give him hope. *Is that what Jesus does?* he thought. *Give people hope?*

He certainly noticed the sparkle in his brother's eyes, even on his deathbed. A question reverberated in his thoughts: *How could a figment of a person's imagination (such as God) provide such relief from the darkness of the world?* It couldn't, he decided, unless he was wrong and God was real. He read the last paragraph of the note.

> With everything said, please accept this gift, a Bible, as a way to discover Christianity, the greatest of faiths.

Jack read the letter a second time. He couldn't help but wonder if he had opened the note over a decade ago things would have been different. It was too late; he believed he had chosen his path and turning back was not an option.

Chapter 33 - River Mersey

After a long ride from Thor's cave, Michael gazed westward up the River Mersey admiring the beautiful golden glow the setting sun cast across the water's calm surface. He considered staying the night this side of the Queen Victoria Bridge in Warrington. Considering the Bobbies would likely be searching both sides of the river, however, he decided to proceed farther north. On the outskirts of Warrington, he knew of a small chapel where they could spend the night. The bridge seemed oddly vacant. He expected more people to be out on such a lovely evening. With a quick jab of his heels, he bought Lancelot to a slow trot. Together, in a triangular formation with Michael at point, Anne on the left, and Sophia on the right, they proceeded to traverse the bridge.

Halfway across the bridge, two men appeared from behind pillars on the far side of the crossing. One, whose navel exposed because his shirt was several sizes too small to cope with his rather flabby belly, held a wooden paling with a nail sticking out the end. The other, firm and athletic in appearance and wearing a black coat and long pants with a sheathed dagger conspicuously attached to his belt, announced: "There is a toll for crossing this bridge!"

"And what is that?" Michael replied. The men strode towards them. Michael glanced over his shoulder to see if retreating was an option. As expected, two men approached from the rear for a possible ambush. Both were rather lean but well-muscled, about six feet tall, with short black hair, similar physical features, and white long-sleeve shirts with navy pants. One held a metal bar as long as a sledgehammer and the other a black Bobby's baton.

The man with the dagger, whom Michael presumed to be the leader, yelled, "Your horses will do."

"Anne, Sophia," Michael said, as he dismounted Lancelot. "Stay on your horses." He looked the man in the eye, said, "We don't want any trouble, Mister."

"Good," the leader said, placing his hand on the hilt of his dagger. "The price of no trouble is three horses, and you three can be on your way."

Michael strode towards the approaching men until stopping an arm's length away. The men approaching from the rear paced around Anne and Sophia to surround Michael. "Nobody needs to get hurt," Michael said, holding his staff vertical with its base resting on the ground. He closed his eyes.

"Funny boy," the leader said. "Thinks he can fight us blind, boys!"

First Michael heard the whooshing sound of the spiked plank the big guy was wielding. In response, Michael twisted his staff and pushed it outward connecting with the guy's flabby stomach and doubled him over in pain. Michael plunged his elbow into the back of the big guy's head, sending him to the ground with a thud. Next, he heard the whirl of the metal bar looping towards him. He thrust his staff a little lower than the direction of the sound. The staff passed between the attacker's legs and proceeded upward with a sharp flick that crushed the fellow's nether regions. The man made a sickly groan, groped at his crotch, and collapsed.

Michael opened his eyes. Two left: the leader with his dagger drawn and the man with the Bobby's baton whose hands were shaking. Michael dropped his staff, clenched his fists while leaving his middle finger and forefinger poking outwards. The leader swung his dagger, and Michael reacted by stabbing him rapidly with his pointed fingers, first directly on a pressure point in the upper-right shoulder that dislodged the blade from his hand. Then he prodded on each side of the man's chest and delivered a quick blow to the base of the leader's neck just below his Adam's apple. The leader grabbed his throat with both hands, gasping for air as he collapsed to the ground. Michael turned to the last aggressor. The man, hand shaking, raised the baton. "Your choice," Michael said, glaring at the man. With a clunk, the attacker's baton fell to the ground and he turned and scurried away.

"Wow!" Anne said, her eyes bulging with admiration for the display of heroism.

Michael picked up his staff. "I know a few moves," he replied, mounting Lancelot. "We best keep moving."

A short while later, as the sun was half past the horizon, they came to the edge of a graveyard strewn with headstones in amongst overgrown grass and knee-high weeds. The small cemetery separated them from a boarded-up ordinary chapel, a simple rectangular box with an elongated triangular roof.

"Looks like nobody's home," Sophia said.

"I expected as much," Michael replied.

After securing the horses, Michael pushed on door of the chapel, but it stubbornly refused to move. With the butt of his shoulder, he strained and shoved harder. A terrible scrawling sound echoed around the chapel as the base of the door clawed across the wooden floor.

Inside, Michael stood his staff up against the wall, which subtly lit the interior of the building. The chapel was a rectangular hall with a row of pews on each side facing a raised pulpit. "Pick a pew for your bed," he said. "We'll be safe here for the night." After wiping the thick dust off a bench, he made his own bed using his haversack as a pillow. Before long, the girls were sitting on a pew, burning off energy playing a game of Pat-a-Cake.

The game started with singing the words "pat-a-cake" as they clapped. Then as they slapped each other's palms they sang "pat-a-cake" a second time, followed by clapping again and singing "baker's man!" They repeated this clapping pattern sometimes crisscrossing their palm strikes while signing the rest of the rhyme, "So I will, master, as fast as I can. Pat it, and prick it, and mark it with T. Put it in the oven for Tommy and me." Each time through the verse, they increased the tempo until one of them missed the other girl's hands. At that point, they would stop and share a laugh and start all over again.

Michael fought back a smile, seeing the child in them. They were children, he mused, forced to grow up rapidly in a broken world. Drawn into a war not of their own making. Both had seen and done things they should never have had to see or do. He closed his eyes and drifted into a memory of a meeting with Mendel.

* * *

Michael slipped into a seat across from Mendel who was sitting behind his desk.

Mendel returned a quill he had used to scrawl on a scroll to its holder. "Michael, congratulations on your White Monk graduation."

"Thank you, sir."

"After careful consideration, we have chosen you as a candidate for an upcoming assignment."

"Assignment?"

"Yes. An escort assignment."

"Of whom?"

"Two young girls."

"Where to?"

"From here to Hermitage Castle on the borders of Scotland."

"When?"

"We're not quite sure. The fact is, we have received information about the assignment from a prophecy in a book."

"In a book?" Michael asked, eyebrow raised.

"Yes," Mendel said, in a measured tone. *The Book Of Esdras*." From his desk drawer, he retrieved the book and passed it to Michael. "Take a read when you get a chance."

Michael accepted the book.

"Ignore the box inside, which is for one of the girls should we meet them."

"Okay."

Mendel pushed the scroll he was writing on over to Michael. "Here is a map you can use as a guide for your journey. On the back you'll see additional instructions and some codes for accessing particular passageways. Memorize the map and notes, then destroy it. We don't want those secrets getting into the wrong hands."

"That is some distance," Michael replied, as he traced the route on the map. A line trailed over hundreds of miles through several marked places—Hyde Park, Stowe House, Birmingham, Thor's Cave,

Warrington—and on it went proceeding in a northerly direction until finishing at Hermitage Castle.

"It's a *suggested* route. Use your intuition to choose stops at your leisure. Variations may be required depending on how your horses hold up and, well, any unforeseen events that might arise."

"Horses?"

"Yes, we are giving you three of our best steeds."

"Are you sure I'm the right person for this assignment?" Michael said, shrugging.

"Not entirely," Mendel said honestly. "But you best fit the description of the one described in the prophecy."

"Oh," Michael said. "Well, I'm not sure. Do I have a choice?"

"Yes, of course. Nobody will force you to take on the assignment if it shall come to pass."

"How old are these girls?"

"The prophecy says around thirteen years of age."

"That is very young to be trekking such a distance."

"One is said to be no ordinary girl. Have a read, you'll find out more."

Michael nodded.

* * *

At first, even after reading the prophecy, Michael was skeptical about the escorting assignment Mendel had given him. On the day of his meeting with Anne and Sophia, he had wanted to ask Mendel to find someone else. Due to the events that occurred during dinner, however, his chance to withdraw passed. Now everything had changed. He was quite honored and justifiably proud that they had chosen him for the assignment.

After finishing their game of Pat-a-Cake, the girls settled on a place in the center aisle of the church and lay down on the floor to sleep side-by-side with Dash curled up at their feet. Seemed to Michael, nothing would be able to separate the two. He sensed that so strong was their love, either one would gladly risk her life for the other. As would he for either of them. He was reminded of Jesus' words in the Gospel of John: "Greater love hath no man than this, that a man lay down his life for his friends."

Chapter 34 - Dunsop Bridge

"Quaint village," Sophia said as they passed over a little hump-backed stone bridge that crossed the river Dunsop in the small town of Dunsop Bridge, which was nestled in the rolling hills of the Forest of Bowland. She fidgeted on her horse. The long rides, typically a day's duration, still managed to displease her bottom such that she had to occasionally reposition her body or stand up in the stirrups for short lengths of time. "Where are we going?" she asked.

"First, to the stables," Michael replied. "We will leave our steeds there. The rest of our journey will be on foot."

"Then?"

"To St Hubert's Church where we'll spend the night."

"Another church?" Anne said. "Why all the churches?"

"Safest place to be when dark forces are about," Michael replied.

"True," she said, nodding.

At the stables, a man in his early thirties with a slim build and blond hair approached as they dismounted. "Good to see you again, Michael."

"And you, too, Marcus," Michael said. He introduced Sophia and Anne.

Sophia turned to Michael, her eyes rolling with curiosity, said, "How do you know so many people?"

"I get around, and many come to visit the Cistercians."

Marcus said, "And what can I do for you, young sir."

"I need these three steeds returned to the Cistercians in London."

"That is certainly something I can arrange," Marcus replied. "Richard would be very proud of these fine stallions."

"And well he should be," Michael said. "They have served us extraordinarily well."

"Who's Richard?" Sophia asked, as he stroked Solitaire's shoulder.

"Richard Eastwood, a horse breeder. The last Bowbearer of the Forest of Bowland," Marcus replied. His voice saddened as he continued. "The old bugger passed away four years ago." He pointed into the distance. "He is buried over at St Hubert's."

Michael nodded. "Condolences, Marcus. He was a fine man and I know you miss him."

"Indeed, but I think he was ready to move on." Marcus glanced towards the sky. "Somewhat looking forward to the afterlife."

"Well, speaking of St Hubert's, that is where we are off to," Michael said, extending his arm. "Thank you for taking care of our steeds."

"Anytime," he replied, firmly shaking Michael's hand.

Sophia whispered to Solitaire, "Goodbye." Her horse nuzzled closer to her. "I'm going to miss you." Solitaire let out a nay, as if to say, "I'll miss you too." Her eyes welled, half from the joy of knowing Solitaire and half from the sense of losing a friend.

"Come, Sophia," Michael said, cutting short the farewell.

On the path to St Hubert's Anne asked, "So who is St Hubert? That's a saint I haven't heard of before."

"Oh," Michael replied. "St Hubert is said to be the patron saint of hunters. Many royal hunters used to hunt in the Forest of Bowland. Some still do. Legend has it that St. Hubert converted to Christianity after seeing a vision of a crucifix between the antlers of a stag while hunting. During the apparition, he heard a voice telling him to seek faith. The event happened on Good Friday. He went on to become a bishop."

On approaching St Hubert's church, Sophia gazed at a life-size statue of a female angel standing on a large stone block adorned with a crucifix. "She's beautiful."

"Indeed," Michael replied. "She stands over the Towneley's family vault."

Anne circled the statute, glancing up and down at it. "I love angels. They are so majestic."

Sophia turned her attention to the surroundings. Various tombstones, randomly placed and each dissimilar to the next, pocked the garden around the church. Some were square slabs with rounded tops, while others were stone crucifixes of varying sizes mounted on masonry bases of every type.

Michael approached the arched entrance of the church, with the girls and Dash close behind. Inside the foyer area, an open wooden doorway provided a way in. "Is anyone here?" Michael shouted. No reply. He stepped through the door. The interior of the church was exceedingly elegant with traditional Roman Catholic appointments—archways edged with golden borders, hand-carved alcoves for statuary, and exposed beams with lovely wood grains. The golden borders were themselves objects of art. Large hexagonal gas lanterns hung from the ceiling by silver chains casting a warm light on the interior. Additional lanterns not lit were mounted on short protruding bars high in the side walls.

Michael pointed to one of the stained glass windows. "There's a depiction of St Hubert." The window consisted of shards of colored glass fashioned in the likeness of a man dressed as a huntsman accompanied by a stag.

"Right, stash your back packs, and find a pew to sleep on," Michael said. "Or, if you like, you can rest on the floor as you did before."

Sophia and Anne slipped off their haversacks and tossed them onto a pew.

"Who wants to come hunting?" Michael said, holding a bow.

"I do," Anne replied.

"Where did you get that bow?" Sophia asked, looking at the striking weapon, string taut and ready for the hunt.

"A church named after the patron saint of hunters was bound to have a few hunting supplies around."

"I'll come along," Sophia said, with a hint of excitement in her voice.

"We're off, then," Michael said. He slung the quiver of arrows he had found in a crate filled with them over his shoulder, and the trio left the place of worship with Dash in tow. After a short walk, they ended up on the bank of the River Dunlop. "Let's follow it upstream." The last light of day grew dimmer and the trees of the forest denser by the step. "We don't have long," Michael whispered. Their pace slowed to a crawl as they attempted to move with stealth through the thick undergrowth. He stopped. "Over there," he whispered, pointing off into the trees.

"I see it," Sophia said, gazing into the distance.

"Where?" Anne said.

"See those two trees beyond that large rock?" Michael said, pointing with his head. "Look a little beyond those to the right."

"Ah, a deer," Anne said, eyes wide. "Are we going to kill it? But she looks so *friendly*."

"Indeed," Michael said. "They are lovely creatures, but so are you two, and to stay that way you need to eat."

The deer raised its head from grazing and gawked in their direction, sensing their presence. Michael ducked behind a tree and motioned for the girls to do the same. He loaded a steel-tipped arrow with a feathered tail into the bow, pulled back the drawstring, stepped out from behind the tree, took his aim, and released the wooden missile. With a thwap, the arrow impaled the left side of the deer, just back from its shoulder. Instantly, the deer collapsed to the ground. "Clean kill," Michael said, "through the heart."

"Oh," Anne said. "One part of me wanted you to miss."

Michael ruffled Anne's hair. "I understand. Taking the life of a beautiful animal can be difficult."

"Didn't you kill the rabbit, Anne?" Sophia asked.

"But that was different. I don't like rabbits."

"Oh... And why is that?"

Anne wriggled her nose, like a rabbit. "They are creepy little creatures."

Sophia laughed, thought about asking why, but decided to let it go.

"Can you girls gather some firewood?" Michael said. "Meet back here at the side of the river. I'll fetch the deer. Dash, you stay with me."

"Okay," Sophia said at the same time Anne said, "Yeppers."

"Plenty of wood around," Sophia said, picking up several dry fallen branches and loading them onto Anne's awaiting arms.

"Sure is."

Several minutes later, they arrived back at the riverbank. "That will certainly be enough wood," Michael said as the girls emptied their arms onto the ground.

"Nice campfire," Sophia said, gazing at the circle of stones around the blazing fire. Next to the fire was a large portion of fresh deer meat. Over on the grassy patch, in a world all her own, Dash gnawed on a large bone. Glancing at the now three-legged deer, Sophia guessed they were eating its hind leg.

"What are we going to do with the rest of the deer?" Anne asked.

"I'll drop it at Marcus' house on the way back to St Hubert Church," Michael said, wrapping the cut meat carefully in some large green leaves. With a stick, he created a clearing in the middle of the flames, placed the covered meat in the open spot, and then roofed the wrapped food with some small rocks and soil. Then he enclosed their uncooked meal with the burning wood of the fire.

Sophia found a fallen log off to the side of the campfire and sat down, still close enough to feel the warmth of the fire kiss her skin. The sound of the river cascading over the rocks and the crackle of the fire combined with the view of the sky changing from day to night with the richest orange hue she had ever seen filled her with profound contentment. "I could sleep right here," she said.

"We could," Michael said, "but we'll be safer at St Hubert Church."

Anne jolted at the sound of a wolf howling somewhere deep within the forest. "I prefer the church," she said.

Michael threw additional sticks onto the fire to fatten the hungry flames. "Shouldn't be long until the meat is cooked." He glanced at Anne. "Don't worry. We'll eat at the church. We'll be long gone by the time that pack of wolves gets here."

"That's a relief," Anne replied.

Chapter 35 - On Foot

The sun crested the eastern hills of the Forest of Bowland and cast a warm golden glow over the landscape. A gentle but chilly wind from the north rattled the trees ever so often. Michael glanced at the clear blue sky thinking the weather could not have been more ideal for the next leg of their journey. "It's a beautiful day," he said, striding across Dunsop Bridge, which they had crossed the day before on horseback, with Anne, Sophia, and Dash alongside him.

"Sure is," Anne replied.

"How far are we going?" Sophia asked.

"Should take us about three, maybe four hours."

"Now I know why you carry that staff," Anne said. "It doubles as a walking stick on long trips."

Michael laughed. "It does serve many purposes." His efforts at holding back his affection for the girls weakened every minute. In some ways that scared him, for he knew too well the agony involved in losing someone you love. The girls had a way of reaching into his heart, deep into his heart, and stirring the tiniest of emotions—from wanting to protect them, to laughing at their wit, to the simple experience of contentment in their company.

Three hours later, after trekking over the rolling grassy hills, they came to the River Ribble. Michael scanned the fast-flowing water, up the waterway and then down. He focused on a shallower area, pointed. "We cross down there."

"Why not cross at the bridge up there?" Sophia said, nodding upstream toward the bridge.

"We don't want to risk meeting any more bandits," Michael replied.

Sophia nodded. "Good point."

At the shallower part of the river, large wet flat stones a broad step apart peeked over the water's surface. "Be careful crossing," Michael cautioned. "The stones will likely be slippery."

"I'll go first," Sophia said. She stepped from the bank onto the closest stone. With a small leap, she crossed to the next. Her foot slipped on making contact with the stone's surface. She tilted back and forth, side to side, struggling to find balance. Her second foot joined her first and found traction giving her a stable foundation. She repositioned the unsteady foot and this time it gripped. "They are slippery," she shouted, over the sound of the rushing rapids.

Michael watched with fingers crossed behind his back as Sophia made the next leap. He did not want to be fishing either girl out of the river downstream. Before long, Sophia was waiting on the other side for Anne to cross. Like a seasoned champion, Anne crossed the stepping stones without a single slip. Michael presumed Sophia probably had broken up the mossy glaze on the rocks. Dash went next, scooting from one stone to the next as if running down a street. *Four legs*, Michael thought, *make things easier.* Michael then crossed without experiencing any trouble.

A short trail led them to a site of ruins. "What is this place?" Sophia asked.

"Sawley Abbey," Michael replied, with a hint of sadness in his voice, "once a home to the Cistercians monks until the sixteenth century."

Only broken, crumbling walls remained forming the outline of once grand structures. Nearby villagers had pillaged the grounds and hauled off stone tiles and other materials for their own homes. Thick green grass now grew in their place. Several archways between walls and a stairwell to a corner area of the upper floor of the abbey remained intact. Michael paced around a few of the walls until one caught his interest. Scanning the wall, he located a larger stone, rectangular, adorned with a pattern of two overlapping circles. He turned about with his back to the engraved brick and paced out ten steps. "Should be right here," he said.

"What?" Sophia replied.

"The way down."

Michael tapped the grassy area with the tip of his staff in various spots. A typical solid-ground thud sounded on the first several strikes, but then a distinctly different sound echoed as if his staff had hit something hard, but hollow. He dragged the end of his staff outwards from the strike until locating a softer patch of grass-covered soil. From there, he ran the end of his staff in a rectangle, tracing the outline of a regular doorframe in the grass.

"How do we open it?" Sophia asked.

A wolf howled. Michael spun around in the direction of the cry. "That's not far away," he said. Another wolf wailed, and then another. All in different directions, seemingly surrounding them.

Anne positioned herself close to Sophia. "I don't like the sound of this," she said.

"Me, either," Sophia replied, squinting into the distant landscape.

This isn't good, Michael thought. It would take at least several minutes to open the hidden entrance. From the sound of their carrying on, the wolves were minutes away. Best prepare. "Quick girls, up the stairs of the old abbey."

Without hesitation, Sophia, Anne, and Dash sprinted up the crumbling stairs. Moments later, Michael joined them at the top of the stairs. They stood in the corner of what was left of the old upper floor of the abbey, an area not larger than two king-size beds. The stairwell provided the only means of access.

"We are trapped up here," Sophia said.

"We are," Michael replied, staff at the ready between both hands. "But that also means the wolves only have one path of approach."

The howls grew louder, closer, echoing throughout the ruined walls of the abbey. Even from his vantage point perched atop a wall, Michael could not located the beasts. They were approaching, however, for the predators howled, out of sight, and circled about stalking their prey. Then, of a sudden, the first grayish wolf appeared from around the corner and stopped at the base of the steps. Anne and Sophia backed as far as they could go without falling off the suspended platform. Dash and Michael moved to the head of the stairs. "Dash, leave this fight to me," Michael said. She growled, baring her teeth while standing by Michael's side.

A second wolf appeared, followed shortly by five more. As a pack, they roamed around the bottom of the stairs, their collective gaze fixed on Michael. Occasionally baring teeth, snarling.

"What are they doing?" Sophia asked.

"Waiting us out," Michael replied.

"How long will they stay?"

"Indefinitely. When we tire, they will attack."

"What are we going to do?" Anne asked, voice quavering.

"I'm thinking," Michael replied. And he was, yet he struggled to come up with a viable plan. If he ran, half the pack would chase him, the other half would attack the girls. Assaulting them is a possibility, but their numbers, he realized, would overwhelm him. He kept playing out the options, trying to formulate a workable strategy.

Anne dropped to her knees and put her palms together. "What are you doing?" Sophia asked.

"Praying for a miracle," she replied. "Sister Mary told me, when all else fails pray for a miracle."

Sophia knelt and joined Anne in prayer. Anne continued, "Dear Heavenly Father, we are in a bit of a bind and would appreciate any help you can afford us. Amen." They both rose and resumed their huddled position. Michael thought: *Short prayer, to the point, and hopefully effective.*

The wolves pranced around the base of the stairs. A little more eager, the leader of the pack occasionally ventured up a few steps followed by two others, and then retreated. Each time the grayish wolf with its head held high and teeth bared inched a little closer, as if to test Michael's resolve, tempting him to meet them half way.

Michael held his stance at the top of the stairs. This was a battle of wills as much as a clash of strength and numbers. Several minutes later, a deep rumbling sounded in the distance. He quickly glanced at the direction of the sound. The sky, clear only moments before, roiled with black cumulus storm clouds and the occasional lightning bolt knifing to earth. "A storm is approaching," he said, turning his attention back at the wolves.

"This is getting worse," Anne said. "So much for our praying."

A flash filled Michael's vision, causing him to blink. He jolted at a deafening crack followed by an explosive boom. "No, this can be a good thing," Michael said, gazing at the wolves.

Some of the wolves began to crouch low, tails between their legs. The rest of the pack took a more neutral stance, easing their aggressive behavior.

Rain began to fall, the drops large and heavy. The girls clustered close to Michael in their huddle as the thunderous storm approached at a rapid pace.

At the bottom of the stairs, the leader of the wolfpack glanced towards the heavens, gazing at the darkening sky. Then he let out a howl and left, followed hastily by the rest of the pack.

"They are going," Anne said, raindrops rolling down her forehead.

"Yes, they do not like storms," Michael said. He put one arm around Sophia and the other around Anne as the storm thundered closer. "Let's give them a few minutes to retreat."

The rain pelted them, drenching their clothes. Wind squalls grew fiercer causing them to huddle tightly as a group. Dash attempted to shelter amidst their legs. Bolts of lightning struck around their position, some only a field away. Storm or not, he had to act. He led them down the stairs and returned to the trapdoor.

Michael continued edging a deeper groove around the rectangular area he had outlined earlier. Once the trench was well defined, he returned to the decorated stone bricks. He focused his attention to the left, and under the stone with the circled patterns, on a brick with a weathered engraving: seven pendant-shaped indents, each growing smaller as they curved around the top half of an indented rectangle standing on its end. Three horizontal raised lines ran down the middle of the rectangle.

Michael recalled the fifteen-digit sequence written in Mendel's notes. Each number represented which line to touch. To remember the code, Michael broke it down into three sections of five.

13211 32213 23121

Michael pressed each raised line in sequence. After touching the last line to complete entry of the code, he pushed on the stone. With a clunk, it recessed slightly then jerked back out.

He returned to the grass-covered trapdoor and wedged the end of the staff into the groove closest to the wall. The narrow trench had filled with water, like little moats, as the rain continued falling. Violent wind squalls torqued through the ruins, strong enough so that the girls had to brace themselves and flex their knees to keep from being blown over.

"What now?" Sophia shouted over the sound of the hammering rain and gusting wind.

"We wait," he shouted, brushing strands of wet hair from his forehead.

"I hope not for long," Anne yelled, leaning into a fresh wind squall.

Just then Michael felt the ground vibrating under his feet. "Here we go," he shouted. The rectangular section he had grooved out began to rise as if something was raising it from underneath. A few moments later, the rectangular slab about as thick as a man's forearm broke free from the surrounding grass cover. The groove Michael had cut cleanly prevented the grass around from tearing as the platform lifted. Under the slab, a marble column that extended from the center of a stone stairwell leading down pushed the stone trapdoor upwards. Once it had risen high enough to allow entry, Michael yelled, "Quick, let's go!"

Chapter 36 - Passage

Sophia followed Michael down the stairs from Sawley Abbey, stepping around the large column supporting the trapdoor above their heads. Light from Michael's staff illuminated the granite passageway. As they progressed farther down, the pillar behind them descended, sealing the entrance. "I'm drenched," Sophia said, wringing out water from her hair.

"Me, too," Anne added, with a shiver. "And cold."

"We'll do something about that shortly," Michael replied.

Dash torqued her body slinging jets of water from her fur onto the walls.

The steps ended with a 180-degree turn that doubled back on themselves descending. "How far down do these steps go?"

"About three stories or so. Two more turns and we should hit the bottom."

Two flights of stairs lower, Sophia heard the sound of running water. "Is there an underground spring here?"

"Indeed," Michael replied. "A river in fact."

At the bottom of the staircase, a stone platform like a wharf ran alongside an underground waterway. Moored to the wharf was a three-seat wooden rowboat rocking in the current. At the far end of the platform, a timber shack with a single glass window protruded from the stonewall. "Let's do something about these wet clothes," Michael said, leading the way to the underground building.

Inside the shack, several wooden crates were set against the walls. It appeared to be more of a storeroom than a place of residence. A single oil lamp hung from the ceiling provided light. Michael ventured over to one of the crates and withdrew two pairs of gray pants and white shirts. "Sorry, girls, nothing flashy, but at least they are dry. Do your best to wring out your clothes before storing them in your haversacks. Your coats should be dry, so you can put them back on. I'll wait outside while you girls get changed."

"What about you, Michael?" Sophia asked. "Your clothes are still soaked."

"They'll be dry soon enough," he said as he turned and left the shack.

After removing her jacket, Sophia slipped out of her dress and pulled on the gray pants, screwing her nose in response to their simple design and rather ugly color. Next, she put on the shirt then examined her coat. Michael was right. The thick inner fleece *was* dry. The leather exterior was still a little damp, but that did not stop her from wearing it. "Ready, Anne?" Sophia asked.

"Yep, all dressed," she replied, stuffing her damp dress into her haversack.

Outside the shack, Sophia saw Michael talking with a stranger. She became fixated on the elderly man's most prominent feature, a long silvery beard that ran down to his waist. His blue eyes gazed in Sophia's direction, breaking her trance. She waved. He nodded in return.

"Ahh," Michael said, turning his attention to the girls. "You're dressed. Come meet Anthony, one of the ferrymen who serve this river system."

Sophia wondered where he had come from, before spotting another boat lashed to a mooring post on the wharf. His boat was longer and narrower than the rowboat and had no oars. The red-painted hull had two cushioned bench seats across the middle. A long thick brown pole protruded from the water at the back of the boat. She recalled having read about a similar vessel called a "gondola" that was used primarily in Venice.

"Nice to meet you, Ladies," the ferryman said. "Please climb aboard." He pointed to the gondola.

She gazed at the boat. Dash was already sitting in the rear of the craft. *How safe is it?* she thought.

"Looks like fun to me," Anne said, stepping into the boat and taking a seat up front. "Come on, Sophia, sit next to me." The boat rocked gently under Anne's movements.

Michael crouched and held the boat steady as Sophia stepped into the gondola. Once she was seated, Michael boarded and sat on the center of the bench behind them. Finally, the ferryman untied the mooring rope and leapt on. After lighting an oil lamp at the back of the boat, he grabbed the long pole. Using the pole, he steered the craft away from the dock.

The gondola picked up speed. "How do the boats get back upstream against this current?" Sophia asked.

"There is a series of locks in a canal that runs parallel to this river through a cavern system of its own, which allows for the return journey. Much slower, though," Michael explained.

Locks fascinated Sophia. They allowed boats to virtually travel uphill. After stopping in a lock, the entrance the boat had come through closed, leaving the boat in a sealed-off section. The exit was then raised a little to let water discharge or enter, causing the water level to rise or drop depending on whether the boat was travelling upstream or downstream. Once finished, the exit fully opened allowing the boat to recommence its journey.

Farther downstream, the river narrowed. The orange glow of the oil lamp tanned the ceiling and sides of the cavern, creating a kind of moving glowing archway. Complete darkness seemed only a stone's throw in front of and behind them. "How long will the boat trip take?" Sophia asked.

"Half a day," Michael replied.

"Half a day," Anne retorted, voice raised. "We're going to be stuck in this dark tunnel for that long?"

"Yes, I'm afraid so," he said, "but at some points you will be able to see the sky. Though it will most likely be night by then. Might be wise to get some sleep."

The ferryman said, "Up front, in that crate, there is some food and drink. Help yourselves when you are hungry."

"Thank you," Michael replied.

"I kind of like this," Sophia said, gazing at the light reflecting on the gentle ripples of the river. "It's incredibly peaceful, quiet, and, in an odd way, romantic."

"Yeah, but you need a boy for romance," Anne said.

"I mean in a spirit-of-adventure kind of way," Sophia replied.

"Beats walking," Anne said. "And softer on my tush than riding."

Sophia chuckled, knowing she meant *bottom*. "I agree." She pondered what kept the current so strong in the underground river and presumed it was most likely from the recent torrential rains feeding the river's source upstream. At the end there was probably a spillway overflowing into a large underground lake, which she knew from her studies played an important part of the ecosystem as they supply water to the many trees above. She wondered if the destruction of the forests would one day make the lake overflow and flood this lovely passage. Though she thought it likely that the lake naturally diffused into the depths of the earth.

Hours elapsed as they coasted down the river with its consistent scenery. In some sections, tree roots in search of water lined the cavern's walls. Every hour or so they passed a wharf similar to the one they had begun at, each with a staircase leading up and out. Sophia wondered where each station staircase led and pondered what sort of elaborate doorway each hidden subterranean entrance provided as a passage into this elegant transport system.

Chapter 37 - Storage

Jack experienced a sense of relief when Mephis said, "We're here, Jack." He wondered why Mephis wanted to come to this dense forest west of Amesbury, days away from Whitechapel. Two days to be exact, travelling by horseback from London through the towns of Slough, Reading, Newbury, Highclere, Ludgershall, and Tidworth.

"Bring our friend with you," Mephis said, dismounting his horse.

Jack dismounted and transferred the rolled-up carpet containing the Shadow-inhabited corpse from his horse's back to his own. He followed Mephis into the trees, moaning silently as his knees throbbed with each step from the additional weight of the corpse draped over his shoulder. "How far, Master?"

"Half a mile or so."

I can make that, Jack thought, straining to keep his eyes open. As they had camped along the way, sleep eluded him. His thoughts tangled in disturbed dreams of the Underworld and Shadows. The comfort of an inn or one of the newer hotels might have made sleep easier to come by, but that was not an option for a pair carrying a reeking corpse on the back of the horse. He had become accustomed to the potent stench of rotting flesh after the first few hours of riding. It appeared the Shadow could not stop the natural decay after all. As a result, Mephis had devised a plan for building his legion of soldiers to defend the grand event—an army of the undead—a plan he was about to reveal.

About a half hour later, they stopped outside a stone corridor that led from a raised section of the earth underground into darkness. *This looks familiar*, Jack thought, remembering reading about ritual inhumation of the dead, which had taken place in British society between 4,000 and

2,400 BC. Long Barrows, tombs for the dead, were the final step in the process of storing the corpses. "Is this a Long Barrow, Master?"

"Yes," Mephis replied, nodding. "A rather large one that will serve our purpose."

A short way inside the entrance, Mephis removed from the wall a wooden torch, which caught ablaze the moment his hand enclosed its stem. The corridor led into a large hexagonal chamber. Passageways extended from each of six angled walls. Jack shivered. The temperature had dropped significantly during the short walk in. "It's freezing in here, Master."

"Why, yes, the cold is desirable for my purpose."

Jack folded his arms across his chest, raised his shoulders a little, and hunched forward. "How can the temperature be so low?"

"Just know that I can do these things, Jack. You have no need to understand *how*."

"Yes, Master," Jack replied, shaking his head. After all this time, he had hoped Mephis might start sharing some of his secrets with him. Freedom from servitude was a distant dream that would become a reality if he could only learn how Mephis healed him.

Mephis strode down the first corridor to the left. Jack set the corpse roll on the floor before following Mephis, warily. The short passage led into a square stonewalled room. On three walls were six recesses about a foot high and seven feet long, coffin size, spaced evenly from floor to ceiling. Some of the alcoves contained skulls and bone fragments. "I want you to clear out this chamber, Jack," Mephis said, "and the other four, which are virtually the same."

"Yes, Master."

"Then I want you to fill each of these recesses with a fresh corpse. By fresh, I mean no more than a week old."

Jack did the math: six per wall, three walls per room, five chambers. "Ninety corpses, Master. Where will I find so many?"

"That's your problem, Jack. Dig them up, as you did with the last one. Steal them from the morgue in a hospital. That is none of my concern. Whatever. As long as they are not more than a week old," Mephis said, eyes narrow, jaw tight. He seemed genuinely upset about the question. "Just don't go on a killing spree. A murder here and there, as you do for our other needs, will be okay. But we don't want to attract the attention of the Bobbies or—dare I be shrewd and utter, Heaven forbid—a higher power."

Jack winced at the thought of a higher power, as his mind thought of Elidin's gift of the Bible and that letter…. A moment later, he said, "That will take quite some time, Master."

"Yes, Jack. No rush. You have a few years, possibly more," Mephis replied. He faced Jack and, squinting, added, "But if you fail me, Jack, it'll be the last mistake you ever make."

"Right you are, Master," Jack replied, believing every word of Mephis' threat.

After they returned to the main chamber, Mephis said, "Let the corpse free."

Jack unrolled the rug and within seconds the corpse stood up and stiffly paced around the room. The familiar cold chill ran down Jack's spine. A walking corpse, even after viewing it several times, still disturbed him.

"Our friend here will defend this place, should anyone come venturing in," Mephis said, followed by his signature evil laugh. "One less corpse you'll have to find."

Jack nodded, as nausea washed over not just his stomach but his whole body and … soul. He was unsure if the nausea was due to the walking undead, the stench of its rotting flesh, the idea of nearly a hundred of these things ambling about, or the prospect of the last judgement before a higher power.

"Oh, and Jack? Arm these corpses. Find swords, shields, medieval weapons. Our Shadow friends are trained to use them."

"Where might I find such armaments?"

"You're a clever lad, Jack. I'm sure you'll scare something up."

Perhaps. At least theft, Jack presumed, would be easier than killing. The warmth of his clothes finally succumbed to the freezing air outside. He rubbed his hands together as his teeth chattered away trying to warm his chilled body.

"Come, Jack. Let's leave this place before I have to defrost you."

Jack now understood the need to keep the tomb below zero—to prevent the corpses from rotting. How Mephis had created the arctic environment was beyond his understanding. *Dark magic*, he thought.

Chapter 38 - Gilnockie Tower

Watching the wharf grow ever larger as they approached, Sophia knew it was only minutes until their gondola ride came to an end. It had been so peaceful and pleasant that she wished it weren't coming to an end—almost. Her legs weren't! She began stretching her legs to relieve the stiffness that had set in on the long trip.

"Who would like to assist in mooring?" ferryman Anthony asked.

Sophia turned to Anne. "You can."

Anne shook her head. "No, I would rather not."

"You can both help," Anthony said.

"Many hands … light work," Sophia said, echoing Sister Catherine.

As the boat pulled alongside the wooden wharf, Anthony passed her the end of a rope, said, "I need you to tie this to an available bollard."

"Is that a post?" Sophia asked, as she accepted the mooring line.

"Yes, it is." He turned to Anne, said, "I'll need *you* to come up back and hold this pole straight so the boat will not turn away from the wharf as I assist Sophia."

"Okay," she replied, a hint of enthusiasm in her voice.

Sophia readied herself as the gondola pulled alongside the wharf. A little leap landed her on the jetty. Quickly, she hooked the rope around a mooring post. "Got it," she shouted. Anthony stepped onto the wharf to help secure the rope. Sophia crouched and held the boat steady. "Anne, Michael, you can step out now."

"Thank you," Michael said, stepping onto the wharf. He turned to Anthony. "And thank you as well."

"You're welcome, my young friend," Anthony replied. Michael hooked one arm around the man's shoulder and shook his hand with the other.

"Come on, Dash," Sophia said, patting her thighs. Dash seemed content to stay behind with Anthony. Curled up on the floor, she looked quite at home. "Seems like she found a friend in you, Anthony."

"Aye," he replied. "My job, however, doesn't allow for a dog. I did enjoy her company."

"Why is she so hesitant?" Anne asked.

"Might have something to do with the lavish attention and regular treats Anthony has been providing her," Michael said.

Anthony grinned. "Guilty as charged."

In a stern voice, Michael said, "Dash, come now!" She rose onto her feet, stretched, then, not as enthusiastic as usual, evident by her stationary tail, leapt from the boat.

Sophia cut her eyes across the platform and, seeing no exit, asked, "How do we get out of here?"

"Follow me," Michael said striding to the end of the dock.

A square section of the floor at the end of the wharf caught Sophia's eye. Made from the same wooden timber, its tone was marginally grayer. A conspicuous gap, wide enough for a hand to fit through, separated it from the rest of the dock. As they stepped onto the area, the platform sank slightly with the sound of a latch releasing. "Huddle together now," Michael said, "away from the edges." A moment later, the floor vibrated and began to rise.

"Wow," Anne said, "we're going up."

Sophia turned her attention to the roof of the cavern. High up, a flickering glow brightened into a square opening in the ceiling. She calculated the space to be slightly larger than the platform they stood on. The light, she presumed, came not from the sun but from a burning lamp. "How is this thing powered?" she asked.

Michael tapped the end of his staff on the platform. "Below, there is a column that rises using the power of the river."

"Like a waterwheel does?" Anne asked.

"Indeed."

"Oh," Sophia said. Technology amazed her. In the last week, she had experienced things she had previously only read about, and even some things that she never knew existed. Anne appeared to be enjoying the discoveries just as much, if not more.

The platform rose through the opening. A tighter fit than she had originally thought. For a short time, solid stone walls enclosed them on all sides until a hallway, as narrow as the platform, appeared on the north side. With a sudden jolt that made their knees buckle, the platform stopped, flush with the floor of the passage. A single lamp dangling from the ceiling by a short piece of rope provided enough ambient light to illuminate a flight of ascending stairs that led straight into the stone ceiling.

"The stairs go nowhere," Sophia said. "We are trapped."

"Give me a second," Michael said, stepping off the platform. At the top of the stairs, he pushed up on the roof. Like a trapdoor, it flipped upwards.

"Wow, you're super strong," Anne said.

"No, that is wood made to look like stone. It's not all that heavy." He climbed higher up the stairs and a few seconds later said, "Okay, girls, all clear, come on up."

"Another graveyard," Sophia said as she stepped off the last step.

Michael closed the trapdoor, which once closed was a covering for a mock grave, complete with its own monument. "You would never guess that is a secret door," Anne said, glancing at the headstone. "I'm guessing there is no Mr. Underme who died in 1745."

"Indeed," Michael replied.

"Where are we?" Sophia asked, gazing into the distance. The sun was not due to rise for at least another half hour and the fog was dense as wood smoke. She squinted, struggling to make out anything more than several arm lengths away.

"In the graveyard of St Michaels Church, in Carlisle."

Long way from home, Sophia thought.

"We had better not hang around," Michael said. "Could be Bobbies on the lookout for the three of us."

Dash barked, and Michael cut his eyes to the dog and added, "The *four* of us, that is."

"Who wants to be in a graveyard at night anyway?" Anne said. "Might be ghosts about."

Sophia laughed. "Could be," she replied, adding an eerie "oooooooh."

Anne punched Sophia gently on the shoulder. "Stop that, you."

An hour later, Michael gazed at the lifting fog that provided a hazy blanket for the rising sun in a clear blue sky. "Beautiful day for a walk."

"Indeed," the girls said simultaneously, doing their best impersonation of Michael's voice. Half his lip curled upwards, the other stayed straight as the girls chuckled. "How far are we walking today?" Sophia asked.

"About half a day."

Sophia did not mind. Walking sounded great after sitting in the boat for such a long period.

Nearly four hours later, they came to the side of a swiftly flowing river. It was too deep and wide to leap across and no stepping stones in sight. "How are we going to cross?" Sophia asked.

"There's a bridge, a little farther up the River Esk, after we cross into Scotland," Michael said. He led them in an easterly direction following the riverbank.

"Ooh, I've never been to Scotland," Anne said.

"Me, either," Sophia added. Before this adventure started, the idea of going to another country seemed but a distant dream. And here they were about to step across the border.

Soon the river turned to a northerly direction and then curved back to the west. At this point, Michael continued north following a grassy path through the trees. Half an hour later, they emerged once again on the banks of the River Esk in front of a narrow bridge, its gray wood well-weathered, that spanned the river.

"Doesn't look very sturdy," Sophia said, gazing across the gently swaying bridge. The "bridge" was not what Sophia had expected. This was no Queen Victoria Bridge where a trio on horseback could get ambushed by bandits, but a rope bridge. It consisted of two thick ropes that spanned the width of the river tethered to the trunks of stout trees on both sides. The walkway was a series of planks of battered gray wood set a step apart that dangled under the ropes supported by thin fraying strands of rope. Sophia took a closer look at the larger rope. "These holding ropes seem a little rotten. You sure they will hold us, Michael?"

"No, I'm not sure at all, but if we do fall, it's only a short way into the water."

She gave a single concerned nod and surveyed the bridge and water below. She figured the highest points of the bridge were about twice her height. Closer to the banks the drop was much less. The short fall would not be deadly, but the great river current would be difficult to fight, especially since the water was likely to be close to freezing. So, death was actually a real possibility, but what choice did they have?

"I'll go first," Michael said. "If the bridge can hold my weight, you girls will be fine." He stepped onto the first plank, which wobbled under his feet. After wedging his staff horizontal under his armpit, he used the ropes either side of him to steady himself.

Sophia held her breath each time he stepped forward to the next plank. About midway, Michael paused, seemingly reluctant to take the next step. From Sophia's vantage, she could not quite make out why he paused, until he transferred his weight to the ensuing plank, which split, sending his leg plunging through the base of the bridge. In an instinctive reaction, his other leg swung forward to the plank ahead, which also snapped like a dried-out old twig....

He went down then, and fast, his only lifeline was his grip on the rope. His fingers clawed at the thick rope but found no traction. He fell and Sophia prepared to witness him splash into the water. But, to her astonishment, he seemed to hover in midair, his shoulders slightly above the base of the bridge. A second later she saw what had happened. The staff under his shoulder wedged itself between the planks behind and farther ahead. Calmly, he allowed himself to drop down until he was holding the staff by his hands. He then shimmied across the rod to the board before the broken one. Once in position, he pulled himself up using the plank and his staff and, after steadying himself, proceeded towards the girls.

"That didn't go so well," Sophia said as Michael stepped off the bridge.

"Indeed."

"Are you hurt?"

"No, I'm fine, a little bruised, ego-wise and physically, if anything."

"Want me to heal you?" She believed confidently she could if she tried. At least his physical discomfort.

"No. I'll be okay. Sometimes our bruises can teach us lessons."

"So how do we cross now?" Anne asked.

"Well I think it's safe to say the bridge is out," Michael replied. "But I did see something upstream that may help." He led them east a short distance. "Down here," he said, following a narrow dirt path that twisted down the side of the riverbank.

On the sandy bank, a raft made from two thick logs and several planks was propped up against a tree. A single rope, at shoulder height to Michael, was stretched taut between two trees and spanned the river. A second thinner rope attached to the back of the raft lay coiled up on the bank fastened to a stake as thick around as Michael's forearm protruding from the ground. "Help me with this," Michael said as he pushed the raft down the bank towards the water.

Sophia and Anne both assisted in shoving the raft into the water. Once afloat, Michael and the girls stepped onto the raft and Dash leapt on board. Michael grabbed the rope spanning the river and pulled. The raft began to move. He continued to draw on the rope, hand over hand, and ferried the raft toward the opposite bank. The current started to turn the raft, attempting to drag it downstream, so Michael dug his heels between the boards of the raft, leant backwards, and heaved with all his strength. A little farther across, the current eased and Michael relaxed to a slower pace.

"This beats the gondola," Anne said, peering up the river, allowing the fresh breeze to swirl her hair.

"Do you have a thing for boats, Anne?" Sophia asked.

Anne grasped Sophia's hand. "I'm starting to. I love the floating sensation."

Several minutes later, the raft ran aground on the other bank. "Everybody off," Michael said. They quickly disembarked. Together they pulled the raft higher up the bank. Michael coiled up the loose rope attached to the raft and fastened to a stake in the ground.

"What is that rope for?" Sophia asked.

"Retrieving the raft if you're on the opposite bank."

"Ah, I see."

"That was much more fun than having to cross that rickety bridge," Anne said.

"A little less of an adventure," Michael said, "but a whole lot safer."

"Too true," Sophia replied. "Where to now, Michael?"

"This way," he replied, leading them north.

A little later, at the top of an embankment, Sophia spotted a tower in the distance. "Is that where we are going?" she said, pointing to the tower.

"Indeed. Gilnockie Tower, originally known as Hollows Tower. It was built in the sixteenth century."

From her vantage point, the tower house appeared simple in design: four greyish stone brick walls, four stories high. Small rectangular nooks on each level provided primitive windows, a parapet bordered the flat top with a central peak that appeared to be a lookout point.

"Not that much farther," Anne said as they proceeded towards Gilnockie Tower. "Good thing, too, because my feet ache and my legs are tired."

Chapter 39 - Reunions

Eager for a place to rest, Anne pushed on the wooden entrance to Gilnockie Tower. It didn't budge. She readied herself to give the stubborn doorway a heartier shove, said, "A battering ram sure would come in handy right about now."

"Right," Sophia said, but then her eye was drawn to a reddish stain around the base of the entry. She pointed down. "Is that blood?"

Michael focused on the spot. His eyebrows raised as he instinctively reached to grab Anne. "Anne, stop!" he shouted. Too late. The door swung open.

Anne froze staring at an armed crossbow mounted on a stack of crates on the far wall, aimed directly at her chest. She watched as a rock tied to the end of a rope dropped onto the crossbow—triggering the arrow's release. She closed her eyes thinking *this is it, I'm going to die* and awaited the impact. The *thwap* of the bolt piercing flesh reached her ears. She awaited the resulting pain. It did not come. She opened her eyes and gazed at the ground. Blood, a lot of dark-red blood, pooled at her feet. Anxiously, she patted down her chest searching for the wound, expecting to feel the stickiness warmth of blood. None. Refocussing on the blood, she traced the source of the growing pool. To her left, lying motionless on the ground with a crossbow bolt protruding from her side, was Dash.

Sophia sprinted into the room and crouched beside Dash. She tightened her grip around the arrow in Dash's side. With both hands, she yanked the cruel dart from the little dog's flesh. Quickly, she laid both palms on the open wound. A brilliant white aurora surrounded her hands. Seconds later, a tear fell from Sophia's eye. The curative light slowly faded. "She's gone. I can't heal her."

Anne's legs went limp and she folded to her knees. Her stomach tensed as if to wring out the sudden pang of grief. "Can't be." She stroked Dash's head. "How?"

"She leapt right in front of the bolt," Michael said. "Her senses picked up on the trap before we did."

"Dash gave her life for me," Anne said, her voice crackling. Grace and sorrow welled in her eyes.

After a good cry, Sophia sniveling, asked. "Why was the door trapped?"

Michael crouched before a skeleton sitting against a wall dressed in a cheap brown gown. "I think this fellow set the snare to protect himself from intruders."

Anne glanced across the room to see what had triggered the trap. A rope fastened to the back of the door led up to the ceiling above the crossbow. From there it threaded through a hoop, from which the rock hung. She figured as the door opened, the rope slackened dropping the rock. The firing mechanism was rigged to activate by the weight of the impact.

Michael picked up a full-length arrow off the floor near the skeleton. "Looks like our fellow here was himself shot by a bow. He most likely came here to await help, which never came. He likely had a few days life left in him. Enough to set the snare a few times."

"What about the bloodstains at the base of the door?" Sophia asked.

"Probably from a previous intruder who sprang the trap."

"Then where is the body?"

Michael shrugged. "Dragged off by wolves, perhaps."

Anne gave Dash a gentle kiss on her cheek. "I'm sorry, girl. I shouldn't have been so eager to rush in."

Michael picked up Dash gently and cradled her lifeless form in his arms. "The best we can do is give her a proper burial." He carried outside.

The girls followed Michael around to the back of the tower. Once there, Anne searched the ground until she found a flattish rock with a sharp edge. On her knees, she used the rock to spade the ground. As she worked, Sophia glanced occasionally at Dash awaiting her final resting place. Each time she did, she blinked to clear welling tears of sorrow from her eyes. She found a thick branch and crouched beside Anne and together they dug the shallow grave. Neither of them said a word, for their expressions of grief revealed everything they needed to say to each other.

The girls wept then, heaving great sobs, as the death of Dash punctuated the other losses they had not had time to stop and bear. All lost because of … them. *For them.*

Anne mourned anew the loss of her parents in the carriage accident. Sisters Catherine, Mary, and Mr. Brumby. People she loved. Gone. Each beat of her heart pulsated a sense of longing to meet them again. "I'm not sure how much more of this I can take," she said.

Sophia put down her stick, embraced Anne. "Me, either," she whispered.

"At least we have each other," Anne said, eyes red and cheek wet with the tears she had tried so hard to hold back. After a minute of solace, they resumed digging in silence.

Michael returned with a collection of stones large and small. He dropped them in a growing pile close to the girls. After his fifth trip, he said, "That should be enough."

"I think we are done, too," Anne said, rising from the shallow grave.

"Indeed," Michael said. He placed Dash gently into the grace. Each of them, one stone at a time placed them over Dash's body. When they were finished, a small rise of various-sized stones covered the burial site. To finish, Sophia took two sticks, one half again as long as the other, and fashioned them into a cross, which she lashed together with threads of rope, the very rope that had triggered the trap that killed Dash. Once finished, she hammered the cross into the ground at the head of the grave with a large stone.

Together, the three of them stood a few steps back from the base of the Dash's resting place. They bowed their heads and closed their eyes as Michael began to pray. "Often we forget how valuable a friend a little animal can be. Dash accompanied us on this journey of her free will and gave her life to protect those she loved. We will be forever grateful for her servitude and we will miss her with each passing breath. Father in Heaven, take care of our companion if it please thee, as she comes back to you. Amen."

Anne and Sophia simultaneously responded, "Amen."

On reopening her eyes, Anne said, "Do you see that?"

"I do," Sophia said.

At the head of the grave, standing behind the makeshift cross, stood a translucent Mr. Brumby with his wife Jill and six-year-old daughter Jane at his side. Next to Jane, tail wagging, Dash sat enjoying a pat. They appeared cheerful, glowing with a radiance of contentment and peace. Mr. Brumby mouthed some words. Anne read his lips as saying, "Thank you." He smiled. Then they were gone.

"She's with her family now," Sophia said.

Two tears—one of grief, one of joy—squirmed down each of Anne's cheeks. "Together again."

"Who?" Michael said, shaking his head. "See what?"

"Do you think that was really them?" Anne asked.

"I don't know," Sophia replied. "Maybe it was a projection from wherever they are now."

"A projection of whom?" Michael asked, eyebrows arched.

"Mr. Brumby and his family," Anne replied, "with Dash."

"Oh." He paused, let his smile build. "Now that would be a pleasant vision."

Anne moved between Michael and Sophia and grasped both of their hands, squeezing them lightly. "We are going to be okay," she said.

Chapter 40 - The Horsemen

"Shouldn't be much longer," Sophia yelled to Michael on his way back to Gilnockie Tower. She dunked her dress into the River Esk for the sixth time and then wrung out the water. "There we go, all lovely and clean. How are you going, Anne?"

"All done," she replied, flapping her dress in the breeze.

The River Esk passed close to the eastern side of Gilnockie Tower, making for a short stroll to and from the water. Together they headed west back to the tower. As they approached, Sophia, shielding her eyes from the fiery glow of the setting sun waved to Michael standing on the eastern parapet above the fourth story of the tower. He waved back. "Michael was quick getting up top," Anne said.

"He sure was," Sophia replied.

Inside the tower, they climbed the spiral staircase to the first floor, taking care to avoid slipping on the loose stone bricks.

"Is Michael coming back down," Anne asked.

"No," Sophia replied, hanging her dress over a rope strung between two rusty iron rods protruding from the wall. "He is keeping lookout throughout the night. Pass me your dress, Anne. I'll hang it for you."

Anne tossed her dress over to Sophia. "Thanks."

"I'm looking forward to getting out of these drab clothes in the morning," Sophia said, hanging Anne's dress. She did not mind the feel of the long gray pants and shirt. In fact, they were comfortable and made movement a little less restricted, but the color was, well, lifeless.

Reminded her of dustmen's clothing, the men who collected the burnt waste ash from the streets of London.

"I'm beat, Anne said, lying on the ground using her haversack as a pillow.

Sophia lay beside her. "Me, too."

"Do you think we truly saw the Brumbys, Sophia?"

"We both saw it, right, so…" She sighed. "I honestly don't know. But I do believe they are in a happier place."

"And Dash?"

"Yes. Dash, too. I'm sure she is."

An hour later, Sophia whispered, "Are you asleep yet?"

"No," Anne replied, rolling over to face Sophia. "I keep thinking about Dash, the Sisters, and Mr. Brumby."

"Me, too."

"Do you believe in Heaven?" Anne asked.

"Yes."

"Why?" Anne asked.

"Because of evil."

"Evil. Huh?"

"Well, it makes sense God has created a place for those who want to be with Him after they die. And a place for those who don't."

"You mean Hell?"

"Guess so."

"Doesn't Hell make God seem like a mean person?"

"No. God gives people a choice to be with him or not. Hell seems more of a place for those who want to do things their own way. Live by their own particular rules. The problem with that, from what I've seen—in my long life of thirteen years—is that each person has his own set of rules, typically to suit their own desires, and they conflict with others. Which cause fights for power."

"Or arguments over toys," Anne said.

"Right. To live in harmony requires everyone to choose by free will to live by one set of laws. Jesus outlines those in the Bible. When we follow them, and the people around us follow them, the result is heavenly. Anyway, that's my thoughts."

Wide-eyed Anne smiled. "Makes sense." She rolled onto her back. "I hope I go to heaven when I die."

"Me, too," Sophia replied. She smiled, imagining a place of harmony where everyone loved each other for who they are. A place of true peace, love, and contentment. "I am the way, the truth, and the life: no man cometh unto the Father, but by me."

"John 14:6," Anne replied. "I know that off by heart. Jesus is more than a ticket to heaven for me. Even if there were no heaven, I would want him in my life, and try my best to obey his teachings. I can do all things through Christ who strengthens me."

"Philippians 4:13," Sophia replied. "I know a little Bible, too."

Anne chuckled. "Growing up with the Sisters helped."

"Sure did," Sophia whispered, rolling onto her side. "Time to get some sleep."

Her mind raced with thoughts, but pleasant thoughts of her happy times in the orphanage. She felt fortunate the Sisters gave her a pretty free rein and exposed her to numerous wonderful experiences. Though the Sisters were strict, they always made her and the other children feel loved. From the dreadful stories she had heard, the kids in some of the other orphanages were not nearly as lucky. Three hours later, she drifted to sleep.

After waking to the sound of the morning birds' chirping, Sophia changed into her dress. She wondered if Michael had managed to get any rest. Once dressed, she gave Anne a gentle nudge to waken her. No response. *Must be in a deep sleep*, she thought. She gave her another nudge. This time Anne's eyes struggled open.

"Morning already?" Anne said, followed by a yawn.

"Yes, I'm afraid so."

"Oh, you put your dress back on," Anne said.

"Yep."

"I'll do the same."

"All right," Sophia said. "I'm going to check on Michael." She climbed the steps to the top of the fourth story and stepped out onto the parapet. "Michael," she called. No reply. She followed the parapet around all four sides. *No Michael*, she thought, shrugging. Quickly, she descended to the first floor. "He wasn't up there, Anne."

"Must be downstairs," Anne replied.

Together they descended the staircase. On reaching the bottom, Sophia heard Michael say, "Good to see you two sleepy heads finally awake."

"We had a late night," Sophia replied.

"Can you hear that?" Anne asked.

Sophia listened. A low rumbling sound, growing louder quickly. "Yes," she said, wondering what it was. The ground began to tremble.

"Sounds like a herd of galloping horses headed this way," Michael said. He ran to the door. "Grab your stuff, we made need to make a quick exit!"

The low thumping rumble grew louder as Sophia and Anne readied their haversacks. Then the sound stopped. A deep male voice shouted: "Michael, White Monk of the Cistercians."

"I guess they are looking for you," Sophia said, stepping back a few paces from the door. "Do you think they are hostile?"

The voice yelled a second time, louder: "Michael, White Monk of the Cistercians!"

"Let's go find out," Michael said, opening the door.

No fewer than fifteen horses gathered around the tower, each mounted by a man in an armored breastplate and leather kilt. The early morning sun glinted off long silver swords sheathed on their belts and round metal shields tied to their backs. All the horses were brown except for one, the black stallion carrying the leader, who seeing Michael, asked: "Michael, White Monk of the Cistercians?"

Michael replied, "Yes. And who might you be?"

"Douglas, from the Order of Esdras. You have come seeking us, aye?"

Michael stepped out of the doorway and paced closer to Douglas. Sophia sighed, feeling great relief flowing through her body. *We have found them*, she thought as she followed Michael. Anne trailed close behind.

"Yes," Michael said. "Jeremial."

"Come. We will take you to him," Douglas said. He turned his attention to another man. "Tavish, release your steed to Michael."

"Aye, Douglas," Tavish replied, dismounting his horse.

Douglas focused his attention on the girls. "Sophia, Anne, you shall ride with Ewan and Hamish." He looked around, seemingly puzzled. "Where is your animal, Dash?"

"She is no longer with us," Michael replied, his brow lowered.

"I'm sorry to hear that," Douglas said, nodding in a gesture of condolence.

Michael faced the girls. "It is safe to go with them."

Ewan trotted up next to Sophia and offered his hand. Sophia grasped his palm and allowed him to swing her effortlessly onto the back of his horse. She watched Anne mount Amish's steed in a similar fashion. Then Michael mounted Tavish's stallion.

"How is Tavish going to travel?" Michael asked.

Douglas glanced at Michael, smiled. "Tavish is a hardy lad. He can walk."

"Aye," Tavish said, nodding. "A jolly brill day for a stroll, too."

"Onwards!" Douglas shouted, jabbing his heels, bringing his stallion to a canter.

Sophia hooked her arms around Ewan's sturdy waist as his horse accelerated. This was her first time being a passenger on a steed. Not being in control made her a wee bit nervous. She glanced at Anne on the back of Hamish's horse. She seemed to be enjoying herself, if the broad smile was a clue. *Why not?* Sophia thought. *This marks the end of a long journey. But … what next?*

Chapter 41 - Hermitage Castle

The water briefly licked the tips of Sophia's toes as Ewan drove his steed through a deeper part of The River Esk. After crossing, the small army continued in a northeasterly direction. Over three hours of riding, they had crossed a few streams, several plains, and narrow grassy trails edging their way through dense forest.

As they drew closer to the castle, Sophia took in the grand structure. Though it was not the largest castle Sophia had seen, it was a reasonable size fort. The stonework was in need of minor repair and the top of one section of the wall had crumbled. To her surprise, the cavalry changed directions and headed northward. "Where are we going?" she shouted to Ewan over the heavy hoof beat of the horses. No reply. He had either not heard her or preferred not to respond. She considered asking a second time but decided not to. Looking ahead, she spotted a tall snow-capped hill in the distance. Ewan shouted, "We are going to Greatmoor Hill." *So he did hear me*, she thought.

They funneled into a small ravine requiring them to ride in rows three abreast. Her row, third from the front, consisted of Anne to her left and Michael to her right. The walls of the ravine grew higher the farther they travelled. She puzzled as to whether this was a natural chasm or a man-made trench cut into the hillside. If the channel was manufactured, it must have been some time ago as vegetation mixed with rocks happily formed the sides. The trench led to a raised iron portcullis mounted in a large stone archway. Behind the gate, two massive wooden doors opened inwards as they approached. An entry into the hollows of Greatmoor Hill.

Inside, the short torch-lit passageway ended at a large stable. Everyone dismounted. Stable hands gathered the horses and drove them into a large underground straw-covered pen where several other steeds of different colors roamed.

Anne, Sophia, and Michael congregated as Douglas approached. "You look surprised, Michael."

"I was expecting us to go to Hermitage Castle, not an underground structure, as grand as this."

"Aye, I expected as much," Douglas said, turning to glance at a wooden doorway in the distance. "Follow me."

The trio did so as he continued to speak. "We do have a few men at Hermitage Castle, but this is our main area of operation. For the time being."

"I see," Michael said.

Sophia gazed in awe of the sheer size of the underground chamber where they kept the horses. She was eager to find out what else awaited them. The door opened into a room with a large round table in the center draped in a pure white cloth and surrounded by twenty-four wooden chairs. On the far side of the table, opposite the door, a white marble throne was the twenty-fifth seat. A chandelier suspended from the ceiling hung above the center of the table and provided a subtle flickering light for the room. From the back of her mind, an image surfaced of the Arthurian legend Knights of the Round Table. The Sisters used to read stories to her and the other children about Excalibur, Lancelot, Guinevere, and Merlin. It first occurred to her then that Michael's mount, Lancelot, might be named after the character of the same name in the legends. *Could this be one of the places they used to meet?* She dismissed the notion. *Nah, those are only legends, not history.*

"Ah, you're finally here," a man said as he entered through a side door. "Come, take a seat at the head of the table." He seated himself in the throne chair. Michael sat to his right and the two girls to his left.

"Is there anything else you require, Jeremial?" Douglas asked.

"Yes, please bring in the wooden box we discussed earlier."

"As you wish," he said, before exiting through the door Jeremial had come through.

Sophia experienced a sense of disappointment in Jeremial's appearance. She was expecting an ideal specimen of masculinity, a well-muscled king in royal garb. Jeremial, however, was approximately six feet tall, in his early thirties, with a lean body. Frankly, there was nothing kingly about him. He was dressed in long pants, the same drab gray color as those pants she and Anne wore on the gondola ride, and a bluish top. He looked ordinary, like an everyday person you would meet on the street. "So you are Jeremial?" she asked, just to be sure.

"Aye," he said, in a rusty Scottish twang.

Sophia's eyebrows twitched in response to the unseemly accent.

"Don't mind my pronunciation," he said. "I'm practicing. They say I sound more like a pirate than a Scot."

"They're right," Anne said, with a little snort.

"Anyway, back to business. My real name is Nemamiah. Douglas decided to call me Jeremial. He says the name helps me fit in better with the locals in this realm. I think the real reason is because the Scots have trouble pronouncing *Nemamiah* properly."

Sophia cupped her hands on the table. The movement helped settle her desire to ask the man a million questions all at once. "Where are you from?"

"Oh, a place distant from here. They don't often let me do field trips. This is unique. But, I go where they deem my services are required."

"Who are *they*?" Sophia asked.

"Higher authorities."

Sophia glanced at Michael. He shrugged. Appeared he was none the wiser as to what Jeremial was talking about.

Douglas returned carrying a rather large polished oak box.

"Here we go," Jeremial said. "Place the treasure trove on the table in front of me."

"What is in the box?" Sophia asked.

"Well," Jeremial said, with a hint of excitement in his eyes, "I suppose we are all eager to find out. Anne here should have the means to open the dastardly locking mechanism."

"Me?" Anne asked, sheepishly.

"Yes. Those four charms on your bracelet. All but the crucifix."

"Oh." She held her wrist up and glanced at the bracelet.

"Take a look at the top of the box," Jeremial said.

They all rose from their seats for a closer look. Etched across the middle of the box top were four small disc shapes, each framing a different picture: planet, star, moon, sun.

"Each of your charms should match one of the symbols," Jeremial said, pointing to each recessed disc in turn. "Quickly now, don't keep us in suspense. Take off each charm and place it in the corresponding spot."

Anne placed the first charm, the planet, on the matching symbol. A second later, the disc began to glow pale green. She continued with the rest. When the fourth charm illuminated a click sounded.

"Right, I've been looking forward to this moment for some time," Jeremial said.

As he lifted the lid, they all leant in to see what buried treasure lay inside. Nestled in silky white cushions were two long thin-bladed silver swords glowing with a soft white light. "One Sword of Light for each of you," Jeremial said.

"Me?" Anne said.

"Yes, you," Jeremial replied.

"Neither of us knows how to use a sword," Sophia said.

"One of my jobs is to teach you."

"Why?" Sophia asked.

"To stop Mephis at the"—he cleared his throat—"grand event. I believe the big guy should just smite him. However, freewill and all that dictates a human out of his or her freewill must stop him. Rules are rules."

"How come they glow?" Anne asked. Sophia thought it odd her first question was not *who is Mephis?*

"They are one of the few weapons in this realm that can send a Shadow back to the Underworld?"

"Shadow? Underworld?" Sophia said, eyebrows bouncing with curiosity.

"Ah, yes. I do have to fill you in on a bit. We can discuss that over dinner."

Sophia nodded. She was curious, but with so many questions running amok in her head, she did not know where to start. Her main concern was the whole business of dragging Anne into a battle with Mephis. Anne cannot fight.

Nemamiah closed the case.

"Oh," Anne said, frowning. "Can't we pick them up?"

"No, no," Jeremial replied. "We don't want you killing yourselves. We'll start with wooden swords to begin with."

"That sounds like fun," Anne said.

Always eager, Sophia thought. But this was to be no game. A distant ultimatum resurfaced in her mind: *Him or me*. This time she did not picture Jack. She visualized Mephis.

"Douglas," Jeremial said, "show the girls and Michael around the facility and then to their rooms."

"Aye," he replied.

"After they are settled in, bring them to the dining room."

Chapter 42 - Training

Sophia yawned, stretched her arms, and swung her legs off the soft bed. She stood up, rubbed the sleep from the corners of her eyes, and strolled to the room next door. On the short walk, she thought back to last evening's dinner—a grand event, equals parts welcoming and briefing. Over the four courses of the meal, Jeremial told them all about the Shadows and the Underworld.

Stepping into Anne's room, she said, "Your room is the same as mine."

"I love the bed," Anne said, bouncing up and down on the goose-down mattress. "Nice and comfy."

"The only thing I don't like," Sophia said, "is there are no windows." She slowly shook her head and made a mock pouting expression. "Feels a bit like a dungeon."

Anne climbed off her bed. "Drawback of being underground, I guess. Would you really want an underground window?"

"Silly," Sophia said, rolling her eyes. "We better get moving. Don't want to keep Jeremial waiting for our first lesson."

They exited Anne's bedroom and proceeded down the stone corridor. Took a left, passed the entrance to Sophia's room, and continued until they reached the room with a wooden sign with the words *Training Room* burnt into the surface in fancy script.

Sophia gently pushed the door half open and stood at the threshold and looked in. A bench spanned the width of the eastern wall. On the wall opposite, a high and wide weapons rack had various types of armaments. The stone floor was covered nearly wall-to-wall with a maroon rug of sturdy pile like a mat. She entered. "Nobody here yet."

"Seems that way," Anne said, following her in.

"Lots of weapons," Sophia said, stepping over to the armaments rack. Medieval long swords, broad swords, two-handed swords, shields, pikes, staffs, spiked ball-and-chain, and various other weaponry hung on the rack.

"A fine selection," Jeremial said, entering the room, "wouldn't you agree?"

"Sure is," Sophia said, spinning about to face him. He wielded two long wooden swords in his hands, of the same length and width as the Swords of Light.

"Sorry I'm late. Our carpenter only just finished crafting these pristine replicas," Jeremial said. "One for you, Anne." He passed her a sword, which she accepted with a beaming grin. "And one for you, Sophia." He held the wooden sword by the blade, allowing Sophia to wrap her hand around the hilt. "They are the same weight as their deadlier counterparts."

Sophia swiveled the blunted weapon in her hand. The blade seemed to be equal in weight to the hilt, making sword movements virtually effortless. Her wild swings, however, consisted of simple random slashing patterns.

"On guard," Anne said, her right leg forward with the knee flexed as she thrust her blade towards Sophia.

With a quick flick of her sword, Sophia knocked Anne's to the side. "Yield or ye shall die," she said through clenched teeth.

Anne laughed. "I yield, Sir Knight, please spare me."

"All right," Jeremial said, sighing, "enough games. From the looks of it, we have loads to teach you in a short period of time."

"Okay," Sophia said, relaxing into a standing position.

Jeremial retrieved from the weapons rack an ordinary wooden staff a little taller than he was. "Okay, I want you two to stand on either side of me and then attack me with your swords."

"Should be easy enough," Sophia said, striding in broad, confident steps to one side of Jeremial.

Anne, in rigid strides, a little less confident, took her place on his other side.

"When you are ready, girls, feel free to attack."

Sophia and Anne simultaneously charged towards Jeremial. They raised their swords and, when within range, both slashed out at his torso. He ducked. Anne and Sophia's swords clashed. Jeremial retreated a step as he swept his staff in a semi arc, at ankle height. His wooden pole first swept Anne's heels off the floor, sending her tumbling backwards. Then the staff collected Sophia's lower shins, knocking her feet from under her. She fell forward onto her palms.

"First lesson. Moving can be a powerful way to defend yourself while opening up a counterattack. Never underestimate the power of a strategic retreat."

Sophia pulled her legs forward to a kneeling position and cleared her throat. "Right," she said, ego smoldering, and shoulders slumping.

"I think I bruised my bottom," Anne said, rubbing her behind.

"There will be plenty more bruises before we are finished," Jeremial said.

Sophia shrugged. *No problem*, she thought. *I can heal them.*

"And you will not be able to carry out any angelic healing, Sophia."

She pouted, wondering whether he had made a lucky guess at her thoughts or had read her mind. Then it occurred to her that he knew she could heal.

"Our first lessons will be to teach you how to move. After you become proficient at those techniques, we will move on and teach basic hand-to-hand combat, for there will surely come times when you are without a weapon. Finally, we will move on to sword training."

Anne attempted to balance her sword by its tip on the ground. "Sounds like a lot to learn."

"A couple of years for the basics."

"Years," Sophia said, rubbing the back of her neck. "What about Mephis?"

"He is busy assembling an army."

"An army?"

"Yes—an army of undead, using necromancy and Shadows. No need to worry. We have people upstairs watching him."

"Upstairs?" Sophia said, scratching her cheek. Douglas' tour of the facility had shown them but a single level with no sign of staircases leading to a higher floor. "Why can't the Order of Esdras, or the people upstairs, stop him?"

"It is said that only a mortal carrying the Angelic Gene using a Sword of Light can defeat him."

Anne rocked backwards on her heals, grinning. "Looks like the fate of the world is in your hands, Sophia."

Sophia's neck muscles tightened as if they had been shortened a few inches. She tilted her head back and forth trying to reduce the strain. *No wonder he wants me dead. I'm a threat to him.* "Are there any others carrying the Angelic Gene?"

"Perhaps," he said, pulling at his chin. "But we don't know who they are. Some who carry the gene never realize their potential, never unleash the associated abilities. In others, the gene is dormant but may be passed on to their children."

"Oh," Sophia replied. "So when I healed Anne … that is when you knew I carried the Angelic Gene?"

"Actually, Mephis has been tracking family tree lines and murdering those who carry the Angelic Gene, dormant or otherwise. The patterns of his murders led us to discover the link. Which ultimately led to you girls."

Girls? He knows we are sisters? Of course he does. She gazed at Anne. No sign of a reaction to Jeremial's words. Either she had not heard what he said or the information went over her head.

"Ah, Michael," Jeremial said, raising his hand in a gesture of greeting. "Good to see you could join us."

The girls turned and faced the entrance.

"Good morning," Michael said, with a tender nod.

"Morning," the girls replied.

"Michael, himself a well-skilled combatant, is going to be observing you girls," Jeremial said.

Michael seated himself on the bench.

"He will also continue your training on days when I'm not available."

Anne, with a beaming smile and rosy cheeks, tapped the tip of her sword on the rug. "I've seen him fight. He is pretty dang good."

"That he is," Jeremial said. "Sophia, do you know how to use your necklace?"

She tossed her head back and squinted. "My necklace?"

"Yes, as a weapon?"

"No," she said, shaking her head and pursing her lips.

"Open the crucifix and retrieve the crosses inside."

She released the clasp on the crucifix and emptied the contents into her left palm.

"What you do is concentrate on a target or targets. Once you clearly have them in your mind, you throw one or more of the little crosses. Like throwing stars, they will glide through the air, slice the target, and then return. They are also capable of dispelling Shadows from this realm."

Jeremial glanced around the room. "Now let's locate a few targets." He pointed towards the ceiling. "Aim at those spiders in the webs in the crevices of the ceiling."

Sophia placed three crosses in her right hand. Her eyes cut across the ceiling to locate the targets. With a short swing of her arm, nowhere near strong enough to propel the crosses to the heights of the ceiling, the crosses left her hand. Contrary to gravity, the spinning crucifixes accelerated towards the marks. Her posture stiffened as she took an awkward step backward. *How is that possible? That's amazing,* she thought. She faced Jeremial. The crucifixes turned sharply, changing targets.

"Don't focus on me!" Jeremial shouted.

"Um, ah," she stuttered in an uncertain tone. Her thoughts froze, transfixed on Jeremial's words. *What?*

Jeremial's gaze darted about as he readied his staff. With three lightning quick swipes, he deflected the course of each cross so that they soared past him. The crosses turned sharply lining up for another offensive run. "Sophia, now would be a good time to stop," he said, his voice conveyed urgency.

Her eyebrows squished together as she swallowed. "How?"

"Think of your hand or look at your palm!" Jeremial said, his eyes darting among the three spinning crosses.

She held her trembling palm out as if to receive a coin. The crucifixes curved in midflight and, less than a second later, landed on her palm. Each glowed a soft white.

"Whew," Jeremial said, wiping sweat from his forehead. "That was close."

Her heart was heavy. She looked down, said, "I'm so sorry."

Anne chuckled. "That was kind of funny."

Sophia glared at Anne, narrowing her eyes.

"I said *kind of.*"

"It's okay," Jeremial said. "Let's try that again."

Sophia swallowed, attempting to dislodge the lump in her throat. "Are you sure?"

"You'll be fine. Just stay focused on the spiders."

"Yeah, kill those spidies," Anne said, clenching her fists. "I don't like hairy eight-legged creatures. Think of those spiders in the Forest of Arden!"

Michael rubbed the left side of his neck where the giant spider had bitten him. "I'm not surprised, after your recent encounter. I can't say I'm too fond of them either."

"Okay," Sophia said. She took a deep breath to steady her racing heart. She took aim. *I must stay focused.* "Here goes."

The crucifixes left her hand, spinning towards the ceiling. This time, her focus stayed on the hairy arachnids. Near their respective targets, the crosses diverged, each pursuing a lone target. Nearly simultaneously, the crucifixes sliced their prey in two before returning to Sophia's awaiting hand.

"Well done," Jeremial said, clapping his hands. "Well done, indeed."

* * *

Many further exercises ensued over the coming seasons. Jeremial conducted some of the training programs, Michael, some others. They trained in unarmed combat, various styles of weapon combat, and worked on increasing general fitness. By diligent effort, Sophia and Anne both acquired superior battle skills at a rapid pace, preparing them for their future engagement with Mephis and his army of undead.

Chapter 43 - Progress

1877 - Two years later.

On a custom-built obstacle course just outside the underground Order of Esdras facility, Sophia readied herself for the day's challenge. She was prepared to beat her best time of six minutes fifty-two seconds. Next to her, Anne, shoulders thrust back, eyes narrowed, lips pursed, appeared more determined than usual. She was yet to reach the target time of seven minutes, however.

Sophia knelt on one knee readying herself for Jeremial to shout, "Go!" Sweat beaded on her forehead, part from the midday warm sun bearing down on her, and part from her earlier jog to the course following Jeremial on horseback. He encouraged them to run everywhere as part of their cardio training—to the dining hall, to the bath, to prayer meeting: everywhere. Out of the corner of her eye she saw Jeremial holding a golden timepiece in his hand. *Anytime now*, she thought.

"Go!" Jeremial shouted.

They both shot forward into a full-out sprint like an arrow from a bow. Sophia dug deep, racing to the first obstacle—a simple enough thigh-high hawthorn hedgerow. In her peripheral vision, she caught a glimpse of Anne just a little behind her. At times, Sophia believed Anne presumed she deliberately slowed down to let her to catch up. Nothing was further from the truth. Anne's fitness and skills over the past two years had advanced beyond what Sophia considered possible. The dramatic progress made her contemplate whether Anne, too, carried the Angelic Gene. There was no present evidence to suggest that carrying the gene was what made Sophia herself stronger or quicker. Her speed, though exceptional for her age, was equivalent to the top one percent of athletes. All the gene appeared to have afforded her was telekinesis, which she avoided using due to the side effects, and a healing ability.

Without slowing, Sophia bounded over the hedge, gliding gracefully through the air. The next obstacle approached abruptly: a dense three-story high wooden wall made of stacked horizontal planks with a rope dangling over the top. A couple of strides away from the barrier, she braked into a forward jump. The height from the leap allowed her to grasp the rope's tail a good six feet off ground. From there, she placed both feet on the planks and leaned backward. With her spine parallel with the ground, she bent her knees and climbed hand over hand up the rope pacing up the wall. By this point in the course, she typically led Anne by several yards. Not today. Anne was just two paces behind.

Standing on top of the wall, Sophia leapt to the ground, flexing her knees as she landed on her feet and shooting into a forward roll to absorb the impact. After the first rotation, she unwound into a sprint. *Now, I should be at least a few yards ahead*, she thought. In the past, Anne had never jumped from the top of the wall. She would lower herself over the top, face toward the wall, and drop to the ground and then turn and recommence running—costing her valuable time. Sophia glanced over her shoulder to gauge her lead. She stumbled slightly. In fine form, Anne was only marginally behind and gaining. A moment later, Anne took advantage of Sophia's misstep and inched ahead. *Impossible,* Sophia thought.

Sophia readied herself for the next obstacle: a platform of stacked logs barely a head's width above the ground. The objective was to crawl under the logs, but crawling was impossible because the low height of the space forced the person into a prone position. An arm's length away from the entrance, she dived forward hoping her momentum would slide her a reasonable distance underneath the logs. The tactic worked, giving her a body length's edge. Beneath the logs, in a prone position, she propelled herself forward using elbows and knees. Her breathing quickened. She could feel the pounding of her pulsating heart in the back of her neck. The armor she wore, a cloth shirt covered with a leather top, and matching skirt made progress ever more difficult. The sweat build up on her chest and belly caused the clothing to rub against her skin like iron wool, creating a burning sensation, and sometimes taking a layer of skin or causing a blister to form. Used to pain, which was all part of her training, she lumbered forward. She hated this part of the course. The restrictive space limited her movement to almost zero. *A little more*, she thought. *I can do this.* An inch at a time, she gnashed along the ground until her shoulders extended past the end of the platform. At this point, she placed her palms on the logs and pushed herself the rest of the way out.

Relieved to be free of the confines of the crawl space—the gnash space, really—she shot off into a sprint. The last part of the course consisted of a half-mile run back to the start. She did not see Anne in front, so she presumed she must be behind. She did not dare look back in fear of a second stumble. Knowing how Anne hated the crawl space even more than she did gave her a little solace. Her heart thumped at maximum. She focused on Jeremial standing at the finish, gold timepiece in hand. In her left ear, she heard heavy breathing and then, in her peripheral vision, saw Anne gaining. A few seconds later, Anne pulled alongside and then passed, leading into the homestretch by several strides. Sophia dug deeper. *She can't beat me*, Sophia thought. *I need to be the faster, stronger, one. To protect her.*

Sophia accelerated, forcing her heart rate past its known maximum. She bore down, shortened Anne's lead. Down to two strides, then one stride. Too late, Anne crossed the finish line—half a stride ahead of her.

"Congratulations Anne," Jeremial said. "You set a new record."

Sophia bent over, hands on knees, gasping for air. Between breaths, she said, "What?"

"Six minutes forty-seven seconds. Shaving five seconds off Sophia's record."

Sophia gazed at Anne, who was lying on her back with her knees in the air, recovering. Her chest rose high and fell hard with each breath. Her most striking feature at the moment: a radiant smile.

Jeremial checked his timing device a second time. "I'm impressed with both of you."

After regaining her breath, dripping in sweat, Sophia asked, "How did you get so fast, Anne?"

"Extra practice with Michael," she replied, rising to a sitting position.

"Oh," Sophia said, "so that is what you guys have been up to in those long hours alone together."

Anne nodded. "Yep."

Sophia presumed there might have been a little romance going on between the two of them. Once or twice a week they would go off walking together and return some hours later. While she knew Michael was a monk, she was not sure whether that ruled out dating, and she felt too embarrassed to ask in case Michael got the wrong idea. She liked him and all, but she was not interested in forming a relationship with him other than friendship. Besides, she knew that deep down Anne had *a thing* for him. "Well, you deserved this win," Sophia said.

"Thanks," Anne replied.

* * *

Two hours later, they stood in front of Jeremial inside the training hall.

"I have something special for you today, girls."

Sophia's lips bowed slowly into a smile. "You do?" she asked, half curious, half wary. Jeremial's surprises sometimes consisted of physically, and sometimes even emotionally, challenging training exercises.

"Well, I'm so pleased with your training with real weapons over the last year that we are ready to move to the next level."

"And that is?"

"Ahh, Douglas," he said, "right on queue."

Sophia and Anne spun to face Douglas, who was walking toward Jeremial carrying the case in which the Swords of Light were stored. A tingle of expectancy shot through Sophia's body. She bounced on her toes like a child who had just won first prize. *Is this the day I get to hold one?* she thought. Anne, biting her bottom lip, appeared just as excited.

Jeremial opened the container. "Sophia, Anne, take a sword each."

"Who's is whose?" Sophia asked.

"Either or. They are both identical."

"You take one, Anne."

"Really?"

"Yes, you deserve to choose first after beating me today on the obstacle course."

Anne reached into the case and retrieved a sword. After admiring the glistening blade in Anne's hand, Sophia reached in and wrapped her palm around the hilt of the remaining Sword of Light. The handle's texture was soft, almost as if the silver melted around her fingers to form the perfect grip. She raised the sword and held the glistening blade vertical before slicing the air to the left, followed by a swipe back to the right. Like the precision-crafted wooden swords, the balance of the blade was remarkable. She softly caressed the flat side of the blade, being careful not to touch the razor-sharp edge, knowing that the merest contact would slit her skin.

"Right," Jeremial said, "let's do the apple test to ensure you have them under control."

Sophia recalled the first time they had done the test. Anne failed, missing the apple completely. As a result, she was not permitted to use a real sword due to lack of control. Eventually, after weeks of additional practice she got the hang of the timing.

Jeremial retrieved two shiny red apples from a bushel basket tacked to the wall. He faced the girls with an apple in each hand, said, "Now, you know the drill. I'll toss these in the air, and you need to cut them in half and then catch them with your left hand."

Both girls nodded, raising their swords.

"One, two, three." Jeremial tossed the apples high towards the ceiling and stepped two paces back. The apples ascended at slight angles, requiring Sophia and Anne to reposition. Their swords moved faster than the eye could register, leaving a blur of light trails as the apples descended into their awaiting left hands.

"Okay," Jeremial said. "Now, show me your apples."

Sophia, with a gleam in her eye, held her palm out with two perfectly cut slices of apple.

"Very good, Sophia. And what about you, Anne?"

Anne swallowed hard, shaking her head side to side as she held her hand out. *Did she fail?* Sophia thought. *Doesn't look good. She'll be heartbroken if she can't keep the sword.*

"You missed," Jeremial said. He sighed heavily. "I expected better."

Then Anne winked and her expression morphed from a frown to a playful grin. With her thumb, she rubbed the top of her apple. "Which piece would you like, sir?" The apple in her hand was split into eight perfectly cut slices.

Sophia's eyes widened as she sucked in a quick breath. "Wow!" she said. "Let me guess something else you have been practicing with Michael."

Anne nodded.

"I think I'm going to have to start coming with you guys on your field trips."

"You're welcome to," Anne replied.

Jeremial stood speechless for a moment with a puzzled look on his face. He rubbed his chin. "Well I'll be. I have never—*never*—seen anyone do that before. Congratulations to the both of you: The swords are yours to keep. Go see the weapon-smith to have custom sheaths constructed with mounting straps."

"Thank you, Jeremial," both girls replied.

"Wear them with pride," he said as they skipped out of the room together.

Chapter 44 - Time To Go

1878 - Nearly one year later

"It's today, isn't it?" Sophia said, standing in her bedroom gazing at Michael's pained eyes under a wrinkled brow.

"Yes. Time to go. Mephis is mobilizing his army."

"Well at least we are armed and dressed for the occasion," she said. "We were on our way to visit Jeremial for the evening training session." She glanced over her leather top and skirt that had been altered recently to suit her growing body. Less than a month earlier, she and Anne had celebrated their sixteenth birthday with the Order of Esdras. Jeremial had surprised them. Sophia and Anne had both laughed hysterically for long minutes when Jeremiah walked into the main dining room holding a chocolate cake in his hands—a cake he had baked himself. His face was covered in random smears of chocolate batter. White flour covered his hair and clothes. To top off the spectacle, he was wearing a goofy lopsided chef's hat and a white, chocolate-stained, apron.

"Jeremial is waiting for us outside," Michael said, his tone somber. "Fetch your jackets. The trip will be chilly."

Anne raced out of the room shouting, "Be right back, I'll get my jacket from next door."

"Do you think Anne will be okay?"

Michael nodded. "Well, she is fighting and performing as well as you."

"I know," Sophia said. She paused, rubbed her eyebrow before continuing. "But it's not me I'm worried about. I worry about *her*. I feel responsible for her well-being."

"That feeling, I believe, is shared. We all feel responsible for each other. We are family."

She smiled gently with a glint in her radiant emerald green eyes. "True enough."

Michael gave her a tender pat on the back.

"I can't say I'm looking forward to several days of riding back to London," Sophia said.

"The way we are going will be much quicker," Michael replied.

"I'm back," Anne said, appearing in the doorway.

"Right then," Michael said, "time to move on." He led them down the hallway towards the main exit.

"Will we ever becoming back here?" Sophia asked as they passed the underground stables.

Michael shook his head. "Unlikely."

Sophia considered what life would be like after Mephis is defeated—if he was defeated. No more hiding out in the southern parts of Scotland. Although, living there had been enjoyable. From trips to the local towns, the dense regional forests, the rich hunting and fishing, and, of course, the training. Though grueling at times, the discipline and fighting skills she had learnt were an invaluable asset. "So where are we going?" she asked.

"You'll see."

"The suspense is killing me," Anne said as they left the underground complex.

Outside the main gate, they climbed a series of sturdy stone stairs recently installed in stadium seating fashion on the side of the chasm. At the top of the short stairway, they followed a worn dirt pathway up the side of Greatmoor Hill. On approaching the top, Sophia's eyes widened. "What is that?"

"Our ride," Michael replied.

A blue spherical balloon rose into the sky and hovered higher than the nearby trees, secured by four ropes, above a square wicker basket tethered to the ground. Douglas was standing inside the basket. Jeremial finished loading sandbags into the basket.

"We get to fly?" Sophia said. Her pulse quickening.

"We do," Michael replied.

"Brilliant," Anne added.

"You're finally here," Jeremial said. "I was about to come looking for you."

"Sorry," Michael said. "My fault. I had to say a few goodbyes. It's unlikely I'll be back here for some time."

"Aye," Jeremial replied, in his awkward burring Scottish accent. "All is set. Douglas here will serve as your well-trained pilot." He gazed at the heavens. "And I've organized favorable winds at three thousand feet to guide you to your destination. Should be about thirty knots."

"Around nine hours then?" Michael said.

Jeremial cleared his throat. "Aye." He frowned. "Do I still sound like a pirate?"

Anne nodded, grinned. "How does the balloon work?"

"It is filled with hydrogen. To descend a valve opens by pulling on a rope that releases the gas. The vessel ascends by throwing the sandbags, ballast, over the side along the way. The less weight, the higher the balloon goes. Don't worry, Douglas knows what to do. And this balloon is no ordinary one."

"The faint white glow?" Sophia asked.

"Yes, you see it?"

She nodded while scanning the glow that lent the ordinary an air of the divine.

"Where are we going?" Anne asked.

Michael faced towards the south and peered into the horizon. "Stonehenge."

"Wait," Sophia said, "I have a question."

"Out with it, then" Jeremial said.

"How do you *organize favorable winds?*"

"Oh, I have my connections."

She was going to question him further, but over the years, she had gotten used to his cryptic replies. He would answer further queries with ever more ambiguous reasoning, resulting in further interrogations. The never-ending cycle made her head hurt. Michael appeared none the wiser and never seemed concerned to ask. In the end, that was good enough for her.

"All aboard," Douglas shouted.

After Anne and Michael boarded, Sophia climbed over the side of the wicker basket. "Not much room in here," she said, slipping between the sandbags stacked along the side and a crate in the center to the only vacant corner.

"Well, girls, this will be goodbye from me." Jeremial said, sniffling.

"Are you crying?" Anne said.

"No, dear, of course not," he said, batting his eyes. "It's just allergies."

"We will miss you," Sophia said. A rush of warmth curled her lips into a smile and sent tingles to the very tips of her fingers and toes. "Thank you for everything."

"The pleasure has been mine," he said, pulling on a length of rope, which tore pegs holding the tethers from the ground. The basket wobbled slightly before beginning to climb.

Sophia, Anne, Michael, and Douglas waved to Jeremial as the balloon carried them into the heights of the sky. Before long, Jeremial appeared no larger than an ant scurrying along the hillside towards the underground compound.

"This is wonderful," Anne said, peering over the side of the basket. "You can see so much. Hermitage Castle looks so different from up here."

"Don't lean so far over the edge," Michael said. "You make me nervous."

Sophia gazed towards the west, watching the sun hover on the horizon. "Enjoy the view while you can. Not long until nightfall." *This is it*, she thought. The final event. No turning back now. Thousands of butterflies flapped their wings in her stomach, not from the flying but from the apprehension of the pending showdown with Mephis. She questioned her own fortitude. *Am I strong enough? Did I do everything I could in training?*

Him or me.

The moon rose and the sky darkened as they sailed southwest, carried in the currents of the favorable winds. The sparkling lights below combined to create beautiful intricate patterns, like a painting, but constantly changing from one mesmerizing scene to the next. Sophia felt the cold wind pure on her face and experienced a great sense of peacefulness. A sense of cohesion with the world. Time passed swiftly as they experienced the ride of their life.

* * *

Eight and half hours later

"Not far now," Douglas said. "Half an hour."

"That's good," Anne said. "My legs are stiff."

"Mine, too," Sophia added. In the corner of her eye, passing in front of the moon she caught a glimpse of something flying by, larger than a bird. Then came ear-piercing shrieks. "What is that noise?" Sophia said, peering into the darkness.

The sound grew louder, accompanied by the noise of great wings flapping. Michael said, "Fiat lux," and his staff came on with a flash of light. Dark shadows revealed the silhouettes of creatures like flying rodents, with arm's-length wingspan, flying towards them. "Bats" he shouted. No ordinary bats, their eyes glowed blood red.

A bat landed on each of the four ropes strung from the corners of the basket to the balloon. Three other bats swooped, in a vee formation, across the top of the basket, narrowly missing their heads. The flying rodents began gnawing on the ropes. Michael swung his staff as if it were a pick-ax and whacked the bat closest to him, sending it spiraling through the air. "Sophia, use your crosses to take out the other three," Michael said.

Sophia quickly retrieved the tiny crucifixes from the locket of her necklace. She scanned the darkness for the bats. They separated. One flew up high, towards the middle of the balloon, the other two-headed straight for her. With a flick of her wrist, she launched the throwing crosses. The first one homed in on its mark. The bat lurched to the left dodging the cross. After a sharp U-turn, the crucifix tailed the bat, accelerating, until ambushing the creature from behind, amputating its left wing. The bat spiraled uncontrollably, tumbling, to the ground far below. The second cross hit the head of its target full-on, slicing the bat into perfect halves, like the apple in the training exercise. The last cross spun through the air tracking its prey midway up the height of the balloon leaving behind a bright white trail. The bat seemed unperturbed by the impending impact. Instead, folding its wings it became like a missile zooming straight for the side of the balloon.

Sophia mumbled, "Oh no," as the cross severed the bat's backend. The front half, teeth bared, continued into the side of the balloon, piercing the material and leaving a sizeable hole. Each crucifix returned to her hand. "We have a problem," Sophia said, gazing at the gas-leaking puncture.

"What?" Michael replied, preparing to take a swing at the last bat gnawing on the rope in Anne's corner of the basket. "Give me a sec'. This is the final one." He swung. The bat swiveled around on the rope. He missed. After repositioning, he took another swipe at the unwelcome guest. This time he hit it cleanly, sending it cascading into the darkness.

Sophia gazed at the rope. Several strands were bitten through. Only one remained. Then the unthinkable happened: The strand snapped. Under Michael's and Anne's weight, the basket pitched in their corner. The sandbags and crate slid towards them exacerbating the lurch. Anne lost her balance, screamed, and vanished over the side. Douglas lost his footing and tripped towards the edge. He attempted to grab onto anything he could to slow his momentum. Unable, he hit the side and tumbled over the side following Anne. Sophia clung to her side of the basket, her weight the only thing keeping the basket from totally tipping sideways into a death roll. She shimmied closer to the edge to peer over the side. Anne, knuckles white as ivory, jaw set in a gritty look of determination, hung onto the cut rope dangling from the side of the basket—the rope-wall training helped. Holding onto her ankle, Douglas gazed up towards them.

Anne's grip slipped an inch down the rope, struggling to support the weight of both of them. "Hang on, Douglas. I can do this," Anne shouted as she tried to pull herself up. In doing so, she slipped an inch or two farther down. She gazed down at Douglas. Their eyes locked. His soft eyes filled with an inner glow that said everything he needed to say before he shouted, "Go, finish this!" He let go of her ankle. "No!" Anne screamed.

Sophia watched Douglas disappear into the darkness below. Nausea rose from her churning gut. She swallowed hard to tame the urge to vomit.

"Sophia, go to the far side of the basket," Michael said, gulping. "Help us balance." She shimmied across to the opposite side of the basket, pushing her body as deep as possible into the corner. The basket refused to level. The combined weight of Michael, Anne, and the sandbags kept it at a sharp tilt. Michael leant over the side, the temporary floor, and extended his arm to Anne.

Anne tried to reach his hand. Fingers outstretched, she reached the tips of his. Not close enough to embrace hands. She gave up and grasped the rope with both hands. Her movements caused her to sway back and forth, dangling from the rope, her only lifeline. After taking a deep breath, she pulled herself up a little. She rested a moment before continuing the threatening climb. A couple of hand-over-hand pull-ups later, she reached out and grabbed Michael's palm.

"I've got you!" he yelled. She released the rope allowing his grip to support her. He lifted her into the lopsided basket. Michael maneuvered across to Sophia's side. The basket stabilized a little as he transferred positions. "Anne, throw some sandbags over this side," he said. One at a time, she grabbed the sandbags and tossed them to Michael. Manipulating their positions and the sandbags, they were able to somewhat level the basket, although it listed constantly like a see-saw.

"Are we descending?" Michael asked.

"Yes, I was about to tell you before, a bat punctured the balloon."

Michael gazed at the moonlit horizon as he tossed a sandbag over the side. "It is time to go down, but not this fast." He threw another, and then another, until there was no more left. "Brace yourselves," he said, "we're going down fast."

No lights illuminated the ground below, so they had no way of judging how far they were from the ground—from impact. A short time later, the pale moonlight provided just enough light to illuminate the tops of the trees. "Here we go," Michael said, screwing his eyes shut.

The bottom of the basket skimmed along the tree canopy, bouncing from one to the next as the wind carried it southwards. Then the trees broke into an open field. A moment of peace, falling, before they slammed into the ground at speed with a thud. A gust of wind, around ten knots, propelled the balloon, dragging them across the field. Sophia, Michael, and Anne huddled with each other in the basket, heads down. Together, they whispered prayers. None of them prayed for themselves, instead they prayed for each other. They slid to a halt. Sophia gazed up at the balloon tangled in the swaying branches of a large oak tree. "We're down."

Chapter 45 - The Final Battle

"Michael, Anne, are you two okay," Sophia said, stretching her arms and legs.

"I think so," Anne replied.

"I'm good," Michael said. "A few bumps and bruises."

"Where are we?" Sophia said, gazing at the torn trail of grass and dirt leading from the wicker basket across the long grass. She realized how lucky they were even to be alive and unhurt. *If this open field had not been here….* She shuddered, thinking what might have been.

Michael rose and offered his hand to help Anne to her feet. "You're bleeding," he said.

"It's nothing," Anne said, wiping a streak of blood from her left temple. "Just a graze."

"Let me look," Sophia said. She clambered to her feet, using the sides of the basket to assist her tense muscles. With her left hand, she brushed Anne's hair off her face for a closer look at the wound. "You're right. It's only a graze. The bleeding has already stopped."

Michael gazed at the moon. "By the position of the moon and stars we need to go this way," he said, pointing into a dark uninviting tree line to the southwest. Holding his staff upright, providing light, he led the way.

The trees reminded Sophia of the forest behind the orphanage where she and Anne used to play and built their treehouse. Those days, their only concern in the world was dreadful weather. She missed those days, longed to have them again, but doubted she—*they*—ever would. The last three years had shown her different sides of humanity—the two polarities. Sister Mary said the paths are shown in Galatians, the dark path consisting of adultery, fornication, uncleanness, lewdness, idolatry, sorcery, hatred, contentions, jealousies, outbursts of wrath, selfish ambitions, dissensions, heresies, envy, murders, drunkenness, revelries, and the like. The light path consists of love, joy, peace, longsuffering, kindness, goodness, faithfulness, gentleness, and self-control.

Sophia had never understood the longsuffering and why that one would be on the light path—until now. The longsuffering came about by learning to patiently endure the wrongs and difficulties in the world. It was a reflection of love. The more she loved, the more able she exercised longsuffering. It was ironically joyful, however, for she knew in the end that the path she was walking would lead her home, to God. She wrapped her hand around her crucifix and whispered, "You fill my troubled heart with joy." Her heart skipped a beat as a bubbling rush of tingles swept over her body causing her arms to breakout in goosebumps.

A short distance into the woods, the harsh rustling of the trees died down to a steady whisper. The light from Michael's staff cast many dark shadows among the trees. More than once, Sophia jerked her sight in the direction of this distortion or that. Only to realize the harrowing figures were plants and trees vines combining to form human-like shapes in the darkness.

Suddenly, they all froze in response to a loud *whooshing* sound. Then a sudden gust of wind rushed in, swaying even the sturdiest of trees and threatening to sweep them off their feet. Through the gaps in the forest, a large red glow became visible. "It's started," Michael said. "Witching hour is already upon us. We are late. We must hurry."

Michael quickened his pace to a slow jog, ducking and weaving through the branches. The girls followed closely behind.

As they stepped out of the forest, Sophia brought her hand to her forehead to wipe away dripping sweat. The sight in front of her sent a wave of cold trepidation from her neck to the base of her spine. A shimmering red oval wide enough to drive a two-horse carriage through hovered in the midst of a ring of grey rectangular stones standing three times the height of an average man on their ends in a circular formation—Stonehenge. Some stones had fallen over while others formed archways. The arches consisted of two stones wide enough apart for a person to walk through. A third stone block, half the size of the standing stones, rested across the top.

Out of the archways, jagged streams of red energy connected to the central oval. Around the outside, stood a host of warriors—at least ninety by rough count—armed with a variety of weapons. Pikes, sword-and-shield combinations, spiked balls-and-chains. Sophia was familiar with all of them. The warriors did not look quite right. On closer inspection, she noticed their skin appeared to be rotting. Some were missing eyes and had only dark sockets. Their heads tilted at angles to their body. They moved awkwardly, jutting about in fast, jerky movements. "What in God's name?" Sophia said.

"An army of undead possessed by Shadows," Michael replied.

"And that red glowing disc?" Sophia asked.

"A gateway to the Underworld."

The gateway began to shimmer, and shadowy figures emerged from within the gateway. They were shaped like humans but black as shadows and two-dimensional as thin as paper. First a group of six, followed by a group of ten. "It's started," Michael said. As the Shadows entered Stonehenge, they scattered, fleeing into the nearby forests. Another group of twenty Shadows marched through.

"Too many undead," Anne said, in a quaking voice.

"For us three, yes," Michael replied. He raised his staff and shouted, "Protinus!" A blinding bright white of light flashed from the top of his staff, like a mini explosion, shooting off in all directions.

From within the tree line to their left and right lights suddenly illuminated, ten on each side. Out of the darkness emerged a line of men dressed in long brown robes and holding illuminated staffs, the same as Michael's with the crucifix on top.

Sophia's skin tingled as she touched her parted lips. "Monks?"

"Yes, my Cistercian brothers."

Anne's eyes watered as a beaming smile swept across her face. "Now we have a chance."

"Indeed," Michael said. Once again, he held his staff in the air and shouted, "Arma!" A long thin blade extended from the base of his staff, and the word "Arma!" echoed across the open field as a chorus from the other monks.

Sophia and Anne withdrew their glowing white Swords of Light from their sheaths. Together, the three of them charged towards the army of undead. The Undead readied themselves forming a line to block the left and right flanks and frontal assault. It occurred to Sophia the duty of the undead was to ensure that nobody stopped Mephis. So they formed a wall of defense.

On her left, Sophia saw a monk fall to the ground, his light extinguishing. Then, to her right, another went down. She scanned the darkness for the source of the assault and found it to be three undead warriors armed with crossbows perched on three of the archways. Without stopping, she opened her cross locket and shook out the tiny crucifixes into the palm of her left hand. She launched three of them with a flick of her wrist. Light trails streamed behind them as they diverged, each homing in on one of the three targets. In mere seconds, they reached their targets, piercing the chests of the undead. A puff of black mist erupted from them before the undead body collapsed and tumbled off their perch to the ground below. As the crucifixes returned, Sophia slipped them back into the locket. The attack put her several strides behind Michael and Anne.

As he approached the wall of undead, Michael turned his staff upright with the cross facing down. A couple of strides out, he plunged the staff into the ground, using the now-flexible pole to vault over the heads of the undead. As he landed, he spun around, and swept his staff in an arc, at knee height, blade extended, amputating both legs of an undead with a single swipe. The creatures fell forward, at which point Michael finished it with a stab through the back. He shouted, "Expello." The carcass shuddered, surrounded in a puff of black smoke.

Anne raised her sword, holding the hilt with both hands over her right shoulder. One sword-length away from the wall of undead she leapt into a spin. At the 180-degree mark, she extended her sword, continuing the spin. The undead appeared to have frozen in confusion or possibly from the sheer speed of Anne's action. Her Sword of Light came around and sliced underneath the undead's chin, releasing a slither of black mist from its neck as the carcass fell to the ground in two pieces.

Sophia dived into the enemy, feet first, slicing an undead from underneath as she passed between its legs. She scampered to her feet and continued her assault. Two undead approached her, one on either side, armed with long swords and round wooden shields. At this point, she wished she had two blades, one in each hand. She thought back to her training as the two undead charged her with swords raised and prepared to swing. As they swung, she ducked, their swords clipping the stray strands of hair on the top of her head. She retreated a step and then swept her sword around in arc, cutting them both down at the shins. They doubled over giving Sophia the perfect opportunity to run them through. In her peripheral vision, she saw one of the monks take a spiked ball in the side of the head, ending his fight. Another monk took a sword through his back, extinguishing his light. As the fight continued, more of her allies fell. At one point, she glimpsed Michael, his face contorted with grief for each of his fallen brothers. After counting twenty kills, she and Michael were the only two-left standing except for two undead.

"Where's Anne?" Sophia said, urgent, scanning the litter of bodies strewn across the battlefield.

"I don't know," Michael said.

The undead approached, each wielding a long two-handed sword. Sophia, sweating, nostrils flared, shouted, "Give up already! I don't have time for this!" She approached the attackers. They swung. She sidestepped their slow laboring swings with ease, circled around their backs, sliced the first one across the neck. Her slice clean, the head stayed in position until the carcass tumbled forward as the Shadow disintegrated within, dispelled to the Underworld. The second undead glanced towards his fallen comrade. His mistake. By the time he refocused, Sophia had pierced him through the chest. "Done."

"I still can't find Anne," Michael said.

They both jerked around toward the gateway on hearing a scream. "It's Anne!" Sophia said. Together, they raced up the small incline into Stonehenge.

"That's close enough," Jack said, holding a glowing red knife against Anne's neck. He held her like a hostage, her back to his front, one arm wrapped around her waist, the other holding a knife poised to slit her throat.

With a frown, Anne said, "I'm sorry. I never saw him coming."

Sophia cut her eyes over to the right until they fixed on Mephis, who was standing several strides in front of the gateway. Jack, holding Anne across from them, was also a number of strides away. Under the shimmering red gateway, a glowing fiery crystal sphere pulsated each second. A single stream of blood-red energy tethered the orb to the base of the gateway. The good news was the Shadows appeared to have stopped coming through. For now at least. Anne's Sword of Light lay on the ground, several strides away from her.

Mephis raised his left hand. Red streams of energy shot out of his fingertips and sparking the short distance to Sophia and Michael. Then the strands began coiling themselves around Sophia like ropes. "I can't move," Sophia said, staring painfully at Anne.

"Me, either," Michael replied.

Mephis bellowed a great vomit of laughter. "My powers are too strong now for mere mortals. You are nothing more than rag dolls. A nuisance waiting to be torn apart." He nodded toward Jack. "Kill her."

Jack cleared his throat. "Are you sure?"

"Yes. Or would you prefer that I kill you both?"

Jack's hand started to shake as he increased the pressure of the blade against Anne's neck. Anne closed her eyes. Sophia realized she did so to avoid having to see the anguish on the faces of her and Michael as, helpless, they were forced to watch her die.

"Don't do this!" Sophia yelled. She gritted her teeth and screamed, her muscles bulging as she tried to break free of the bonds. No good. Her stomach felt like someone was spinning it around in tight circles at the end of a rope.

Over near Jack, a bright snowy flash lit the sky followed by a white oval shaped doorway of light appearing in its place. A man stepped from the glow.

"Diniel," Sophia said, at the same time as Jack said, "Elidin."

Jack shook his head. "Brother? How is this possible?"

"Ah, yes," Mephis said, squinting. "Diniel, Elidin—one of the same. A thorn in my side for quite some time."

Sophia quickly realized that rearranging the letters of Elidin spelt Diniel. *Jack's Brother?*

Mephis raised his right hand. From his fingertips erupted a dark stream of black energy. Diniel responded raising his hand firing a white surge of energy. The blackness consumed the white like water squelching a fire. The dark energy encircled Diniel. Mephis raised his hand, lifting Diniel who was cocooned in the shadowy dark energy, off the ground. "Your powers are weak compared to mine, Diniel. Do you have any last words for your brother, Jack?"

Jack squealed, "Wait."

"Why, Jack, he is of no use to us, or to you."

"But," Jack stammered. "But…."

"Time to meet your maker, Diniel," Mephis said, closing his fist. Diniel's face contorted as he bellowed a primal scream. The black energy tightened around him, like a hungry boa constrictor squeezing the life from its prey. Tremors wracked his body. His eyes began to bulge.

Jack released Anne. He wound up and with all his might heaved the glowing red dagger at Mephis. Handle over blade the dagger spun through the air. Mephis was concentrating so completely on Diniel that he did not see it coming. The blade sliced through the cotton of his thin coat and sank deep into the flesh of his chest until it stopped with a significant thud as the dagger's handle prevented further penetration.

The black energy holding Diniel vanished, and he dropped like a stone to the ground. Sophia's and Michael's bindings released.

Mephis threw back his hood. The veins in his eyes were bright red. He grabbed the handle of the dagger with both hands and pried the blade loose. Blood spilt out of the gaping wound. He fell to his knees, yelling, "Jack! What have you done?" On his knees, he tried to stem the tide of blood flowing from his wound. Moments later, he clawed at his face with his fingertips leaving behind trails of blood—black blood. His eyelids closed. He fell onto his back as he released a final rageful scream.

Sophia turned her gaze to Jack. He stood there shaking.

"Thank you, brother," Diniel said, rising to his feet, and swaying on wobbly legs.

Jack saved us, Sophia thought. Not exactly what she had expected. Nor was coming to understand that Diniel was Jack's brother. A strange pair, that was. Diniel was quite an amiable person; Jack, quite the opposite.

After grasping her sword, Anne ran over to Sophia and hugged her tightly. "Thank God, it's over."

"Not yet," Michael said. "We still have to close this gateway before more Shadows cross into this realm. I suspect that enough have already made it through to influence humanity to war, the greatest of evils. We don't need more."

"How?" Sophia asked, gazing at the shimmering gateway.

Diniel strode over in front of the gateway. "This orb has to be destroyed."

"That's easy enough," Sophia said, raising her sword.

"On the *other* side," Diniel added. His voice lowered: "On the *Underworld* side."

Sophia frowned, feeling a sense of defeat. She lowered her sword. "Oh."

"Once destroyed, the gateway will close. But whoever goes through will not be able to come back."

Sophia, Anne, and Michael positioned themselves in front of the gateway, where they stood staring into the spiraling energy.

"Well, we can't leave the gateway open," Anne said.

"I'll do it," Michael said.

"No, you can't," Sophia said, extending her arm in front of him.

"I have to," he replied pushing her arm away.

"Wait," Jack said, trudging to his brother's side. "I'll go. I'm destined there anyway."

Diniel faced him. "God will forgive you if you ask."

"I would have to forgive myself first," he replied, his eyes dim and serious.

Sophia felt an ache of sorrow as she observed the grim twist of Jack's mouth. He appeared to want to punish himself for his sins.

"Then," Diniel said, nodding, "I'll come with you." He bent over and picked up the glowing orb in his left hand. "Come, Jack, where there is will there is hope." He extended his right hand. Jack reached out and took his palm. Together they stepped through the gateway, vanishing in the swirling mist. A moment later, the gate began to flicker, slowly at first, and then increasing to a rapid pace. The streams of red energy shooting off to the surrounding stones snapped, one at a time. The gateway then swiftly shrunk in on itself before vanishing in a vibrant compact glimmer of light.

"They did it," Anne said.

Sophia relaxed her shoulders. "It's fini—" Her voice stopped mid-sentence replaced with a gasp. Pain ripped through her upper right chest. She gulped for air as if someone had knocked the wind out of her.

Anne turned to her. A stream of blood ran from the corner of Sophia's mouth.

"It's not finished until *I* say it is," Mephis said, standing behind Sophia. In his hand, halfway up Sophia's back, he held the handle of the glowing red dagger. He jerked upwards on the handle. Sophia gasped a second time, her eyes rolling upwards, and Mephis smirked, said, "You are not the only one who can heal." He jerked the dagger again.

Michael raised his staff. Mephis responded by shooting a bolt of red energy from his hand that hit Michael squarely in the chest sending him tumbling backwards. Before Anne could raise her sword, Mephis shot another bolt in her direction—another direct hit that sent her spinning backwards into the side of a stone block.

Between deep gasps of breath, Sophia said, "There is one thing that separates the likes of you from the likes of people like me."

"And what pray tell is that, my dear?" Mephis said sarcastically, twisting the knife yet again in her flesh.

"We believe." She rotated her sword in her hand to turn the blade in on herself. "Greater love hath no man than this…" She thrust her blade slightly upward through her chest, narrowly missing her rapidly beating heart. The blade continued through her body and out of her back then into Mephis' chest where it impaled his evil heart. "…that a man lay down his life for his friends." She withdrew the sword.

Mephis shuddered violently. He attempted to scream but no sound emitted. Black mist flowed from his eyes, his ears, his nostrils. A second later, his body disintegrated into dust. His bodiless cloak fell to the ground.

Sophia collapsed to her knees, reached behind her back, held her breath, and withdrew the dagger. She turned pale as fresh snow.

* * *

Anne staggered to her feet and raced to Sophia. She dropped to her knees and caught Sophia in her arms as she fell. Michael shook his head and stretched his eyes as he pushed himself off the ground, then stumbled over to them.

"Heal yourself," Anne said.

Sophia's eyes closed and then reopened slowly. "I can't."

"Why?" Anne said, her brow falling under the weight of concern.

"The dagger," she said. "it was poisoned with the same toxin that killed my mother."

"*Our* mother," Anne said, her eyes welling tears of love and impending loss. She tightened her embrace around Sophia.

"How did you know?" Sophia whispered, her voice fading.

"Jack told me. Looking at our reflections in the mirror as we stood together, seeing our identical eyes, I knew it to be truthful."

"Why didn't you say something?" Sophia asked.

"Why didn't you?" Anne responded.

Sophia forced a tiny smile as her eyes battled to stay open.

"You can't leave me, Sophia." She shook her. "You promised you would never leave me."

"I'm sorry," Sophia whispered. Her eyes gave up and the fight and closed as her smile faded.

"No, no," Anne cried, staring at Sophia's pale face through a tear-filled blur. "Don't go. Please don't leave me. You can't." The dam burst now, sending a torrent of tears cascading down her cheeks.

In an instant, Sophia's body turned to dust, leaving Anne holding nothing more than Sophia's leather armor.

Sophia's armor slipped from Anne's lap as she rose. She charged towards Michael and landed in the pit of his chest where she thumped, first with her left fist, then with her right, hard at first, but then weaker with each subsequent blow, yelling, "No, this can't be!" between great sobs. Michael embraced her the best he could, allowing her to pound away on his chest.

Eventually, minutes later, she stopped and rested her head in the nook at the base of Michael's neck. The flow of her tears began to stem, each droplet taking a little longer than the last to flow down her face. The wind kicked up then, and with each gust parts of Sophia's dusty remains took flight, carried across the pastures of Stonehenge. Anne noticed the particles, and thought, *At least now she is free from this agonizing world.* Through bloodshot eyes, she gazed at Michael, her stomach aching as she had not eaten for a month. A deep pit of nothingness. Every time she swallowed, she felt a lump of disbelief in her throat the size of an apple. "How am I going to go on?" she said.

"Longsuffering," Michael replied. He paused, pulled her close, hugged her tightly. "By patiently enduring the wrongs and difficulties in the world." He stroked the back of her head, running his hand through her long raven black hair. "It'll be okay. You'll get through this." She continued to weep, long slow tears of pain. The only sister she had was gone. She was all alone—again—feeling that familiar aching she had experienced at age four when she lost her parents in the carriage crash. Only this was worse, heavier, deeper, tearing at her soul.

Thirty minutes later, Anne broke away from Michael. She wiped her eyes with the back of her hand. She dropped to her knees and picked up Sophia's cross necklace. After unhitching the new wooden latch on

the necklace that the carpenter at the Order of Esdras had made to lengthen the string, she said, "Michael, can you put this on me, please?"

Michael knelt down, took the necklace, and draped the cross over her shoulders and let it dangle between her bosoms. He then proceeded to clasp the latch at the back of her neck. Next, Anne picked up Sophia's sword and its sheath. Rising to her feet, she slung Sophia's sheath over her left shoulder where it crisscrossed her own. She grasped both Swords of Light in her trembling hands. "These will now be called *The Sisters of Light* in memory of my sister, Sophia." A fresh outburst of tears caused her to pause. With a rapid movement, she sheathed both blades simultaneously behind her back. "You'll live in my heart forever, Sophia. From this moment forward, I will fight for you. Every Shadow I destroy will be in your name. Every evil I conquer will be in your honor. Every battle I overcome will be drawn from the strength of knowing you." She gazed to the heavens. "I will live for God."

She grasped Michael's hand. "Which way are we headed?"

Michael squeezed her hand gently. "East, to Amesbury. Once there we can arrange burials for Sophia and my fallen brothers. Afterwards, we can procure steeds to take us to London. I will be returning to the Cistercians. You are welcome to join me."

Anne forced a smile. They strode eastward together, holding hands, under the moonlight.

Before entering the tree line, Anne glanced over her shoulder, towards Stonehenge. A tear in her eye, she whispered, "Goodbye, Sophia. May the wings of angels carry you safely to Heaven."

Chapter 46 - Possible

1879 - 1 year later

Michael slipped into the chair across from Mendel who was sitting at his desk.

"Well, Michael," Mendel said, sealing an envelope, "do we have any news on Anne's whereabouts?"

"You mean *Sophia*—on *Sophia's* whereabouts."

"Ah, yes," Mendel said. "I keep forgetting that she changed her name in honor of her mother and sister."

"Indeed. I believe her mother's engraved gold bracelet was the tipping point."

"Right. Good work in finding that." Mendel adjusted his glasses to rest higher on his nose.

Michael nodded. "In the lost property bin in St Thomas Hospital, of all places."

"Anyway, back on topic. Have you heard from her, Michael?"

"No. Only rumors and whispers."

"Such as?"

"She is creating a bit of a legend for herself." Michael rubbed the back of his neck. "The saying goes that Sophia, perched high up on the top of church spires, listens to the night for screams. On hearing a cry, she goes to the person's aid, so everyone's guardian angel is only a call away. She stalks the Shadows, feeds the hungry, and cares for the lonely."

"Has anyone actually seen her?"

"There are many reports of people saying they saw a girl with raven-black hair and emerald green eyes. None are verifiable."

"Seems she picked up on her stealthy training from the Order of Esdras quite well."

"She did, indeed." Michael rubbed his chin, reflecting on his own experiences with the Esdras.

"Just as well with the Bobbies still looking for her. We got the charges against you dropped but were not able to get hers dropped. From everything that happened, did you ever find out if she carries the Angelic Gene like her sister?"

"No," Michael said, shaking his head. "I never saw her do anything that would confirm she does. But you know what?"

"What?"

"While she may not carry an Angelic Gene she certainly has an angelic heart."

Mendel smiled. "From your reports, I would certainly agree."

"Did I tell you the last thing she said to me in person? She had one heartfelt idea."

"What's that?"

Michael thought back to his last meeting with Sophia, who was still known as Anne at the time.

* * *

Michael climbed the last rung of the ladder onto the roof of the St Mary Abbots church in London. He stepped onto the roof and crawled up the angled shingling. "You are lucky I'm not scared of heights," Michael said, glancing towards Anne. She sat on the apex of the roof, perched like an eagle ready to take flight. Her black hair contrasted with her pale complexion and glinted with soft moon glow. The pupils of her emerald green eyes reflected the glittering stars. Her lips were not smiling, nor sad. A mixture of hope and pain. An arresting look.

"Beautiful night," Anne replied.

Michael seated himself on the roof's apex next to her. "I have something for you." After reaching into his pocket, he held out a golden bracelet in his hand.

Her eyes widened as she accepted the gift.

"It was your mother's," Michael said.

"It is beautiful," she said, reading the inscription *Sophia*. She wiped a forming tear from her eye.

"Your mother's and sister's name."

"I've been thinking," she said.

"About what?"

"About changing my name from Anne to Sophia in honor of them."

Michael nodded. He saw no problem with the idea. There were no official records to change, and only a handful of people called her Anne.

She slipped the bracelet onto her wrist. "Then it's decided. From now on, please call me *Sophia*."

"Okay, I will." He paused for a second, smiled, and then continued, "Sophia." His heart warmed saying the name as it brought back many fond memories of the two girls he had come to love as family.

Anne slid the silver bracelet off her arm. She then unclipped the crucifix charm. "I want you to have this," she said, holding out the cross.

Michael gazed at it. "But … Are you sure?"

"Yes, very. You never know, one day the cross may help you to find me. Like a bond between us or something."

"Thank you," he said, squinting at her, accepting the gracious gift. "I'll take very good care of it." He placed the cross into a pocket on the inside of his monk's robe. "Do you miss her?"

"You want to hear the strangest thing?"

"Sure."

"She came to me in a dream, said she had made the decision to go home. To be with God."

"That is not strange."

"She went on to give me the impression that God created her for the purpose of protecting me so we could defeat Mephis together. And once the task was accomplished, she would return home."

"I see. That is a little strange. But I guess each of us truly does have a purpose in life."

Anne scraped on the shingles with her fingernails. "She said that Mendel was right: God does not sit idly by when his world is in distress."

Michael cocked his head, nodded slowly.

"She introduced me to Jesus." Anne paused, wiping a second tear from her eye. "She was like an angel to me."

"To both of us."

"You know what?" Anne said.

"No." He shook his head. "What?"

"When I die, if possible," she paused, taking in a deep breath. "I want to continue the fight against the Shadows and answer the screams of children in the night." She clutched the crucifix around her neck.

"Go on," Michael said, watching her captivating emerald green eyes refract the moonlight in the night sky as she gazed towards the heavens. "Don't keep me in suspense."

"I'm going to pass on Heaven and become an angel instead."

The End

"For with God nothing shall be impossible" – Luke 1:37 (KJV)

Other Novels by Steve Goodwin

Elijah Hael - The Last Judgement

A thought provoking story of love, life and death, the afterlife, and spiritual warfare.

I am dead. This is my funeral.

Elijah turned to look at Castiel who looked back at him and nodded gently.

And in that instant everything changed, in ways that Elijah Hael and those who read his story could never anticipate or imagine.

Enter a world of intrigue, suspense, wonder and living energy where our souls are battled over, unseen by many but experienced by all.

Don't miss the opportunity to join Elijah Hael on his spellbinding, dazzling and unforgettable journey through his life to his destiny. An adventure, infused with Christian values, you'll never forget. Those who enjoy an uplifting, challenging, touching story will adore this novel.

Elijah Hael - The Genetic Code

A dazzling, thought provoking, combination of faith versus secular beliefs, science fiction, spiritual warfare, action adventure and romance.

Yesterday's gone. Tomorrow is a distant hope. Now means everything...

Nya struggled to believe her accomplishment. Nearly a decade's work was all coming together. This was her moment. The Nobel Prize would be hers for the taking. Her work was going to change the face of bioscience forever.

The only problem, someone with an exceptionally dark desire wanted to twist her work for sinister purposes that would change the face of life on earth forever. And he was prepared to go to any lengths to get it.

Thus began a chain of startling events that would force Nya to place her trust in an unknown man whom she discovered from archived news reports ... **died years ago**.

Journey with Nya, a believer, as her faith is tested. Join Isaac, a non-believer, who questions his existence. Discover how they face death together in a remarkable journey. An emotionally rich escapade which will delight those who quest personally challenging and thought provoking reads.

Keep up to date with Steve Goodwin's novels at

Official Web Sites

www.ElijahHael.com
www.TheAngelicGene.com

Author's Blog

www.stevegoodwin.org

Facebook

www.facebook.com/TheAngelicGene
www.facebook.com/ElijahHaelTheLastJudgement
www.facebook.com/ElijahHaelTheGeneticCode

www.ingramcontent.com/pod-product-compliance
Lightning Source LLC
Chambersburg PA
CBHW061316170626
46817CB00001B/203